RED
CARPET
KISS

Also by Melissa Brown

Love of My Life series
Bouquet Toss
Champagne Toast
Picturing Perfect
Unwanted Stars

The Compound series
Wife Number Seven
His Only Wife

Sorority of Three: Freshman 101

RED CARPET KISS

MELISSA BROWN

Montlake
Romance

Published by Montlake Romance, Seattle

www.apub.com

Amazon, the Amazon logo, and Montlake Romance are trademarks of Amazon.com, Inc., or its affiliates.

ISBN-13: 9781477830963
ISBN-10: 1477830960

Cover design by Regina Wamba

Printed in the United States of America

For my mom, Deb,

who helped shape my love for the Beatles

and compelling television dramas.

Thank you for all of your help with this story.

I love you, Mom.

Prologue

"Don't look at me like that." Gina glared at Nolan, her eyes searing into his. Her hair fell in loose waves, tumbling past her tan shoulders.

"Like what?" Nolan crossed his arms in front of his broad chest, smirking at her, blocking the doorway she was determined to cross.

"Like you have me all figured out," she snapped. "You don't and you *never* will."

Right on cue, Gina pushed against the taut muscles of Nolan's arm, attempting to leave the room, the tension, the heat. But instead, she walked right into his embrace. Nolan angled himself properly and wrapped one arm around her tiny waist. She gasped, avoiding his prying stare.

"I think I do, baby. And it scares the hell out of you." His hand pushed into the curve of her lower back, bringing her closer.

Gina's eyes softened, and her hands wrapped around Nolan's neck. Nolan's lips curled into a satisfied smile before making contact with Gina. He turned her slightly to the left, pressing her into the door frame as he kissed her. Hard.

"Annnnd . . . cut!" Rob, the director, hollered from his chair. "Nice work, people. Let's do it one more time." He stood and walked to the actors, rubbing the blond scruff on his chin. "This time, Nolan, be a little more forceful when you turn her. We want the audience to feel the urgency."

"Got it," Nolan responded, saluting Rob and returning to his spot beneath the open door frame, standing on the tape stuck to the floor. Members of the makeup team appeared at his side to wipe the lipstick from his skin and to freshen Gina's appearance.

Everything had to be just right.

Elle Riley wouldn't have it any other way.

Eleanor "Elle" Riley was the creator, head writer, and show runner of *Follow the Sun,* the most popular television drama to hit the airwaves in over a decade.

She was also a perfectionist—a complete and total perfectionist. Her director knew it, her producers and crew knew it, and the actors were reminded with each take that Elle would not accept anything but the very best performances for her show. Dozens of names were listed in the closing credits, but the show was based on her novels. It was her baby, her pride and joy—it meant everything to her.

In its first season, *Follow the Sun* had earned three Emmy nominations, including one for Outstanding Drama Series. When they were cast as the leads, Nolan Rivera and Gina Romano were relative unknowns in Hollywood. But after just a few months on the air, they were plastered across gossip magazines, followed by paparazzi, and raised to celebrity status. Gina embraced her fame—posing for fitness magazines, conducting interviews between takes, and dining at the trendiest restaurants.

Nolan had chosen to be more private, retreating from the attention—he led a quiet life in the Hollywood Hills, only appearing publicly when necessary. Both actors lit up the screen, captivating audiences. Combined with Elle's writing, *Follow the Sun* had become the show to beat. And Elle was determined to maintain its spot at the top.

When filming resumed, she pulled her attention away from the actors and thumbed through the script to the next scene to be filmed. Rob returned to his seat next to Elle and leaned his elbow on the wooden arm of his chair. "Thoughts?"

"I'm not sure she's ready for the next scene."

They'd been going strong for over ten hours, and Elle was contemplating skipping the scene until the next day. After all, it was a tricky one, and she worried Gina might be too exhausted to nail the emotion required to pull it off.

Rob shook his head and Elle tilted hers, looking at him over her wire-rimmed glasses.

"What?" she asked, crossing her arms in front of her chest as her knee bobbed up and down.

"You're too hard on her."

"I disagree." Her tone was harsh, dismissive.

"She can handle it, Elle. She always does."

Gina was a good actress. In fact, most of the time, Elle thought she was the perfect match for the character. But there were specific scenes that gave Elle pause. Those were the scenes based on *him*. Based on the man who had inspired the entire concept for *Follow the Sun*. The man who had left her heart wounded and exposed.

In the quiet moments, the thoughtful moments, the moments when Elle could tune out the noise of Hollywood, she let her mind drift back to the chapel in Las Vegas. To the man whose heart she had broken, who then stifled hers in retaliation.

Their love affair was her inspiration.

Her muse.

The hidden scar that sat tucked beneath her chest.

And because she didn't know where he was, having avoided social media like the plague, and because he might be sitting on a couch somewhere, snuggling up to a girlfriend or wife who insisted they watch her show week after week, Elle knew those scenes needed to be just right. Every last one.

If he was watching, he had to know she was strong, that she didn't need him—or anyone, for that matter—to make her whole, fulfilled, or satisfied.

And that, despite the scar, her heart was, and would continue to be, just fine.

Chapter 1

Thick, white buttercream frosting covered the tips of Elle's fingernails. She popped each finger in her mouth for one last lick and savored the sugary-sweet, intoxicating taste of celebration.

Solo celebration.

Aside from Linus, her sweet terrier, who lay next to her on the couch, and the soothing sound of her beloved Beatles in the background, Elle was celebrating her birthday alone. Her parents raised her on Beatles records, and they quickly became the soundtrack of her life. She listened to different albums for different moods, and her birthday was no exception. She was thirty-five years old and single. And for reasons all her own, she preferred to commemorate this day completely by herself.

Ten years ago, on this very day, she had married. But it didn't last long.

Thirty-six hours, to be precise.

Because of that impulsive decision, her birthday would be forever linked to *him*. She didn't speak his name, especially since moving to California. No one knew him here, their past, their history. Their mutual friends and classmates knew not to bring up his name or ask how long it had been since she'd seen him. She was able to control her curiosity if no one mentioned him. If she caved and learned about his life, inevitably she'd learn he'd moved on when she still could not.

And she preferred it that way.

Her best friend, Whitney, the casting director for *Follow the Sun*, simply referred to him as "Vegas," knowing that Elle couldn't handle discussing her past with Troy Saladino. Even her best friend was on a need-to-know basis about that chapter in her life.

"That was delicious," Elle said, wiping her mouth and hands with a napkin. She then placed the cupcake liner back into the box from Sprinkles Cupcakes. "Totally worth the money."

Linus peeked out from the nook he'd created in the pillow next to Elle and tipped his little head to the side.

Elle shrugged before petting him on his snout and giggling. "Okay, fine, maybe not."

Her laptop beckoned from across the room. She needed to get a head start on the new season, but the impending love scene between Desmond and Molly was stressing her out. She and the network rarely agreed on a suitable level of steam for prime-time television. Elle was all about pushing the envelope, allowing her characters to act on their sexual impulses in what Rob, her director, called "interesting" locales such as utility closets, parking garages, and even a hotel day spa. But the resistance she received often muzzled her creativity. "Do you think I should write that love scene, Linus?"

Linus tipped his head to the side again, looking adorable. She loved when he did that.

"I didn't think so." She smiled. "No one likes working on their birthday."

Elle laughed and reached for the *Entertainment Weekly* on her coffee table. She smiled as she stared at the cover, savoring the photo of Gina and Nolan, standing back-to-back, with arms crossed. Pride stretched from her head to her feet, knowing her characters were sitting on thousands of coffee tables across the country. Her characters. Her show. Her creation. For just a moment, her normal birthday sadness drifted away as she paged through the magazine and landed on the article devoted completely to *Follow the Sun.* Her moment was interrupted when her purse began to ring. She retrieved her cell phone and reluctantly answered the call.

"This is Elle," she said, pressing the phone to her ear.

"Elle, listen, it's Rob. We're having a little trouble down at the studio. Any chance you can come down and help us out?"

Elle resisted the urge to roll her eyes. Rob was a terrible liar. Between the cracking and hesitation lingering in his voice, all signs pointed to some sort of surprise birthday celebration at the studio. Which was nice. Really nice, actually.

But she didn't want to be around anyone. She wanted to waste away in her own disconnected memories, which had become a tradition over the years. Elle listened to the Beatles' *Revolver* album while wallowing in her memories of Troy—the years they'd spent together both as friends and lovers. Over and over again, she replayed the sweet moments as well as the ones that brought nothing but sadness and regret. Despite the pain, it was comforting somehow—as if her memories, and the songs that played in the background, kept them connected. She was listening to the album for a second time when Rob's call came through.

Elle decided to push the issue, to see how far she could take it.

"Um . . . I'm already in my comfies. Any chance we can do this in the morning?"

Rob paused, and then the connection grew muffled. Elle smiled, knowing he'd covered the phone to talk to another conspirator.

"Just get over here," another voice chimed in, this one feminine, yet snippy . . . and all too familiar. Whitney.

"I knew it," Elle said, shaking her head, petting Linus as he rubbed up against her leg, and hoping Whitney wouldn't recognize the album in the background. *Revolver*, although it was her favorite album, was the album that made her think the most of Troy. "You *know* I don't like to make a big deal out of this."

Whitney sighed. "I know, and it isn't, I promise. Just get down here."

"Fine, give me twenty."

"I'll do you one better. Take thirty."

"Wow, feeling generous?" Elle said, placing her pumps, one by one, back onto her tired feet.

"Nah. Waiting on the food delivery."

"I already ate," Elle whined.

"Tough." Whitney snapped, "And run a comb through your hair."

"I resent that," Elle responded, catching a glimpse of herself in the mirror. She did look disheveled after a long day at the studio. Her normally curly blonde locks were flat to the sides of her face. She grimaced, gazing at her reflection. "But whatever, fine, I'll be there in a half hour."

· · · · ·

Elle loved the way her hair felt when it blew through the tranquil California breeze. The crisp scent of the ocean enveloped her in its serenity. Her left elbow rested on the leather interior of her brand-new convertible.

She'd once owned a convertible back in Chicago, where she had spent the majority of her life. In fact, Troy had encouraged her to buy that first convertible. They'd dated for a year in college after meeting and becoming friends in ninth grade. Attached to one another's sides for most of their teen years, despite the fact that they bickered more than the average friends, they'd spent a few summers driving in Elle's bright red Sebring, the top down, the Chicago wind destroying Elle's hair no matter how she tried to avoid it.

When she first moved to Santa Monica, she'd refused to purchase anything that reminded her of him—including a vehicle in which they'd made so many memories. But when *Follow the Sun* was nominated for its first Emmys, and the producers renewed it for three more seasons, Elle was feeling unstoppable and she managed to forget about him briefly to purchase a brand-new silver Mercedes E-Class convertible.

Each time she slid into the warm leather seat, Elle ran her fingers up and down the cool steering wheel, and a small contented sigh left her lips. She was living the dream.

The twenty-five-minute drive to the studio in Los Angeles was easy and uneventful. When she reached the peach-colored booth at the entrance of the studio, Larry the attendant raised an inquisitive, yet playful, brow.

"Didn't think I'd be seeing you again tonight."

"I guess I'm needed." Elle shrugged.

"Have a piece of cake for me," Larry replied, giving her a wink. His tan skin, worn and aged like leather, pulled at his cheeks with his smile. In contrast, his silver hair glistened from the top of his head.

"You too?" Elle asked, not completely surprised by the reach of Whitney's sneaky planning.

"Afraid so." Larry chuckled.

"I'll bring you a slice on my way out. How's that?"

Larry laughed again, raised the gate, and nodded. "Sounds great. Enjoy yourself, Ms. Riley."

Whitney was waiting for Elle at her designated parking space. Her chocolate-brown curls were pulled up in a loose ponytail. Her nose was scrunched and her arms were crossed in front of her chest.

Elle was confused by her attitude. "What? Am I late?" She glanced at her watch.

"C'mon, let's go. Everyone's waiting." Whitney opened the car door, allowing Elle to step out of the vehicle.

"Seriously, what's the matter?" Elle was distracted by Whitney's mood and couldn't concentrate on the party until she knew her friend was all right.

"It's nothing, I just—I hate that we have to trick you."

"You mean about my birthday?"

"Yes," Whitney snapped, slamming the door shut. "You're thirty-five today. Thirty-freaking-five! You deserve a celebration and I wish you'd stop convincing yourself that you don't."

Elle nodded. She understood where Whitney was coming from. "Sorry." Her shoulders sank. "Old habits die hard, I guess."

"Well, I, for one, am officially tired of it. I want you to *live* your life, Elle, not tiptoe through it."

Uncomfortable with the frankness of the discussion, as she often was, Elle pressed two fingers into a salute, attempting to defuse the situation. "Sir, yes sir."

Whitney's pale cheeks turned red and Elle knew her best friend was ready to blow at any second. Whitney loved her and wanted her to be happy. She didn't want to piss Elle off when there were at least twenty people upstairs waiting to celebrate the day she was born.

"Seriously, I'm sorry. I know you're right. And I'm working on it, I promise."

Whitney's arms uncrossed, and she took a deep breath. "Okay, good."

"Are we okay?"

"Yes, of course." Whitney linked her arm through Elle's. "We're always okay."

"Good. Because I am seriously in the mood for some cake."

"That's coming, but there's a surprise first."

"What is it?" Elle dug a finger into Whitney's side.

"You'll see."

When they reached the large conference room, Elle was pleasantly surprised. No lights were turned off, no one hunched behind countertops and tables. Her cast and crew were mingling throughout the room, cocktails and plates in hand.

"Hey, happy birthday," Rob said, wrapping one arm around Elle's shoulder. "Did we get ya?"

Elle glanced at Whitney, raising one eyebrow. Whitney closed her eyes, puckered her lips, and nodded.

"You sure did," Elle said, playing along.

Rob's smile widened and his chest broadened. Elle couldn't believe he actually thought she'd been duped. Did he not remember the phone call that took place less than an hour earlier?

Elle turned back to Whitney. "So you mentioned a surprise . . ." Her words trailed off, as she hoped Whitney would end the suspense.

Whitney guided Elle to a long table across the room. Elle thought she smelled marinara sauce. "Ah, yes, well, we have Gina to thank for that."

"Gina?"

"She told me about this hole-in-the-wall restaurant ten minutes from here, and they specialize in . . ." Whitney stepped to the side, revealing the most delectable table of food Elle had ever seen.

"Chicago-style pizza?" Elle squealed, eyes wide. "Here in Los Angeles? How do *I* not know about this place?"

"Because it's a dump," Gina said, jumping into the conversation. "But it's the real deal. It's just as good as anything I've had in Chicago."

Gina Romano had fully embraced her life and stardom in Los Angeles. Most people didn't know she was a Midwestern girl just like Elle. She was raised in Milwaukee, but dropped out of high school to pursue a career in acting. After several cosmetics commercials, and two failed pilots, she'd been cast as the female lead in *Follow the Sun*. Since rising to stardom, she'd gone out of her way to distance herself from her Wisconsin upbringing, even hiring a dialect coach to assist her in abandoning her persistent Milwaukee accent.

"Here, let me get you a piece. Sausage and mushroom, right?" Whitney grinned, retrieving a spatula from the table and pushing into the steaming pie covered in thick tomato sauce. The spatula cut through layers of cheese and toppings until it made contact with the thick crust. Elle's mouth began to water.

"My favorite," she said as Whitney placed the dish in her hand before grabbing two glasses of red wine.

"Come, let's sit."

Elle cut into the hefty slice, steam spilling from the thick layers of mozzarella. She blew on the generous bite before placing it in her mouth. Her eyes closed as she took in the flavors. The flavors of home.

"This," she said, licking her pink lips. "This was worth changing out of my yoga pants for."

Whitney lit up, her smile genuine and proud. "I knew it would be." She raised her glass. "To you, my friend. Happy birthday. I'm blessed to know you." She glanced around the room, bustling with actors, cameramen, and makeup artists. "We all are."

Elle placed her hand on Whitney's wrist, her eyes misting. She pushed her blonde hair behind her ear and locked eyes with her best friend. "Thank you. Seriously, thank you." She took another hearty bite, pushing away all the feelings of sadness that had gripped her heart earlier that evening. "And I seriously need the name of this place. This is freaking delicious."

The ladies clinked their glasses together as Elle pondered all the ways in which she would change her attitude to improve her life. She was finished clinging to her past like she had planned to do that night. She was thirty-five now. It was time for her to enjoy the blessings of her life and she vowed to begin the very next day.

Chapter 2

You *what?*" Elle shrieked, rising to her feet. One of her fists crashed into her coffee cup, and it plummeted to the floor. The ceramic cracked into several pieces and the piping-hot beverage spewed onto her floral office rug.

Her assistant, Nicole, flung her notepad and pen into the air and sprinted out the door. Elle and Rob watched as she flew from the room.

"What the hell?" Rob mumbled under his breath, his mouth hanging open as he stared at the open door.

"Focus, Rob," Elle snapped before glaring at Nolan Rivera, who sat in her office chair, avoiding eye contact. His tan cheeks were turning a dark shade of crimson as his fingers tapped against the arm of his chair. "Nolan, what on earth—"

"Unfortunately, Nolan simply has too many offers on the table," Shane Crawley, Nolan's agent, interrupted, instead of allowing Nolan to speak for himself and defend his bombshell of a decision.

Nolan was leaving the show, and there was nothing Elle could do to stop it. Hollywood was a machine—one that was constantly changing, evolving, and screwing over television writers like herself.

"What kind of offers?"

"Film mostly." Shane crossed his arms in front of his chest. He was a portly man with more hair on his arms than the top of his head. His smug demeanor sent Elle's anger through the roof. She ignored him, turning her attention back to Nolan, who was watching her from the corner of his eye.

"I don't understand. You're a *star*. This show *gave* you a name."

"I'm sorry." He shrugged, pursing his lips together. "It's time for me to move on."

"That was a scripted answer. Just be honest with me."

"My *client* owes you no explanation. His contract is up this spring and he's choosing to explore other opportunities. End of story."

Elle looked to Rob for support. When he offered a meager shrug, Elle was instantly irritated that he didn't seem nearly as shaken up by this as she was. He was the director of the show—he should have been incensed!

Elle plopped back into her leather chair, her breathing ragged as she struggled to calm down. Nicole whirled back into the room, rolls of paper towels in her lanky, tan arms. She threw herself to the carpet and covered the coffee with towels.

"Sorry I took so long," she whispered.

"It's fine, don't worry," Elle responded, holding her hand to her chest, her eyes pressed tight as she struggled to focus. "Well, gentlemen, I guess we're done here." Elle stood, walked to the door, and opened it, ready to usher Nolan and his agent out of her office. Her gesture was received loud and clear. Nolan and Shane said their good-byes and left the office. Just before closing the door, Nolan peeked back inside.

"I really am sorry, Elle."

"Just go." She knew his apology was genuine, but it was impossible for her not to take his departure personally. This show was her baby, her creation, and he was threatening its success.

"So what do we do?" Elle asked Rob. The idea of Nolan Rivera leaving *Follow the Sun* made Elle's skin sweat, her heart race, and her mind swirl. The fourth season was set to start filming in just a few short weeks.

Panic.

Total and utter panic.

"He's obligated to stay until the end of the season. Then, we'll just write him off," Rob said.

"He's the *main* character," Elle snapped, glaring at Rob. Did he not realize that losing the male lead would completely destroy the storyline?

Rob rose from his chair and walked to Elle's desk, easing his bottom onto the corner of the mahogany wood. He crossed his arms in front of his thin chest and crossed one leg over the other, leaning in toward Elle. She was used to this routine. He'd perch on her desk and act like a wise sage, guiding her to a resolution, then convince her she'd come up with it all on her own. He meant well, but sometimes, Elle just wanted him to be real with her—have a frank conversation, not a politically correct one from a Hollywood script.

"If anyone can fix this, it's you."

Yep, right on cue.

Elle inhaled and exhaled deeply, forcing the panic from her chest and out through her mouth. "So I have to change the story? That's what you're telling me, right?"

"We have time to bring someone else in . . . let the audience get used to him . . ." His voice trailed off, allowing Elle to process his suggestion. And she did.

"A love triangle," she murmured, her mind racing. She did her best thinking when she tuned out the world around her.

"Brilliant," Rob stated and rose to his feet. "I knew you'd figure it out."

Elle rolled her eyes, knowing Rob had planted the seed. They both knew it.

She searched her brain for another character from her books, but no one came to mind.

The novels and television series were all set in Las Vegas. The two main characters, Desmond and Molly, worked for a hotel and casino—both striving to replace the owner when he retired. The two bickered, argued, and sabotaged one another to impress the boss. Hijinks ensued and their chemistry was undeniable. The couple dated, broke up, tried to be friends, dated again, etc. The characters *belonged* together. And everyone could see it but them.

There were twists and turns, of course. Side characters tempted the two leads and increased the drama. But in her novels, the two had never cheated while together, and neither had ever walked away completely. And part of her felt that was the appeal of the novels. People wanted to believe in soul mates, in true love, in forever. So how the hell would she maintain that appeal if she had to replace the male lead?

"Can we recast him?" Elle said, deliberately veering off course from her original idea.

Rob sighed, and she knew he was disappointed in her sudden change of heart. "The network won't allow it. It's in their contracts. Nolan and Gina are the only two who can portray Desmond and Molly."

"Ughhh." Elle pushed back in her chair, which teetered up and down, up and down.

"But that love triangle thing. That could work."

Of course it could work. But it would deviate from the story Elle

17

had written. It would no longer be a variation on *their* story. Then again, maybe that was exactly what she *and* the show needed.

A fresh start.

Elle stood, walked around Nicole, who was still blotting the already ruined rug, and began to pace. As the ideas built within her brain, the office seemed to grow bigger, allowing her the space to brainstorm, to create a character out of thin air.

"There was this one character—"

Her thoughts were interrupted by a harsh knock at the door. Whitney peeked her head in before Elle could respond. Her cheeks were flushed. She knew.

"I just heard." Whitney walked to Elle's side and wrapped one arm around her friend's waist. "We'll figure this out."

"Elle was doing just that," Rob interrupted. Elle glared at him. Didn't he realize by now she didn't want, or need, her ass to be kissed on a regular basis? She was just a writer from the Midwest— despite her new Hollywood name and image, she was just a normal person who appreciated honesty and authenticity—two things Rob lacked. He was way too Hollywood for Elle to handle sometimes.

"*We* were figuring it out, yes," she corrected him.

"What can I do?" asked Whitney, a look of worry painted on her face. Her cinnamon eyes narrowed, her cheeks still flaring with heat, and sweat forming on her brow. Elle knew Whitney had run from her office downstairs.

Elle took another deep breath before placing her hands on her hips and summoning all the confidence she could muster. "Find me the hottest actor you can. One who can act circles around Nolan."

Whitney drew back in surprise. She crossed her arms in front of her, but the corner of her mouth perked up into a slight smile. "I love when you talk dirty to me."

"I'm serious. I'll create the character—you get me the actor."

"On it." Whitney nodded. "One condition."

"What's that?"

"You attend the auditions." Whitney knew full well Elle never missed an audition. Aside from the extras who were chosen for brief moments on screen, Whitney and Elle had always agreed on every actor who was cast in *Follow the Sun*.

"You got it." Elle smiled. "We're going to have the biggest love triangle this network has ever seen."

• • • • •

Thumbing through the head shots of the actors who'd auditioned that week, Elle wasn't convinced any of them could portray the new character of David. They were all attractive, that she could admit. She'd seen a few of them in commercials and sitcoms. But none of them were speaking to her as David, and none of them were good enough to read with Gina. Only the best of the best would reach that stage, and at this point none of them would. Not one had the appeal of someone like Nolan. He was difficult to top.

After seeing dozens of men that week, she'd been hopeful that morning.

Today's the day, she'd said to herself. But the morning proved to be a bust.

The first actor of the day was gorgeous—seriously attractive. But when he read with Elle, his delivery was flat, seriously lacking any type of charisma. Elle and Whitney had shared a glance of agreement. He would need an acting coach to make himself convincing as David, and even then Elle was hesitant.

The next guy was average looking—attractive in all the typical ways, but nothing head-turning—nothing that made him stand out from any of the other secondary characters on the show. His delivery was fine. His voice was fine and his demeanor was (once again) fine. He wasn't a definite "no," but they would need to consult the makeup department to spruce up his overall appearance and he'd need several coaching sessions to improve his delivery. Elle didn't want fine, she wanted fantastic.

By the time they'd tested seven more actors that day, they were feeling defeated. Elle didn't want to settle and she knew Whitney was in complete agreement. They needed to find the perfect combination of devastatingly handsome and ridiculously talented. And if that meant they needed to see dozens more candidates, then that was fine. It was worth it to find the perfect fit.

When actor number seven left the room, Whitney followed him out to check in with her secretary. Actors were notorious for jumping in on auditions at the last minute and they were willing to stay late if needed.

"Add one more to the pile," Whitney said after returning to the room, handing a head shot to Elle. "He'll be here in a few."

Elle's breath caught as she looked at the eight-by-ten head shot of Luke Kingston. He was handsome, appealing, sexy. Wavy hair, square jaw, a perfectly shaped nose. His smug grin made adrenaline spike in her abdomen.

He was perfect.

But could he act?

Elle attempted to play it cool. "What has he done?" She flipped the shot, revealing the actor's resume filled with commercials and a handful of pilots that had never aired. It was severely lacking compared to the other actors on the docket.

"Not much," Whitney answered. "But there's something about him, don't you think?"

Elle flipped the resume over to stare, once again, at the strikingly handsome actor. "Yeah. Something."

"Well, he's on his way now. So we'll see if he has that 'something' in person."

"God, I hope so. The others have been so lackluster."

"Yeah." Whitney bit on the edge of her pen. "Let's hope Mr. Gorgeous can act."

Elle let put a chuckle while secretly hoping Mr. Gorgeous could, in fact, knock their socks off. No matter how handsome he might be, there was no way she'd hire him if his delivery was wooden or forced. The charisma he emanated in the photo needed to translate in his acting. There would be no compromise, as far as she was concerned.

A man cleared his throat and Elle turned her attention to the now-open door. "Excuse me, ladies. I'm here to audition for the role of David McKenzie."

Elle swallowed hard, taking in the sensation of his voice: deep, soothing, smooth. She felt her cheeks warm as Whitney responded, urging him into the room.

"Yes, do you need a minute to prepare?"

Luke closed the door behind him and walked to the table where Elle and Whitney sat. He placed another head shot on the table before his lips pulled to one side. "No, I'm ready. I practiced all the way here."

Whitney stood and extended her hand. "I'm Whitney Bartolina, casting director."

Luke shook her hand. "Pleasure."

Elle rose to her feet. "Nice to meet you, I'm—"

"Elle Riley, creator of the show," Luke interrupted, meeting her eyes. "I know who you are."

Elle felt her cheeks redden. Of course she knew he'd obviously done his research on the show. After all, her picture was on the network's website; she'd walked the red carpet. She wasn't exactly a household name, but many in the industry knew who she was.

Her brain knew her body should resist reacting to the actor's gesture. But she couldn't contain the excitement that stirred deep in her abdomen. Luke extended his hand to Elle and she reciprocated the gesture. But unlike his simple handshake with Whitney, he placed his left hand over hers as they moved their hands slowly up and down.

Luke shook his head. "Such a pleasure to meet you, you have no idea."

"Thank you."

Reluctantly, she pulled her hand away and returned to her seat. She avoided Whitney's eyes, knowing her friend would see right through her act of normalcy. She was attracted to an actor . . . in the middle of an audition. She'd never hear the end of it.

"Elle will read through the scene with you."

"Great."

Luke stood a few feet from the table, ran his fingers through his wavy brown hair, and took a deep breath. And for just a brief moment, his nerves were obvious to Elle. He took one last glance at the script, then directed his gaze at her. Elle was startled by the color of his eyes. The black-and-white head shot didn't do them justice. They were blue, bright sky blue. She wondered if they were real or colored contacts. It wouldn't be the first time an actor had covered up his own eyes for dazzling baby blues.

"Now, keep in mind, this role is still in the creative stages. But David is the head of security for the hotel. He's tough, obviously, but he's also smart. Smart in a way Molly doesn't expect. This character is going to surprise her at every turn."

"Got it." Luke's confidence had returned. He stood up tall, a cocky grin on his face, dimples appearing on his cheeks. "I'm ready."

As Elle and Luke read through the scene, it was clear to her they'd found the man for the part. He was sexy, charismatic, and his delivery of David's lines was effortless.

"Thank you, Luke. We'll be in touch." Elle maintained her poker face, despite the sizzling nerves beneath her skin.

"It was an honor, ladies. Thank you." Luke flashed Elle and Whitney a dazzling smile layered with confidence before shaking their hands. Just before his hand grasped the doorknob, he turned back to Elle and smiled one last time. It was a sweet and soft smile, a seemingly genuine expression from the handsome actor. Butterflies swarmed her belly.

"I think we found our David."

Elle stared at the closed door before finally finding her voice. "Yep." She cleared her throat, and forced her eyes away. "We'll need to do a read-through with Gina, just to make sure there's chemistry."

"True. But Gina has chemistry with everyone." Whitney laughed. When Elle didn't join in, Whitney continued. "Are you okay?"

"Are you kidding, I'm thrilled." Elle sorted the papers, tapping them gently on the desk, still avoiding the eyes of her friend.

"Liar. What's going on?"

Elle was silent.

"Oh my God, you like him."

Still, Elle was silent.

"Well, *this* should be interesting."

"Shut up." Elle nudged Whitney with her elbow. "He's just . . . sexy as hell. Don't you think? I mean, those eyes . . ."

Whitney nodded, making a face as if to say "duh."

"Maybe we should keep looking, I mean—"

"No way." Whitney huffed. "He's the right man for the role. Period."

"You're right."

"Besides, there is no rule about sleeping with the cast. We're all adults. Hell, I slept with Nolan three months ago."

Elle turned to Whitney, her mouth agape. "What? How could you not tell me?"

Whitney shrugged. "It was no big deal. We'd had a bit too much to drink. We started going at it at the wrap party. I really thought you saw us."

"No, I left early." Elle's eyes widened in realization of the series of events that had taken place over the last couple of months, all culminating in the need to hire a new male lead. "Oh my God, Whit. Is that why he's leaving?"

"Don't be silly, of course not. He's going to be a movie star, remember?"

Elle wasn't convinced. "I still can't believe you didn't tell me."

"It was a one-night thing. No big deal. Besides, he and I are fine. We're still friends."

"Interesting," Elle said, pondering her friend's revelation. She didn't believe in mixing business with pleasure. And she knew it was best if she got her hormones under control when in Luke's presence. Her show, her baby, her career was at stake. Not only did she have to make her audience fall in love with the character of David McKenzie, she had to make him lovable enough that they abandoned the character of Desmond. She wasn't convinced she could pull it off, and if she got involved with the new character, she'd only muddle the waters even more.

She would write his lines, create his character. He would make David come to life on the small screen.

And that was it.

Anything more would only lead to trouble.

And Elle Riley didn't do trouble.

Chapter 3

When Elle arrived at the studio gate the following morning, she was astonished to see a crowd of photographers swarming the booth.

"What the hell?" she murmured, pulling the car over. She quickly dialed Whitney, who answered on the first ring.

"It's TMZ, someone leaked it." Her voice was flat. She didn't seem at all surprised. She'd been in the business much longer than Elle and, for the most part, was better at handling the curveballs Hollywood often threw their way. Elle, not so much.

"About Nolan? Seriously? It's been less than twenty-four hours, for God's sake!" Her arm leaned against the door as her hand cradled her forehead in defeat. "What should I do, Whit?"

"Don't let the bloodsuckers get to you. Ignore them and eventually they'll go away." She paused. "Eventually."

Elle ignored Whitney's calm instructions, focusing on the questions swirling in her brain. "Do you think his people leaked it?"

Without hesitation, Whitney answered. "You bet I do."

Elle sighed, throwing her head back to crash against the headrest. "When is this going to get easier?"

"For you? Maybe never." Elle thought she heard a chuckle.

"Not funny."

"Sorry, but seriously, you have to let these things roll. It's all part of it. Listen, this should cheer you up—I just spoke with Luke's agent. He's coming by this afternoon to read with Gina."

Just the mention of his name made Elle's nerves stand at attention. Within seconds, she was no longer concerned about the huddled mass of photographers blocking the gate. Instead, she was listening to the hum of her body, the buzzing in her brain. She knew she'd have to get herself under control, but his presence did something to her—the very thought of him was exhilarating. She couldn't wait to watch him read with Gina, watch his masculine jaw move as he delivered his lines. Yesterday, she'd read with him and was too nervous to watch him—afraid she'd lose her place in the script and look like a fool. This time, she could lean back in her chair and admire the man who affected her in a way no one had since she'd relocated to California.

"Elle? Elle?"

Her hand jumped to cover her mouth. She'd spaced out and forgotten Whitney was still on the phone with her. What in the world was happening to her? She was acting like a teenager—and a foolish one at that. She was Elle Riley, known for her professionalism and steady hand. She had to snap out of it.

But those eyes . . .

"I'm here, sorry, I dropped the phone."

"Fine, whatever, just . . . get through the gate and get in here. Rob wants to meet with you."

"Why?"

"Oh, I don't know—maybe something about needing an entire season of scripts that now include a new character and new story-line?"

"Oh, *that*. Okay, I'll be in in five."

Slowly, Elle pulled up to the studio booth, doing her best not to flinch at the blinding camera flashes or her name being shouted.

"Elle, can we talk to you?"

"Elle, are the rumors true? Is Nolan no longer under contract?"

"Elle, can we get a statement? Can we get a picture?"

It annoyed her that every single shout began with her name, as if she and the gossip-hounds were on some sort of intimate basis. Where she came from, calling someone by his or her first name was something you earned—a friendly form of intimacy. She had a lot to adjust to in this new land of gossip magazines, starlets, and celebrity.

Larry waved her in, opening the gate so she didn't have to open her window. She could hear the photographers yelling louder as her car pulled into the lot and away from the mania. Once she was out of sight, her pulse returned to its normal rate and she was able to breathe easy. For the time being.

• • • • •

"Okay, let's be realistic here. We need to film the first twelve epi-sodes before we go on hiatus. How many have you already written for this season?"

"Six, but we have to rewrite almost all of them to include Luke."

"Not necessarily." Rob stood and paced the length of his office. There was no desk-perching today. His shaky arms and fidgeting hands gave away his nerves. He was just as concerned as Elle. "You could write him in on episode seven. That leaves sixteen more epi-sodes to develop the love triangle."

"I'm not sure that's enough—"

"Sure it is. If we start building it too soon, viewers will complain. They'll say it's dragging. This way, if you introduce him midway through the fall season, you can leave them hanging right before hiatus."

Elle took a moment to process Rob's idea—she had to give Rob credit, he was a problem-solver, and a hell of a brainstormer. Despite his Hollywood attitude, he had bailed her out of several situations already during her short career. He was a seasoned television director who'd worked on two other television dramas before *Follow the Sun* and his track record was stellar.

"Okay—but we need to establish some sort of cracks in Desmond and Molly's relationship. They're on-again in the season opener . . . we have to make it believable."

"Of course, make additions, changes, whatever. Just don't rewrite. Luke will join the cast in episode seven." Elle appreciated Rob's no-nonsense discussion. It was a breath of fresh air compared to the wise sage she'd dealt with the day before.

"Got it, chief," she joked. Rob's face contorted in confusion and Elle worried she'd made him self-conscious about his approach. "Seriously, though, thank you. You're going to save me a *lot* of time."

"Reinventing the wheel never benefitted anyone. We'll make this work, and I have a feeling it'll be just what the show needs."

Elle nodded. "I hope you're right."

Closing the door behind her, Elle said hello to Rob's secretary and continued toward the open hallway lined with framed posters of the cast. She had a few hours to work on developing episode seven before the read-through that afternoon with Gina and Luke. She could only hope to make some progress so both she and Rob could relax. She hadn't yet spoken to Nolan since the news broke. Whitney had urged her to let some time pass first. This show was so important to her, it was impossible to separate business from personal. His decision to leave the show bruised not only her fragile ego, but it placed a very large damper on her confidence in future seasons. Was Gina next? Would *Follow the Sun* become a rotating cast? It was difficult to predict if his departure would have a ripple effect, or if the pebble would just land in the pond, sinking quietly to the bottom.

When she rounded the corner to the hallway leading to her office, she was greeted by an unexpected face. An unexpected handsome face with a relaxed smile, and bright, friendly, sexy eyes.

Luke.

"Hey." Luke ran his fingers through his hair and Elle wondered what it would be like to do that. To stroke his wavy locks while lying in bed together, completely naked after an intense lovemaking session.

"Uh, hey, I mean, hi. Hi." Elle stumbled over her words and was instantly mortified. She had to get herself in check or he would suspect she was developing a crush. She was his boss; she had to act like it.

Luke ran his tongue slowly across his bottom lip as he inspected her face, and she felt naked, exposed, as if he could read her thoughts. As if he could see them splayed on her bed, covers and sheets falling toward the cool floor. Both naked. Both flushed and sated from their activities in the bedroom. The bedroom in her brain.

As much as she wanted to deny it, this man did things to her. When she was around him, every cell of her body awoke from a deep sleep. And she liked that feeling; she missed it. In fact, every time she was near Luke, she craved that feeling of being startled awake—of adrenaline coursing through every nerve of her body.

Luke placed one lazy hand on his hip, just below the worn leather belt that fit snugly around his waist. "I know I'm a little early. Thought you might let me take you to lunch."

Elle glanced at her watch. It was barely nine a.m. When her eyes reconnected with his, she noticed his tan cheeks turn the slightest shade of red. He shrugged and chuckled as he corrected himself. "Or breakfast."

"I'd love that, really I would, but . . ." She looked around for someone or something to guide her stammering thoughts. "I have so much to do. I have to add you, I mean, David, into the script for episode seven, and I have some backstory to create. I'm just swamped at the moment. You understand, right?"

Why was she turning this gorgeous man away? She had no idea.

"Rain check, then?" Luke persisted, his eyebrows raised, making his eyes appear vulnerable, almost needy. Elle felt her resolve weakening as he stepped closer to her, invading her personal space. Normally, that would've bothered her. But when Luke's arm brushed gently against hers, Elle was intoxicated rather than uncomfortable. She wanted more.

"Yes, of course." Elle's expression softened as she leaned in closer. "I'd like that."

Luke looked appeased, calm. He must have understood she wasn't closing that door completely. His fingers grazed her forearm and his eyes locked with hers as a satisfied smile crossed his face. Elle felt naked, exposed, as if Luke could read her mind, see the fantasies brewing in her head. "Good."

Elle's skin tingled at his touch. "But I'll, um, I'll see you at the read-through."

"Yes, I'll get to meet the famous Gina Romano." His fingers remained on her skin, moving slowly back and forth along her arm, which was covered in goose bumps. Elle resisted the urge to move away from his touch. It seemed brazen and inappropriate, but she didn't want him to stop. So she swallowed hard, doing her best to ignore the dry, cotton-like feel of her throat. "She's not so bad. I'm sure you'll like her."

"So far, I've been nothing but impressed." Luke narrowed his eyes, his fingers slowly moving to grip Elle's forearm ever so slightly. His message was clear. With that simple gesture, it was obvious to Elle he was just as drawn to her as she was to him.

How they would handle their attraction was another story. For that, Elle had no answers—only more questions. Questions she couldn't allow herself to entertain. She had a storyline to develop, a character to create, and a show to save.

Her attraction to Luke Kingston would have to wait.

At least for a day or two.

Chapter 4

Never had Elle been so turned on, yet so annoyed in all of her adult years. She watched as Gina and Luke read through the lines of a scene she'd written for David.

"David, what are you doing here?" Gina flipped her jet-black tresses behind her shoulder and toyed with the buttons of her silk top as she delivered her lines. Elle cringed, knowing Gina had quite an effect on nearly every man she met. She didn't want Luke to succumb to Gina's charms, but the show runner in her was impressed with Gina's obvious acting skills. She could only hope Gina wasn't actually interested in Luke.

Luke's gaze darted to Gina's more than ample chest and Elle's heart rate increased. "I can't stay long," the actor recited. "I'm needed back at the casino." Luke smiled at Gina and instantly Elle was pissed off.

Their chemistry permeated the room. This was a *good* thing, she attempted to remind herself. It was powerful for the show.

Their obvious attraction amped up the scene and she knew it would work. Audiences would buy it. They'd root for David and eventually accept Desmond's departure. Luke and Gina would be the new faces of *Follow the Sun*. She saw everything brimming inside her head: success, high Nielsen ratings, bragging rights, possible awards. She saw it all. But she also saw the undeniable spark between the two actors, and it manifested itself in a rush of adrenaline in her gut.

She couldn't take it anymore. She had to end the reading. "That's great, thanks. I think we have all we need."

Luke nodded, shook Gina's hand, and paused briefly to look back at Elle. Heat filled her cheeks as his lips turned into a half smile, before he left the room. She didn't want him to go, but she knew it was necessary in order for her to regain her composure.

"Well, isn't he a hottie?" Gina said, winking at Elle. Elle pursed her lips and nodded, dismissing the actress from the room.

Elle nodded to Whitney, giving her the all clear to finalize Luke's offer of a contract.

"You okay?" Whitney tilted her head. "You seem out of sorts."

"I am."

"Wanna talk about it?"

"Not really."

"Is it Mr. Gorgeous?"

Elle smiled begrudgingly. "Maybe. I hate that I barely know him and I'm already feeling like this. It's why I avoid getting involved! I feel unglued already and we just met."

"Don't self-sabotage, Elle. I can tell you want to. You get this look in your eye."

Whitney was right. Since arriving in California, Elle had sabotaged every relationship she'd begun. Every last one. As much as she tried to decipher her patterns, and as much as she allowed Whitney to psychoanalyze her, she didn't know why she did it. She didn't know why she was this way. But if she was being honest, none of the men she'd dated since moving to California had made adrenaline course through her veins the way Luke did. It was why her self-saboteur status was in full effect.

"I can't make any promises."

"I mean it. You like him—don't cut it off before it even begins. You can't control everything in life—you can't keep yourself from getting attached, from getting hurt. That's just life."

"It's better for the show if I avoid an affair with one of my actors, Whit. This has the potential to get extremely messy and you *know* it."

"Whatever. You've spent years worrying about the show. The show is just fine. What about you? When will you start taking care of Elle?"

"Someday." She offered a weak smile.

She retreated to her office, telling her friend she was swamped with scriptwriting. Everyone knew she was on a time crunch as filming began the following week. She'd managed to alter the first six episodes, and had completed episode seven, but she had over a dozen yet to complete. She had a team of writers to assist her, but being the perfectionist she was, she wasn't ready to give them control when it came to the addition of David's character. Rob had bristled at her possessive outlook on the season, but backed off eventually when Elle promised to step back slightly after episode ten, allowing the other writers to contribute to the storyline.

When she reached her office, she was surprised to see Luke waiting in a chair, studying his cell phone. He rose to his feet as she approached, his cocky smile returning to his square jaw. Aside from his flushed cheeks, his overall demeanor screamed of confidence—his broad shoulders, the one hand resting on his hip as he pushed the phone into his back pocket, and the way he stared at her as if she were a delectable dish he was dying to consume.

"Can I help you?" She didn't mean to sound brusque, but she was starting to wonder if this was all a game—a game meant to mess with her head.

"I need to talk to you," he said, closing the gap between them. She could smell his scent—woodsy and light, nothing too harsh. She liked that natural smell and was relieved he wasn't one of those actors who covered themselves in the latest trendy scent. Luke leaned in, his nose tickling the skin of her ear. She shuddered.

"In private," he whispered.

Elle turned to close the door. When it clicked shut, she pushed him against the cold wood, her finger pressed to his chest. She watched as he glanced down at her hand pressed against the button of his shirt. An uneven smile formed on his face.

"What are you doing?" she said. "Are you trying to make trouble?"

"I don't understand—"

She narrowed her eyes and peered into his unapologetic stare. "Yes, you do."

"According to my agent, this is perfectly acceptable. We're adults."

"Right," she scoffed. "Is this a ploy? Because if it is, you don't need to worry about that. Whitney's already giving them the go-ahead, they're drawing up your contract now. You don't need to do this just to get the job."

His hand squeezed hers tightly as his head moved slowly from side to side. "Not a ploy."

"And I'm supposed to believe this why?" Elle tipped her chin toward Luke, but beneath it, her heart was racing so fast, she felt weak.

"I haven't been able to stop thinking about you—not since we met last week."

Elle rolled her eyes. "Hardly."

When Luke responded with a look of confusion, Elle continued. "I'm not blind. I saw the way you looked at Gina." Her voice was faltering beneath her words. She sounded weak, attached . . . everything she didn't want to appear to Luke Kingston.

"She is pretty cute . . ." He shrugged before taking her hand in his and lowering it to rest on her hip. "But she's not who I want."

Elle released her hand from his grip, crossing her arms in front of her chest. Silence hung in the air.

"I loved reading with her, I'm not gonna lie about that. But you're the one I think about. Yours is the face that keeps me up at night."

Still, Elle remained silent, not sure what to say.

"And what happens when this," she said, motioning between their two bodies, "doesn't work out? Your contract won't be up for two seasons. We'll be spending a lot of time together, Luke. *Think this through*."

Elle didn't do awkward. She didn't want to avoid a member of her cast, let alone have to resist the urge to kill off his character. There would be table reads, and hundreds of takes during production. She needed to keep her work environment a safe one—one without conflict. Why couldn't he understand that?

"One date." He stepped closer, running his hand down her cheek. She closed her eyes, enjoying the sensation of his soft hands and forgetting all about the work environment that seemed to matter so much only seconds earlier.

"One night, you mean," she replied, feeling she had nothing to lose. She was ready to lay her cards out on the table. If Luke was looking for a one-night stand, he'd need to look somewhere else.

"If that's what *you* choose," he corrected her. "But I'm not looking for that."

"Neither am I." It was the truth. It'd been quite some time since Elle had been in a romantic relationship, but she knew herself well. She was the type who grew attached. Casual flings were not her thing.

Luke took one more step toward Elle. Her breath caught as she awaited his next move. Leaning in, his lips brushed against hers, not in a kiss, but in a teasing motion, stirring something within her. Back and then forth, he moved his lips ever so slightly to tickle hers. Her chest rose and fell with each second. She longed for him to stop teasing her. Luke moved his feathery touches to her jaw and then to her neck, never kissing her, only touching her just enough to send shivers down her spine.

"Give me a chance, Elle. I'm not that guy, seriously."

Despite the nagging feeling that this was, in fact, a mistake, Elle closed her eyes and whispered her answer, "One date."

Luke stood tall and ran his fingers through his hair. "That's all I'm asking for. Tonight?"

"What time?"

"Whenever you're free."

"You're certainly making this easy."

"I can't help it." He wrapped his arm around her waist, pulling her close, their chests pressed to one another. "This is what you do to me."

"Seven o'clock?" Elle asked, avoiding the intimacy of their embrace as her heart pumped furiously inside her body.

"Perfect. There's this wonderful restaurant . . . Angelini Osteria. Have you been?"

"I think so."

"Great. I'll pick you up."

Elle scrunched her lips together before responding. "Actually, I'll meet you there."

Luke broke eye contact briefly. "That works too."

He then placed a chaste kiss on her forehead, released her from his grasp, and walked out the office door. Elle, lost in thought, walked to her office chair, slumping down inside the comfort of the worn leather. Her skin tingled, her heart pounded, and her mind wandered. She was in trouble. Yep. Lots and lots of trouble.

• • • • •

"What the hell is the matter with you?" Whitney screeched into the phone. Elle stood in her bra and panties, cell phone pressed to her ear as she held a black lace cocktail dress to her body. Her hair was pulled up into a tight bun, her bangs swept loosely across her forehead. Her makeup was completed, but she had no idea what to wear. She tilted her head, trying to envision what was appropriate for this date. She didn't want to be overdressed or too sexy. But then again, not being sexy enough was not an option. Luke had made it clear he was attracted to her, that he couldn't stop thinking about her . . . and despite her snarky attitude earlier that afternoon, the feelings were completely mutual. She wanted to be just the right amount of sexy.

"I'm fine," she choked out, placing the black dress back in her closet, trading it for a strapless denim dress with a large brown leather belt.

"I can hear *The White Album*. You only listen to that when you're freaking out. Talk to me, Elle."

Elle cringed at how well Whitney knew her and her habits. Whitney hit the nail on the head when she recognized *The White Album*—an album with songs laced with creativity and storytelling that eased Elle's mind when she was feeling anxious and contemplative. By the time she reached "Blackbird" she was usually able to calm herself down. But she was way past "Blackbird" and the adrenaline coursing through her body still hadn't subsided.

"I have a date. One I'm not so sure about."

"A date? And you didn't tell me?"

"It's complicated."

"Oh my God, you caved, didn't you?"

Elle groaned into the phone. "I couldn't help it. He's . . . persistent."

Whitney laughed.

"Don't laugh at me. Seriously, this is probably a huge mistake. We both know it."

"You and Luke or you and me?" Whitney pressed.

"You and me. He has no idea. The guy's done a few pilots and commercials. He hasn't done anything long-term yet. He has no idea how awkward this will get when the shit hits the fan."

"And what if it doesn't?"

"Be serious. As soon as fans recognize him on the street, I'm toast."

"That's a possibility, I guess. But not a given," Whitney suggested. "And as usual, you're selling yourself short."

"No, I'm just a realist. Stardom affects everyone, just in different ways. And I have no idea how it'll affect him." Her fingers grazed over the earrings in her jewelry box, finally stopping on a pair of silver hoops.

"So then why bother? Just put your sweats on and hang out with Linus. Avoid, sabotage, and self-destruct." Elle hated the tone of Whitney's voice and the condescension reverberating through it.

"Don't be an asshole," she replied, slipping one earring through her ear. Quickly, she transferred the phone to that ear and repeated the process with the second earring.

"Whatever. There's a reason you're thirty-five and single. No offense."

"Hey," Elle said. "I'm not the only one who's single in this conversation."

"Okay, first of all," Whitney began, "I'm thirty-two."

"Irrelevant."

"And secondly, I date, and often. I'm perfectly content with my life."

"And so am I."

Silence hung in the air. It was a blatant lie. Elle knew it, and she was fully aware her best friend did too. They'd shared too much for Whitney to play the fool.

Whitney sighed. "C'mon, Eleanor. We both know that's not true."

Most people in Los Angeles were not allowed to refer to Elle by her given name, but Whitney was the exception. Even though it graced the covers of her romance novels, since moving to the Los Angeles spotlight, she'd chosen to modernize all aspects of her life, including her name. When Whitney used her true first name, Elle knew she was serious. She'd had enough and needed to make her point, so Elle decided to concede.

"Fine. I understand. I need to loosen up."

"Thank you. What time are you meeting him?"

Elle glanced down at her watch. "In twenty minutes."

"Well, shit, I'll let you go then. Let your hair down, have some fun!"

Elle promised Whitney she'd do her best to enjoy herself. She hung up the phone, placed it on the counter, and pulled the pins from her hair, causing the bun to tumble past her shoulders, her blonde locks forming loose curls that spilled down her back. She took a deep breath and walked back to her closet to finish getting dressed. Then she walked back to the sink, retrieved the pins, and placed them between her teeth. She looked at herself in the mirror, shook her head, and spent five more minutes placing her hair back in a bun.

• • • • •

Luke was already sitting at a small, cozy table at Angelini Osteria when Elle finally arrived, ten minutes later than their reservation. Elle was never late, but Luke Kingston seemed to flip her version of normal on its head. She couldn't get past her hesitation. She still couldn't decide if this was all a game to him, a way of making a name for himself in the beginning.

It was easy to say she had trust issues. Since Troy broke her heart ten years earlier, she'd dated . . . sporadically. Whitney had a point when she compared their love lives. The best word to describe Elle's relationships would be . . . also *sporadic*. She had dated a few men in Chicago, and a few more since moving to Santa Monica, but none had stuck. Mostly because it was difficult for Elle to separate herself from her show. And to stop sabotaging any chance she had at happiness. When things grew serious with any of the men she'd dated, she found reasons to end each relationship abruptly and without explanation. She couldn't let go of the past long enough to be happy.

Letting go was hard . . . she hadn't let go in ten straight years.

When Elle reached the table, Luke, looking all kinds of handsome, set his menu on the table, and rose to meet her. He placed a chaste kiss on her cheek. "You made it."

"Did you think I wouldn't?"

He shrugged, giving her a tight, toothless smile. "After our discussion earlier, I thought maybe not."

"I honor my commitments."

She didn't intend to come off as cold, but she wasn't quite sure about him—his intentions, his interest in her, it was still murky in her brain.

"As do I." He handed her a menu. "Have you been here before? The porchetta will change your life." He took a quick sip of his red wine.

"Porchetta?"

"You've never had it? Seriously, it's to die for, so rich and delicious. You have to try it."

"Maybe I will." She felt herself easing up, relaxing into his carefree demeanor.

"Let's get you a drink. Red or white?"

"Red, please. Pinot noir."

"Perfect."

Luke signaled the waiter and promptly ordered a bottle of pinot noir. She hated to admit it, but she loved that he ordered for her. She'd yet to be on a date in Los Angeles where a man acted in such an old-fashioned manner. Secretly, she wondered if he'd been watching reruns of *Mad Men*. In Elle's opinion, Don Draper may have been part douchebag, but he knew how to treat a lady in public.

"Where are you from . . . you know, originally?" Luke asked before taking another sip of his drink.

The waiter arrived with the wine and poured a glass for Elle. She thanked him graciously, and took a sip to calm her nerves.

"Chicago. I moved here a few years ago when the network bought the rights to the show."

"Oh, that's right, I think I knew that." Luke chuckled, scratching lightly at the skin of his forehead.

"Did you Internet stalk me?" Elle teased. She liked that he was showing just a hint of vulnerability. It was obvious to her Luke hadn't meant to ask that question since he already knew the answer. But she'd play along.

"Guilty as charged." He shrugged. "Couldn't help myself, I had to know more."

Elle was flattered. Beyond flattered, actually. But she was trying too hard to keep her poker face intact. She couldn't let him see how he affected her, especially since she was still smack-dab in the middle of figuring him out.

"Interesting," she replied, staying coy. "And you, where are you from?"

Luke's eyes widened in response and he nudged her on the shoulder. "You didn't read my resume?"

Busted.

No, Elle wanted to answer, I was too busy staring at your gorgeous head shot. The resume only received a tiny glance. "I did, but I don't remember seeing a hometown listed, only your work in Los Angeles."

"That's because I've lived here my entire life."

"Ah, well, that makes sense, doesn't it?" Elle looked at her empty glass, wondering how she polished off an entire glass of wine during such a short period of time. Luke offered to pour her another glass, but she shook her head. She couldn't lose control. "Thank you, but I'll wait for our food to arrive."

"Sure."

Silence took up residence at their table, and, feeling awkward, Elle picked up her menu and stared at the dishes, unsure of what to order. Luke followed her lead and glanced at his as well.

"I'm not really a fan of pork, so—"

"The pasta's great too."

"Mmm." She bit into her upper lip as she studied the dishes. "I think I'll try the sole."

"Nice choice."

Menus were placed back on the table and silence reared its ugly head once again. Luke chuckled to himself and poured another glass of wine, raising it to his lips.

"So . . ." He paused, studying her face with narrowed eyes, as if he was trying to solve her like a puzzle. "How is my character coming along?"

There it was. Work talk. She'd waited for that, wondering when he'd cut to the chase. She took a rather large breath in, pursing her lips before speaking. "He's fine."

Again, silence.

"I'm sorry, did I . . . did I piss you off or something?"

Elle crossed her arms in front of her chest. "No, why would you think that?"

"Well, I mentioned the show and you shut down. It's like you built this wall right here." He motioned with his arm, an invisible line down the center of the table. Elle sensed concern in his knitted brow. She was hurting his feelings—she hadn't expected that.

She'd come in contact with many self-serving actors in the past. Guys would chat her up at a bar while she was out with Whitney. They'd buy her drinks, ask a few questions about her life, her work, and then parlay it into talking about their careers. Before she knew it, they'd be pulling out a business card or a head shot and she'd feel like a complete fool. Was it fair to assume Luke was the same as those who'd fooled her in the past? Not necessarily, but she couldn't help it. Yes, he had the role already, but this was his big break, and having an "in" with the creator and head writer of the show could definitely serve him well.

When Elle sat frozen, completely lost in her own quizzical thoughts, Luke spoke softly. "Listen, Elle, I like you. But if you'd rather just . . . I don't know, have a drink and call it a night, that's okay."

"I—I." She stumbled on her words. She hadn't expected such a reaction from him.

You're screwing this up, she thought to herself. She shook her head and reached across the table to take his hand in hers.

"No, I'm sorry. Just frazzled, I guess. I didn't mean to take it out on you."

She watched as his face relaxed; he squeezed her hand in return, then raised it to his lips and placed a kiss inside her palm.

"Forgiven."

Elle didn't know that one word could reduce her to a pile of mush. But that one did. She sat, stunned as Luke cradled her hand in his.

"I asked about my character because, frankly, I'm excited. I've been hitting the pavement for years in audition after audition. This is a big deal for me."

Elle had never thought about this from Luke's point of view. His resume was filled with measly projects that probably failed to pay his bills each month. Securing a supporting role on television's hottest show was life changing for him. She needed to recognize that.

"That makes sense." She squeezed his hand. "I get it."

"Look, I know you think I'm some opportunist or something. But that couldn't be further from the truth. If you give me a chance, you'll see that. When I'm here with you, I see you—that's all."

"And what do you see?"

"The most beautiful woman I've ever seen."

Elle closed her eyes tight, tilting her head in disbelief. There was no way she could believe this gorgeous man was that affected by her appearance. She knew she was attractive, but she was also a realist and knew he'd probably dated his fair share of actresses and models.

"Not only that," he continued, "I've watched the show since it began. It's smart. Really smart. I'd dare say it borders on brilliance."

She'd received countless compliments on the show up until this point, but the word *brilliance* had never been used. She silenced the little voice in her head that told her not to believe him. She found herself swept up in that word, in the sentiment of his compliment.

"Thank you."

The waiter returned and Luke placed their order. She sat, stirring in her own conflicting thoughts. Part of her wanted to follow Whitney's advice, walk to the ladies' room and take her hair down, return to the table and allow Luke to see she was just as captivated by him as he appeared to be by her. But the other part, the dominant part of her psyche, rejected that as foolishness. Pure and utter foolishness.

She had to stay strong, stay smart. She had to remind herself that no matter how intoxicating this man might be, she was, for all intents and purposes, his superior, his *boss*.

She had a reputation to uphold, and the last thing she needed was a scandal on her already very full plate.

When their meal came to an end, Luke refused her offer to split the check.

"Don't be silly, I invited you to dinner."

She felt guilty, knowing his paychecks for *Follow the Sun* had yet to begin, and he was probably strapped for cash based on the sparse employment listed on his resume. But the last thing she wanted to do was insult his manhood or ability to provide. So she simply thanked him and they walked slowly to her car.

"So . . ." He looked up at the evening sky. "Where to?"

The foolish part of her brain wanted to invite him back to her place, to allow herself to get lost in his touch, to lose herself in the seduction that was Luke. But she just didn't have it in her. Her hair was still up tight in its bun, with no plans for it to be released.

Elle felt her body tense as she delivered what she knew would be interpreted as a dismissal. "I'm going to call it a night."

"Oh." Luke exhaled and nodded, pursing his lips in obvious disappointment. Elle wanted to change her mind, to extend an invitation to her place, but she had to be careful, no matter how attractive he was.

"I guess I'll see you later this week? Costume department needs my measurements. Maybe I'll stop by your office or something."

"That'd be nice."

Luke leaned in, his eyebrows pressed toward one another in a pensive glance. His lips brushed against hers and, although her immediate reaction was to turn her head, to only give him access to a cheek, she just couldn't do that. Desire was building within her, and even though a kiss was not nearly enough to satisfy that desire, it would have to do for now.

Her lips touched his with subtle urgency. He smiled before placing a hand behind her neck and kissing her deeply, his tongue gaining entry inside her welcoming mouth. Her arms wrapped around his back, pulling him closer, her tongue completely at his mercy. Her heart was racing inside her chest. Just when she thought of leading him back to her car, and driving quickly back to her place, he pulled away. He took his lips away from her, and immediately she craved him, wanted him to return. Her lips pressed to his, the hunger inside her demanding to be fed. After several seconds, he pulled away, teasing her with feathery touches to her upper lip. And then he kissed her again, pushing her to the brink before pulling away once more.

Her hands found his shoulders, and she pressed into them with frustration. Her words came out in a throaty moan. "What are you doing?"

"Just checking."

She was confused. "Checking what?"

"You had me all confused. But now I know."

"I don't understand."

"This"—he gestured between them—"is just as mutual as I thought it was."

Her body stiffened at his words. She felt exposed, silly, and ridiculous. She hated that her carnal behavior had revealed her true feelings toward him. She craved control, and she felt it slipping from her grasp.

"So what if it is?" She puckered her lips and stood straight and tall.

He ran his fingers through her hair, releasing the bun, and allowing her hair to spill down her shoulders. She gasped, peering into his eyes.

Luke ignored her question. His fingers weaved in and out through the loose curls that tumbled down her back. "I like your hair like this. It suits you."

He kissed her one last time on the lips before pressing his lips to her exposed shoulder, sending shivers down her spine.

"Just so you know, I have no intention of backing down. I want you, Elle. And I *know* you want me too."

She swallowed hard and licked her lips. She was terribly uncomfortable yet aroused by his words. She wanted him in her bed, desperately.

"Good," she whispered, the corners of her mouth curling up in satisfaction.

He grinned at her response, before saying good night. Her body tingled as she drove back home, unable to escape thoughts of that kiss, of the way he'd teased her, of how he made her come apart. Their chemistry was no longer something she could deny. She only hoped she could maintain her professionalism despite her building need for Luke Kingston.

Chapter 5

Elle awoke, yet again, with sweat dripping down her neck and an ache between her legs. For four straight nights, she'd dreamed of Luke—above her, beneath her, behind her. On the bed, the couch, against the wall—the fantasies made her yearn every single morning. She despised her alarm clock for pulling her from the encounters.

She wiped the sleep from her eyes, attempting to focus her vision as she shifted to a seated position. How long could she resist him? Of that, she was unsure. He was invading her psyche in more ways than she was comfortable. For work, it was having a more than positive effect on her productivity. Writing David was simple—scenes poured from her brain and out through her fingers as she typed. The sexual tension between David and Molly was screaming from the pages. Rob was delighted at episodes eight and nine. She'd delivered them just yesterday and he praised her up and down—predicting all sorts of grandeur for the upcoming season. Luke was proving to be quite the muse.

But when she wasn't hard at work on another script, her mind was wandering and, like a smitten teenager, she'd been counting down the days until Luke would arrive for his appointment with Barb, the head costume designer. And today, it had finally arrived.

After a refreshing shower, Elle pondered the clothing in her closet. Her schedule for the morning was a table read with Nolan, Gina, and several members of the supporting cast, followed by lunch, and an afternoon of writing. Tomorrow, they would begin shooting the very first episode of the season. Her nerves were aflame with anticipation of both the official start of the season and her hopeful run-in with the possible leading man in her life.

She opted for a simple pencil skirt with a pale yellow chiffon blouse. Nothing extravagant or ostentatious, but classy, fun, and just a little bit sexy. Butterflies swarmed her abdomen as she groomed herself for the day ahead. She expected it would be quite a busy week, but she welcomed the excitement.

• • • • •

What Elle didn't expect upon settling in at the sizable table in the conference room was the rising tension between her two leads. Typically, table reads were a relaxed experience for all involved. The actors had received their scripts the previous week and were given plenty of time to study their own lines. Then, the table read allowed them to work on delivery and ask for direction from both Elle and Rob.

The normally relaxed environment, however, was anything but. Tension hovered above the table and Elle struggled to decipher the source of the strain as her actors struggled through the scene. She knew it wasn't the writing. This was the first episode of the season and had picked up immediately after the cliff-hanger of the season finale. No, it was the actors. Specifically Gina Romano.

"I've been looking for you everywhere." Nolan delivered his line, his eyes sincere, his voice conveying the desperation Desmond was feeling.

Gina rolled her eyes as Nolan read the line and her response was wooden and stiff, without any of the emotion the script demanded. "I've been looking for you too."

Elle couldn't take it anymore. She had to interrupt the read. Gina's unprofessional behavior was unacceptable.

"I'm sorry, is there a problem here?" She pushed her reading glasses down to the tip of her nose and glared at Gina.

Gina wouldn't look her in the eye. "Nope, no problem here."

"Maybe we should take a break," Nolan suggested, clearing his throat and tapping his copy of the script on the table.

"Fine, whatever." Gina dropped her attention to the floor, retrieving her phone from her purse.

Elle stared at the two, each refusing to look one another in the eye. She had to get to the bottom of this. Sure, Nolan would eventually be written out of the show, but they had twenty-three episodes to shoot before that would become a reality.

Elle stood and walked to the door. "Nolan, care to step outside for a minute?"

Nolan inhaled deeply, glaring at Gina before pushing his chair back. The bottoms squeaked against the linoleum floor. He huffed, ran his hand through his dark hair, and followed Elle into the hall-way, closing the door behind him.

"What was that all about?"

"I don't know." He avoided her eyes just as Gina had at the table. *What the hell is going on?*

"I can stand out here all day, so . . ."

"Fine, but . . . you can't tell her I told you."

Elle's annoyance level was reaching a new high. "What are we, five? No, I make no promises. You two are messing with my show."

Nolan's shoulders slumped as he stuffed his hands into the pockets of his worn jeans. He looked down at the floor.

"It's no big deal."

"Obviously." Elle had quite the habit of handling conflict with sarcasm. She knew it made her seem tough as nails, and she didn't care. She was irritated they'd managed to ruin the excitement she'd had flurrying in her belly all morning. Now, she was breaking up a fight between two adults who were acting like kindergarteners.

"She's pissed off, that's all."

"About?"

"My leaving." Elle continued to stare at Nolan, waiting for him to finish his sentence. He looked at her like she was a raving lunatic. "The show. She's pissed I'm leaving the show."

Elle crossed her arms in front of her chest. "Sorry, not buying it."

Nolan's eyes rose to meet Elle's. The whites of his eyes became more prevalent as he widened them in disbelief.

"She read with Luke Kingston last week and she was fine. Whatever this is, it's recent."

"She found out . . . about me and—me and someone on staff."

Whitney. Of course. They'd slept together, but . . . why would Gina care? Then it dawned on her.

"Wait . . . you and Gina? You're . . . a couple? How in the world did I not know this?" Elle was shocked. She'd worked with the two for years and had always assumed their chemistry was simply that—on-screen chemistry. She never imagined they were actually involved when they were no longer delivering the lines of Molly and Desmond.

Nolan walked quickly from Elle, pacing the length of the hall-way, his arms stretched out to rest behind his neck. "No one knows. It was . . . a casual thing. At least, *I* thought it was. I guess I was sorely mistaken."

"So you and Whi—I mean, this *other person*, was it a one-time thing?" Elle pressed, mostly out of curiosity. She hadn't reacted so well when Whitney had mentioned their fling a few weeks earlier. She wasn't sure if it had continued without Whitney sharing the details.

"Yes, of course. It was just . . . I don't know, a drunken thing. No big deal. I'm still friends with her and everything."

"But Gina . . . she found out."

"Yes. And as you can see, she's pissed." He gestured toward the room.

"Well, obviously you two have some things to discuss."

"Obviously." Nolan leaned his hips against the wall, looking up to the ceiling in defeat.

"But here's the thing. Right now, you're on my watch and this can't affect your work."

"Believe me, I know. I'm doing my best."

Elle glanced back inside the conference room. Gina was watch-ing them through the tiny pane of glass in the solid wood door. Her eyes were glassy and her fingernails tapped against the top of the table.

"Come with me."

Elle led Nolan back into the room, where he resumed his seat. She, however, stood tall in front of the two actors. "Everyone, except for our two leads, you can take a ten-minute break. Meet back here at nine forty-five, all right?"

Papers shuffled and chairs squeaked as the supporting cast gath-ered their things and left the room. Gina placed her phone in her purse and looked to Elle, her fingers continued to tap against the wooden table.

"I'm going to make this brief." Elle paced behind the table, looking between the two actors holding up the workday. "Whatever drama is happening between you two, you can figure it out on your own time. Right now, you need to pull yourselves together and focus on the task at hand. I've been working like a maniac on this season and I will *not* watch my show go down in flames because you two are having some sort of ridiculous fight."

Gina's nose flared and her eyes widened. Her attention snapped to Nolan, daggers peaked from her brown eyes.

"You *told* her? I can't believe you, Nolan. Seriously." She stared down at the table, biting her lower lip as her cheeks turned a deep shade of crimson.

"He told me very little—the rest is blatantly obvious."

"Right."

"I really don't have time for this. Now, get over yourself and get into character. For the next two hours, you're Molly, *not* Gina. Have I made myself clear?" Her fingernail tapped the table as she pressed it down to make her point.

"Yes," they said in unison.

"Thank you. I'm going to grab another cup of coffee. When I get back, I expect this cloud of tension to be gone."

The two actors glared at one another and Elle knew she had to leave that room. If she didn't she'd end up using the rest of the ten minutes lecturing them. Her cup was empty and she desperately needed a boost. She walked down the hall to the kitchen. A fresh pot of coffee filled the room with the bitter yet inviting scent she craved so deeply. Elle inhaled deeply while filling her cup to the brim. She resisted the urge to stop by Whitney's office, knowing it would just fan the flames of drama. There was nothing Whitney could say or do to fix the situation Nolan had created with Gina. It just had to play itself out.

A text rang in: Just finished my costume measurements. Meet me for coffee before I head out?

Luke.

Disappointment swarmed her belly as she knew she had no time to see him. She had two minutes before she was needed back for the table read. There was no way for her to steal away with him for any amount of time before he would leave the building.

Table read, I'm sorry. I wish I could . . .

How about dinner?

Elle smiled, excited to see the man she couldn't evict from her thoughts.

Sounds good. Pick me up?

You got it. Send me your address later.

Seven o'clock?

Perfect.

With a new air of confidence, Elle strolled back to the conference room, knowing even Gina Romano couldn't spoil her good mood. That evening would be spent with Luke, and she could hardly wait.

• • • • •

Elle's fingers were growing hot as they darted between the keys. Furiously the script for episode ten spilled from her brain and onto the screen of her laptop. She was satisfied with the way the storyline was building, and even though she'd promised Rob she'd allow the other writers to assist with this episode, she was determined to get the "bones" written before they gave their input. They had all reviewed the episodes she'd written thus far and had sent their approval and praise via e-mail, which made her feel all the more confident about building the David McKenzie storyline.

A knock on her office door brought her back to reality. Within seconds of the knock, Whitney slid herself inside Elle's office, closing the door behind her. She closed her eyes and knocked the back of her head softly into the door. Obviously the conflict between Nolan and Gina had spread throughout the staff.

"Whit, I love you, but I really don't have time—"

"Did you know they were a couple? Because I swear I didn't!" Whitney took a seat facing Elle, who, realizing she would not be getting any more writing done, closed her laptop and focused her attention on her distraught best friend.

"Nolan told me today. Gina was pretty pissed during the table read."

"Seriously, I never would have done that had I known. I'm *not* a home wrecker."

Elle sat back in her chair, realizing just how upset Whitney was. "Of course you're not. Nolan said it was casual."

"Not according to Gina. She just bitched me out in my office!"

"How did she even find out?"

"Tabloid. I guess someone had a picture of us making out in his car after the wrap party. They're trying to pass it off as recent."

Whitney's dark hair spilled down her arms as she pretended to bash her head slowly into Elle's desk.

"Ugh, that happens all the time, though, right?"

"I know, but Gina's not buying it. And I guess they started heating up this summer . . . way after Nolan and I hooked up."

"I'm assuming you told her this?"

"Of course I did. But apparently they've been sleeping together off and on for months . . . like since we started filming last season."

"You've got to be kidding me. I had no clue." Elle wondered how so much could be happening right under her nose. Was she oblivious? Or were they just talented at sneaking around?

"No one did. They were like ninjas. So stealth."

"Stealth sex ninjas," Elle added with a chuckle before diving into her drawer for reinforcements. Her hand dug through several stacked packages of candy.

"Please tell me you have Swedish Fish."

Elle grabbed one of the yellow boxes with the signature red writing. It was their favorite, the very first thing that bonded them. Years earlier, during their first one-on-one meeting, Elle had offered Whitney some Swedish Fish. They'd bonded over sweets ever since. She poked a finger into the side of the box, tearing off the top and popping the inside bag to reveal the delectable smell of syrupy sugar in the form of little fish. She offered them to Whitney first, who grabbed the box and held them close to her chest as she scooped them in.

Elle rolled her eyes. "No worries, I'm not hungry or anything."

"Oh." Whitney glanced down at the candy box security blanket as she shoveled two more fish into her mouth. "Sowwy."

"Don't talk with your mouth full, dork. Now listen, this is all going to blow over. Nolan and Gina will talk it through and she'll calm down."

"And if not?"

Elle did her best to ease Whitney's stress. "And if not, he'll still be gone by the end of the season."

The two ladies allowed themselves to erupt into devious laughter.

"You're so bad," Whitney said between bites of bright red candy.

Elle nodded. "And that's why you love me."

"Speaking of bad . . ." Whitney's words trailed off as she wiggled her wicked eyebrows at Elle. "How's Mr. Gorgeous? Sleep with him yet?"

"Not yet. But I'm seeing him tonight."

Whitney popped one last piece of candy in her mouth before handing the almost-empty box back to Elle. Elle peered into the box before giving Whitney a look of surprise. How on earth did she remain so skinny with that appetite? She was like a tornado of hunger.

"So . . . is tonight the night?"

"Maybe." Now it was Elle's turn to clutch the box of candy like a fiend. She bit the head off one of the innocent candies, savoring the mixture of cherry and strawberry sweetness in her mouth.

"You know you want to. Let your hair down, Elle. I know you can do it."

Elle dropped the box of candy back into her emergency drawer, grabbing a wet wipe for her hands. She smirked at her best friend. "Whatever, home wrecker."

• • • • •

Luke arrived promptly that evening, buzzing at the iron gate at the base of her driveway. Originally, she'd owned a condo when she moved to Santa Monica, but when the show rose in popularity, she was horrified to find photographers peeping into her windows. She knew they stalked the actors, but she couldn't wrap her mind around why they'd have any interest in her personal life. Regardless of her lack of understanding, however, their persistence forced her hand. She purchased a four-bedroom Spanish-style home in a gated community, her hands trembling as she signed the ridiculously expensive mortgage agreement. But after settling in, and receiving several bonuses for the success of the show, she never looked back. She'd come to cherish and appreciate her privacy and couldn't imagine retreating back to living somewhere where her private life could be preyed upon. And with the new star of her show pursuing her in a romantic way, she knew her privacy would be necessary more than ever before.

He pulled into her brick driveway, aviator sunglasses on the bridge of his nose. Elle watched from the window as he exited his SUV, flowers in hand, and strolled to the door with confidence. Quickly, she moved behind the curtain, so as not to reveal she was watching him. She glanced quickly into the mirror in the butler pantry next to the dining room before answering the doorbell.

"Hey there," he said, his woodsy scent pervading her senses. The sound of his voice, his smell, his confidence—everything about Luke Kingston turned her on. He placed the bouquet of gladiola in her arms and she wanted to burst, to break apart into a thousand tiny pieces. Memories of their encounter in the parking lot swarmed her brain and made her skin throb, aching for his touch.

Whitney was right. Elle wanted this, and she needed to own it.

"Come in," she said, letting her apprehension slide from her shoulders.

Linus yapped at Luke's feet, hopping on his hind legs and sniffing Luke's pants.

"Who's this little guy?"

"That's Linus. Sorry, he's a little jumpy."

Luke smiled, crouching down to pet the exuberant terrier. "It's no problem. I love dogs."

For just a moment, Elle watched as Luke showered her companion with affection. A sweet ache developed in her gut as Luke scratched behind Linus' ears and Linus soaked it up.

"He's so cute," Luke said, rising to his feet.

Elle snapped her fingers. "C'mon, Linus. Let's get you a treat."

Reluctantly, Linus followed Elle into the kitchen, torn between his new best friend and a snack. She retrieved a handful of treats and placed them on the floor. As Linus gobbled his goodies, she returned to Luke, who was taking in his surroundings.

"Wow, this place . . ." His voice trailed off as he walked around the circular, two-story foyer. A large glass table sat in the middle of the room. Elle placed the bouquet on the table and then watched as Luke studied her home.

"It's pretty new. I'm still getting settled in," she lied. She'd been there for over a year, but for some reason she didn't want him to know just how wealthy she was. But who was she kidding? He knew.

"It's really charming . . . which is fitting." He removed his sunglasses, placing them in the pocket of his jacket.

"Would you like a drink?" Elle offered, not quite ready to have Luke leave her home. She was craving the privacy only a residence could provide.

"Sure, what do you have?"

Elle gestured for him to follow her back to the butler's pantry where he could view her selection of spirits. Luke inspected the bottles, before lifting her untouched bottle of Johnnie Walker Platinum. Her heart sank for just a moment in the realization the bottle would finally be opened.

"Scotch would be great." He cleared his throat. "On the rocks, please."

Elle took a deep breath and gave him the most confident smile she could produce. She couldn't let him see her silly reaction to opening a simple bottle of scotch. "You got it."

She poured a glass for herself, making it a double and adding a twist of lemon.

"No ice?" Luke asked, perking up an eyebrow.

"Nope," she said.

"I'm impressed. My kinda woman." He raised his glass to hers, and clinked. They each took a sip, although secretly Elle wanted to down the entire glass. It wouldn't be her first time doing that, but she didn't want to give the wrong impression. The last thing she needed was Luke assuming she had some sort of drinking problem.

"Should we sit?" she asked, leading him to the firm gray couch in the formal living room. Luke followed behind her, and when they reached the couch, he waited for her to sit, then eased himself next to her, his arm perched atop the back of the couch.

"I'm glad you were willing to see me tonight."

"Willing?" She challenged him, raising her eyebrows and hooking her bottom teeth under her lip. "That's an interesting word choice."

"Leave it to the writer to analyze my vocabulary."

Elle blushed slightly, but waited for him to explain what he meant by "willing." When she was quiet moments later, Luke shrugged. "Well, you know, after our first date, I wasn't sure."

Elle decided to challenge him, remembering the feel of his lips on her skin. "You seemed pretty confident in the parking lot."

"Ah." He gave her a cocky smirk before taking a sip. "I guess you're right."

Elle finished her scotch, and, feeling her apprehension slide away, she placed the empty glass on the coffee table, embracing the desire coursing through her veins.

"So acting . . . was it always a dream of yours or were you just seduced by the charms of your environment?" Without hesitation, she placed her hand on Luke's thigh, her fingers delighted at the thick fibers beneath his pants. His quads were tight and firm.

"I guess you could say that. I think, when I was like five or six, I wanted to be a vet. Our dog died and I wanted to fix him."

Elle's fingers stroked the fabric of his pants and Luke took a deep breath. "Well, that's sweet." She embraced the feeling of control infusing her senses. He wanted her; of this she was certain. And she wanted him. God, she wanted him. It's not that she didn't want to take a walk down memory lane with Luke, to learn about his childhood and the name of the family dog. But at that moment, it was no longer high on her list of priorities. She wanted him above her, drinking her in with his touch. She wanted his hands everywhere, touching each and every inch of her body. She wanted him inside her, driving her to the incredible release she knew he could provide.

Luke polished off the rest of his scotch, leaning forward to place the glass firmly on the table. He turned to Elle, his eyes wide and blazing. The muscles of his jaw flexed as he swallowed. His hands reached to cup her face, his eyes locked with hers.

"You're so beautiful." It came out in a hoarse whisper.

Elle said nothing, but licked her lips in a slow, sensual motion, moving her hand from his thigh, to the growing bulge in his pants. She was done holding back with Luke. She wanted his lips on her . . . everywhere. She cupped him, never breaking eye contact and watched as the corners of Luke's mouth pulled into a smile.

He smiled and then he kissed her. No more teasing, feathery motion. This kiss was demanding and full of desire. His hand drifted to wrap around the back of her neck as his lips and tongue explored her mouth. She opened for him, wanting him to deepen the kiss as she stroked him through the fabric of his pants.

"Bedroom?" Luke asked, his voice smooth and unwavering as he moved his attention to her neck. His lips caressed and his tongue stroked the sensitive skin beneath her chin. Elle nodded, broke herself from his embrace, took his hand, and led him upstairs to the master bedroom.

Elle hadn't planned for him to see her bedroom. Unintentionally, the Beatles' *Abbey Road* album had been left to play on repeat after she'd gotten ready for their date. Elle hurried to her CD player to silence the music.

"No, it's okay," Luke said, following her to the stereo. His fingers danced down the skin of her shoulders, making her shiver. "You can leave it on."

A moment of hesitation clouded Elle's thoughts. She wasn't so sure she was ready to share her beloved Beatles. As odd as that sounded, even to her, they were special—and such a part of her past with Troy. Quickly, she thought of a solution by grabbing another disc—a neutral band that meant absolutely nothing to her. She swapped it for the current CD, and returned her attention to Luke.

"This is better."

"Whatever you say. You're in charge." Luke dragged one finger down past her temple and cheek, stopping at her chin. He gripped the skin and bone, pulling her back to him. His lips consumed hers once again, and he turned her, walking her back toward the bed. His nimble fingers eased her out of her dress with next to no effort. Her black silk dress pooled around her ankles, leaving her in only her red lace bra and panties. Slowly, he lowered her down onto the soft mattress, his hands roaming her body as his lips did the same. His hands moved back and forth over her exposed abdomen, dipping down to stroke her over her panties.

Arousal built within her, so much so she felt she might explode if not given the release she so desperately needed. Her fingers grasped his hair, pulling him back to her mouth. Her tongue twisted and turned, dancing with his, and her hands fumbled with the buttons of his shirt. Luke pulled away slightly, smiled, and unfastened the buttons quickly, stripping his shirt from his body. Elle's eyes widened as she took in the sight of his tan pecs. Beneath them, his ridged muscles formed delectable washboard abs. He was astonishing.

Next came the belt. He removed it quickly before dropping his pants to the floor, revealing forest green boxers that clung to the sinewy muscles of his thighs. Although Elle was more than impressed by what she saw, she wanted those briefs to join his pants on her floor. She slid herself toward him, hooking her fingers beneath the waistband of the briefs, and eased them down. She stared at his naked body with satisfaction as her heart hammered beneath her chest. Her desire for Luke was mounting. She needed him, all of him.

Luke stripped her of her bra, staring at her breasts with appreciation before taking one nipple into his mouth. Electricity spread throughout her body. His fingers dipped beneath the waistband of her panties and he tugged until they tumbled to the carpet below, tickling her calves as they fell.

Luke released her nipple from his mouth, and Elle found herself yearning for him to return to the now-hardened peak that longed for his touch. His eyes were hooded and dark. "Lie back."

She obeyed, laying herself down on the bed, pulling him to lie above her, enjoying the weight of his body against her own. They fit together so naturally, the curves of her body easing into his. Comfortable yet sexy. Their kisses sweet yet passionate. A condom wrapper crinkled beneath his closed fist. His desire for protected sex aroused her even more. She pressed her lips to the firm muscles of his chest. "I want you. Now."

A satisfied smile crossed Luke's face before he ripped open the condom wrapper and rolled the sheath down. Instead of entering her and pressing her against the firm mattress, Luke rolled to his back, pulling Elle to straddle above him. When Elle looked down with confusion, he raised his eyebrows and gripped her hips.

"I told you, you're in charge."

How did Luke know how much Elle craved the power of being in control? It didn't matter. All that mattered was he was lying beneath her, hard and ready. She eased herself onto him, her muscles stretching with each delectable inch. Her hands stretched to press into his shoulders as she moved up and down, letting him enter her again and again. Pressure built quickly within her, her hips twisted in a circular motion and her head hung down, allowing the tips of her blonde hair to tickle Luke's chest. He grunted and moaned beneath her, his fingertips digging into the skin of her hips.

Elle's arousal climbed and climbed until she knew she'd break apart at any second. Her orgasm rippled through her and she cried out, throwing her head back in bliss. "Oh God!"

Once Elle had found her release, Luke began to thrust harder beneath her, lifting his hips off the bed as he pounded into her again and again until his climax manifested itself in several loud grunts, his fingers still digging into her skin. The mixture of pleasure and pain swirled within Elle, forming pure satisfaction within her body.

Elle separated her body from his, lying down next to him, her head resting comfortably on his bicep. Luke played with her hair as his breath evened. Normally Elle would be mortified their "date" had been nothing but a roll in her sheets, but her mind was so blissfully numb, she just didn't care.

"Wow," Luke exhaled, "didn't expect that."

"Yeah, well . . . it's been a long four days."

"Indeed." His fingers left her hair and drifted to trace the line of her silhouette, moving in soothing motions along her ignited skin. "Are you hungry?"

"Starving."

"Should we get dressed? Go out?"

Elle pondered the question, then realized she'd much rather enjoy dinner with Luke inside the sexy confines of her bedroom. "Takeout?"

Luke grinned before nuzzling into her neck. "I was hoping you'd say that."

"There's a great Chinese place a few miles away that delivers."

"Perfect. I'll eat anything, so—"

"I'll surprise you."

Reluctantly, Elle pulled away from Luke to stand, retrieving her bathrobe from the hook of her bathroom door. The fluffy cotton enveloped her in comfort as her body still hummed from their encounter. She loved how easy everything was thus far. This easygoing, highly sexual, and ridiculously gorgeous Adonis was lying in her bed, seemingly just as crazy about her as she was about him. Never had a relationship (or something resembling one) been so easy, so effortless. She'd had passion before, but this time it was combined with comfort, rather than constant chaos and miscommunication.

She strolled down the winding staircase to reach her kitchen. Flipping through the menus, she found the one for China Palace and quickly dialed the number on the front flap. After ordering half the dishes on the menu, unsure of what she was in the mood for, she heard footsteps. Warm lips met the skin of her ear and soft hands weaved through her hair, pushing it to the side to give his mouth better access to her skin. Elle turned to face Luke.

"It'll be here in thirty minutes."

"That's just about enough time . . ." Luke's words trailed off as he resumed the seduction of her neck. Elle giggled before allowing herself to be swept up, once again, in the man named Luke Kingston.

Chapter 6

Elle and Troy Saladino had had a tumultuous friendship filled with sexual tension that reached an all-time high on a camping trip during the fall of their sophomore year in college.

Elle sat at a picnic table with her friend, Staci, watching the six guys construct the various tents. Troy's muscles flexed beneath his polo shirt while he attempted to snap two of the metal pieces together. As it was her tent, Elle rolled her eyes, knowing Troy was doing it completely wrong.

"Um, Troy, I think you—" she began, her tone snide. She always enjoyed giving him a hard time.

"Keep it to yourself, Rigby. It's under control," he answered, not even giving her a second glance. When she and Troy became friends, they realized they had both been raised on the Beatles. Each Sunday morning, their families listened to 105.9 WCKG's *Breakfast with the Beatles*. Elle's father would make pancakes and bacon and the radio would stay on the entire program. Troy's parents had done the same. When she revealed she was named after the song "Eleanor Rigby," Troy's nickname for her was born. Secretly, she loved it and hoped he'd never call her by her actual name.

"I'm serious, you may want to look at the *instructions*."

Troy grabbed a sleeping bag and tossed it her way. "If I wanted your opinion—"

"You'd give it to me," Elle interrupted, finishing his statement with a quick roll of her eyes. "Whatever."

"Ugh," Staci lamented, throwing her hair behind her shoulder. "Why don't you two just *do it* already?"

Elle's heart rate sped out of control. She swatted Staci across the arm and avoided eye contact with Troy, but she felt his soulful brown eyes on her. They'd never discussed the sexual tension looming between them. They'd never dissected their banter to find its source. In fact, despite their constant flirtation, Elle had no idea if Troy thought about her in that way. Did he fantasize about her the way she did about him?

He was recently single. He'd broken up with Amanda Bauer—again—a girl who lived in Eleanor's dorm, just two weeks prior. Aside from her obvious good looks, long blonde hair, beaming green eyes, and alabaster skin, Amanda was the most boring human being Elle had met in her nineteen years. She was one of those girls who waited to hear your preferences before answering a question.

For example, Elle had joined Troy and Amanda for a quick lunch between classes.

"So, Amanda, what's your favorite show?" Elle was always interested in television series.

The blonde took a deep breath, her eyes pained. She looked physically stressed and Elle couldn't understand what could be so perplexing about such a question. All she wanted to do was know this girl a little bit better, to understand what Troy found so appealing.

"Um, I don't really watch that much television. How about you?" Her eyes perked up, looking relieved to have placed the "pressure" on Elle's shoulders.

"*Dawson's Creek*. I'm addicted." Elle scooped a large bite of salad into her mouth.

Amanda's face brightened. "Yes! Dawson! He's so hot."

"Actually, I prefer Pacey."

"Oh, well, yeah. He's totally hot, too."

Interesting, Elle had thought. Conversations like this one had taken place frequently during Troy's agonizing four months linked to Amanda. Elle felt he deserved better—someone with more than just a pretty face and flawless complexion. He needed someone who challenged him, someone who made him think. Someone who corrected him when he was putting a tent together improperly . . .

A minute passed after Staci's remark and finally Troy returned to the tent. Elle busied herself by organizing the drinks in the cooler. With each can she moved, she knew his eyes were still on her, daring her to look in his direction. But she couldn't. If she *did* look his way, he'd know the truth. He'd know how she felt about him—he'd know she'd fantasized about the two of them together, that she wanted to know how his lips felt against hers.

Troy cleared his throat. "Hey, Rigby, will you give me a hand?"

Elle froze, dropped a can of cola into the cooler, shut the top, and walked to Troy, coaching herself mentally.

Be strong. Show no fear.

"I thought you'd never ask." She nudged him in the ribs, and his lips perked up into a half smile. "My poor tent, I'm surprised it's not in shambles by now."

Elle shook her head as she picked up pieces of the tent, trying to mask the smile creeping up on her face. She loved giving Troy a hard time but had trouble developing a poker face when around him. He always saw right through any facade she attempted to create.

Troy shook his head slowly. His top teeth dug into his bottom lip. Elle loved when he did that. On Troy, sarcasm was sexy.

"Such a smart ass." He grabbed the tent back from her. "Forget I asked."

From anyone else, this attitude would have been a major turn-off, but with Troy it was an odd form of foreplay. They fed off of one another's snark. No, this wasn't a turnoff; it was an invitation.

Together, they built the tent successfully while continuously ribbing one another. When it was complete, however, he wrapped an arm around her, his hand hanging down from her shoulder.

"We did good."

Elle turned to look him in the eye. "Yeah, I suppose we did."

"We're a good team, Rigby."

This time, when Troy looked at her, his snark was long gone. He swallowed hard while his eyes peered into hers. Part of her wanted to break the eye contact, but she couldn't—it was too powerful. Her hair was up in a ponytail, but during construction of the tent, a few large strands had fallen. They sat in front of her eyes. Troy turned his body, removing his arm from her shoulder, and pushed her hair from her eyes. He pressed the strands behind her ear.

"There," he said, his words soft. "That's better."

• • • • •

The sun had set and the small group of campers gathered around the fire. Their bellies were full with hot dogs and marshmallows cooked by the fire. Beer was passed around and dirty jokes were spewing from the guys' mouths.

Elle and Troy sat together, nestled under a blanket. Troy cracked jokes with the guys, but she noticed how attentive he was. During dinner, he served her first before eating. When she cracked up at the jokes, he fixed the blanket to make sure she was covered and comfortable. Yes, they were little things. But to Elle, the little things were enormous. Troy had always been a thoughtful friend, but this felt like more, like something was building between them.

"Hey," he whispered into her ear. "Wanna go for a walk?"

"Sure."

Troy grabbed two flashlights, and they walked down the path. The campground they were staying in was patrolled and monitored at night, so Elle felt safe walking around the grounds with him.

"I used to go camping all the time as a kid. Did I tell you that?"

"No," Elle replied. She liked that Troy was revealing more of himself to her. She wanted to know everything about him.

"My dad was an Eagle Scout and thought it was important, I guess. I learned all those knots, how to make a fire—"

"Obviously, he skipped tent-building."

Troy shook his head. "Can't let one by, huh?"

"Not with you."

Troy stopped and he crossed his arms in front of his broad chest. "Why is that?"

Elle was confused. "What do you mean?"

"You and me. We're always, I don't know, giving each other crap. Why is that?"

Elle was more than confused—she was stunned. She thought that was a positive thing in their relationship. He kept her on her toes and she had assumed she did the same for him. Was she wrong?

"That's just how we are, I guess." She shrugged, not knowing what else to say.

"I'm not like that with anyone else. Not even my little sister."

Thank God, Elle thought. The last person she wanted to be compared to was Troy's sister. But she didn't like how this conversation was going. During their short stay on the campgrounds, she had felt her denial start to slip away—if Troy was letting her down easy, she would be crushed.

"You didn't like Amanda, did you?" he asked.

"Does it matter?"

"Yes."

"Why? Who you date is your business, not mine."

Troy stopped. He kicked the rocks beneath his feet. Even beneath the dark night sky, Elle could see the frustration in his knitted brow. "I guess."

They walked together, following the gravel path away from the campground and into a wooded area. The only sound was the crackling of the gravel beneath their feet. Elle wanted to push him, to discover what on earth he was trying to say, and to understand why he was frustrated.

Frustration and silence were not a healthy combination. Elle's chest ached as she pondered her next move. She wanted terribly to drag the stagnant conversation back to a place she understood. Normally, she'd give him a hard time to reel him back into their banter, but apparently Troy was conflicted about the state of their relationship. Banter was not the answer.

The sound of crackling twigs could be heard behind the bushes near the gravel path. Troy froze and held his hand out to block Elle from walking forward. "Did you hear that?"

"Yes." It came out in a choked whisper. She was so wrapped up in her emotions, she'd forgotten they were two teenagers walking alone at night. Normally, Elle would have voiced concern over leaving the safety of the supervised grounds, but the reticence between them stifled the cool air and she didn't want to increase their already strained conversation.

Troy grasped her forearm and held a finger up to his lips. She nodded, indicating she wouldn't make a sound. She stood like stone, looking from side to side, hoping a small animal, like a rabbit or chipmunk, would reveal itself and remove the fear surrounding them in the darkness.

Troy moved toward the bush, shining his flashlight and lifting the branches to inspect what could possibly be hiding behind the layers of evergreen. A muffled growl came from the ground beneath the bush and Troy stepped back.

"We should go. C'mon," he said, placing his hand on the small of Elle's back and guiding her to walk quickly down the path, back to the safety of the campground.

"What was that?" Her lungs were heaving.

"Just keep moving." Troy looked behind them several times, his arm wrapped completely around her waist as they increased their pace. The familiar glow of campfires welcomed them and Elle felt at ease. They would be fine. Troy, however, didn't look so relieved.

"Troy?" Elle asked, turning to place a hand on his shoulder. "Are you all right?"

"I would never let anything hurt you. You know that, right?" His nostrils flared, and his chocolate-brown eyes gleamed in the moonlight. Protective Troy made something stir in Elle. She pressed her hands behind his neck and pulled him to her.

He crushed her lips with his, wrapping his arms around her waist and pulling her toward his firm chest. Elle could feel his heart pounding. She opened her mouth, inviting him to deepen the kiss. He moaned into her mouth as his tongue met hers. They moved together in unison—it was everything Elle had thought it could be. He pulled the elastic from her ponytail, allowing her hair to tumble past her shoulders. He ran his fingers from the roots to the tips before dragging his fingernails down her back. His hands then roamed underneath her cotton shirt and she arched in response to the slight sting of his fingernails grazing her skin. His mouth moved to her neck as his hands continued to climb up her back. She looked up at the starry sky, wondering where this was headed and what it all meant. Even at times like these, it was impossible for her to turn off her brain, to truly lose herself in someone else. She craved control. But with Troy, she could never quite get it. The push, the pull was always in control of both of them.

"Should we . . . head back?" It wasn't what she wanted. But the need to control was a strong one—and a part of her personality difficult to suppress.

"Is that what you want?" Troy murmured between kisses. Her skin tingled with each kiss.

"I don't know."

Troy pulled back, placing both hands on her waist. "That's not true. You know. Tell me what you want."

Elle hesitated before telling the truth. Before risking everything. "You. I want you."

He shook his head with a smile. "You have me."

"Do I?" Elle narrowed her eyes, conveying her doubt with a simple glance. She didn't just want one night with Troy. She wanted so much more than that. At least, she *thought* she did.

Troy nodded; his expression turned serious. He ran his fingers through her hair before running the side of his hand down her cheek. "If you only knew, Rigby."

Relief flooded Elle and she pressed her lips to his once again, pulling him close to her, making the decision to let go of her need to control. Her hand dipped down to grip him beneath his jeans.

She murmured into his neck. "Should we go to my tent?"

Troy licked his lips before pursing them together. "Are you ready for that? I mean, I know you haven't—"

Troy was fully aware of Elle's virginity, but she didn't have any intention of discussing it. Regardless of what happened after that night, she knew right then, right there, she wanted Troy to be her first.

"Shh." She placed a finger on his lips. "I'm ready."

They walked hand in hand back to the tent. The others had already gone to sleep and Elle realized just how long they'd been gone on their walk. Troy unzipped the flap of the tent, revealing an empty space just for them. He unzipped the rest of the flap and gestured for her to enter. The tent was warm and her sleeping bag was open and ready. She sat down on the cool fabric, removing her shirt and unsnapping her jeans. Troy zipped the flap of the tent and knelt down next to her on the sleeping bag.

"Rigby," he whispered. "Are you sure?"

Elle nodded, pulling his shirt from his body. She ran her fingertips down his chest, enjoying the warmth of his skin on her fingertips.

"I'm sure."

• • • • •

The next morning, she bristled at his touch. When he attempted to snuggle with her beneath the sleeping bag, she pulled away, explaining she needed to use the bathroom. She avoided his eyes, knowing he'd see right through her lies.

When they'd finished making love just hours before, Troy had stroked her back gently before he dozed off to sleep. And although she enjoyed herself immensely, and knew he cared for her and they were meant to be together, Elle cried herself to sleep, silent tears streaming down her face.

The truth was, she was terrified.

She wasn't ready.

And she was a self-saboteur. The epitome of a self-saboteur.

Troy was everything she'd wanted, but she was petrified of actually having him—of actually being happy. Happiness required vulnerability—something Elle was terribly uncomfortable with, because vulnerability meant giving up control and that was something Elle just couldn't do no matter what her heart wanted. She sobbed in the shower stall of the campground ladies' room. When Staci attempted to comfort her, she asked her to leave.

When she returned to the campsite, Troy stood next to the deconstructed tent. Again, she avoided his eyes, not sure of what to say. She knew it was over before it even started. And she knew it was her fault.

"Hey," he said, leaning in close. "What's going on?"

Elle faked a smile. "Nothing, I'm fine. How are you? Did you sleep okay?"

"Rigby, c'mon. Did I . . . did I hurt you or something?" He ran one hand down her arm. She flinched at his touch and his eyes widened in disbelief.

"No, I . . ." She glanced around the campsite, worried their friends were watching the awkward interaction. "I just need to get back. I have a lot of studying to do."

"Okay, I'll drive you."

"No." She shook her head, retrieving the tent from his arms. "You stay, hang out with the guys. I'll ask Staci."

Troy rubbed his hand against his forehead. "I don't understand what's happening. I mean, last night—"

"It was nothing. We're fine, just like always." She shrugged.

She hated herself for being so dismissive. Troy's pained expression made her heart ache, but she was on autopilot, running away in a complete panic. Running away from the only guy she'd ever really wanted.

What in the hell is the matter with me?

● ● ● ● ●

Troy didn't speak to her for two weeks. She'd almost given up on their friendship completely when she found out he'd gone back to dating Amanda. He'd done that to spite her; she was fully aware of that. Troy never shied away from making a point.

But in the strangest of ways, his dating the woman who'd grated so terribly on Elle's nerves became their truce. He dated Amanda for another year, and slowly Elle eased her way back into a friendship with the man she secretly desired, but knew she couldn't quite handle. She knew if she fell for Troy, he could break her heart. She couldn't control their relationship. She couldn't avoid heartbreak or disappointment.

She told herself that Troy was better off with someone like Amanda. Someone who hung on his every word, who never said anything contrary to his beliefs or opinions. Someone the opposite of her. Someone who wasn't so afraid of falling in love.

And after a while, she believed the lie that when it came to Troy Saladino, she was friend material and nothing more. The self-saboteur inside her had won.

Chapter 7

Elle awoke to the soft pads of Luke's fingertips making circles on her skin. It was an ordinary Tuesday morning, and Luke had spent the night, just as he had several nights before over the past few weeks. The difference about this morning was he was needed in a makeup chair by 7:00 a.m. Elle glanced at the clock, relieved they had plenty of time to arrive at the studio.

It was Luke's first episode as David McKenzie. Episode seven. Elle would, officially, be overseeing his acting. She hoped he'd nail his scenes—the last thing she wanted to do was correct him in front of the cast. She had no desire to emasculate him like that in front of his peers. But this character and the coming episodes were pivotal—absolutely crucial to the success of the show.

"Morning." His voice was raspy. "Time for breakfast?"

"Sure. What'd you have in mind?"

"I'm easy, you know that. Whatever my lady wants is fine." He planted soft kisses on her shoulder and goose bumps rose to meet his lips.

"I'm fine with coffee . . . and you have to be on set in just over an hour. Rain check?" Elle rolled over to face him. He'd spent the night often enough that she no longer worried about bed head or morning breath. Luke didn't seem to mind either anyway . . . at least not on her.

"I have an idea. How about dinner . . . tonight? We can celebrate my first day on set." His grin was infectious and Elle found herself smiling right back at the handsome actor in her bed.

"Deal. Ooh, I'll ask Gina for the name of that place."

Luke hopped out of bed; his tan pecs flexed as he threw his shirt back on. "What place?"

"A restaurant that serves Chicago-style pizza."

Luke shrugged. "Never had it."

"Seriously?" Elle threw the back of her hand over her forehead, dramatically sighing for Luke's benefit. "Oh, the horror!"

"Don't quit your day job. You're a terrible actress."

Elle smirked, knowing he was right. "You have to try this pizza, Luke, I'm serious. It's . . . well, for me it's home."

He leaned down, digging his hands into the mattress, his face only inches from hers. "Well, then I can't wait to try it."

He placed a delicate kiss on her forehead before retreating to the guest bathroom to shower and prepare for the day. Elle appreciated that he gave her the space she required in the morning. Her bathroom, her closet—he knew it was off-limits to him between the hours of six and eight a.m. He was such an easygoing guy—things like that just didn't bother Luke. And Elle loved that about him.

In fact, their relationship was full of sex, laughter, and not much else. He relaxed her, helped her mind drift away from the stresses of work. She even wondered if one day he could possibly help her become less of a control freak, although that was still very much up in the air.

• • • • •

The set was all abuzz about episode seven. Rob was pacing the soundstage and Whitney, normally not a fixture on the set, was wandering through the dressing rooms wishing everyone luck. This episode was more than important; it was positively essential for the success of the season. It would air in just over three weeks and audiences had to accept not only the character of David, but also the actor who played him.

Luke had to make a positive impression on millions of viewers.
No pressure.

If Luke was feeling the stress of it all, he hid it rather well. Elle had watched as he took his place on set. He was dressed to the nines in an Armani suit and scarlet-red tie. Since the role of David McKenzie was of the head of security for the casino, he would consistently be seen in such a dapper state. Luke's normally wavy locks were smoothed back with just enough gel to make him look sophisticated without coming across as creepy. She watched him as he fixed his cuff links with ease and took direction from Rob, who continued to stalk the stage. He appeared to be ready for his close-up. Ready to be welcomed into the homes of millions of home viewers and if his demeanor was any indication, it was going to be a huge success.

Whitney glided from the dressing rooms, holding a magazine, a huge smile plastered across her face. When she reached Elle, she thrust the copy of *Us Weekly* into her hands.

"Great news. Turn to page thirty-five."

Elle thumbed through the magazine and landed on the page where the editors polled their readers. This week's poll focused on the character of Desmond.

"*Desmond of* Follow the Sun *has been making waves during season four and rumor has it Nolan Rivera is leaving the show. Do you think Desmond deserves to win Molly's heart?*" Elle read the poll aloud.

"Eighty percent, Elle! Eighty percent of readers don't like Nolan's character anymore. That's golden. Golden!"

Elle was delighted, looking at the pie chart that depicted just how out of favor Nolan's character had become. The viewers were ready for a change, and she was ready to give them one. She hugged the magazine to her chest.

"This . . . is even better than I'd hoped."

"Eighty percent is something to celebrate!" Whitney slid into Rob's chair, right next to Elle.

"Well, not yet. First, they have to fall in love with *him*." Her eyes drifted back to Luke, who was nodding along to Rob's directions.

Whitney followed Elle's stare before leaning back in her chair, placing her hands behind her head. "Somehow I don't think that'll be a problem."

"God, I hope you're right." Elle's bottom teeth dug into her lip.

"You're still worried he clouded your judgment?"

Elle nodded, closing her eyes with embarrassment.

"I was there, too, remember?" Whitney insisted. "He's a good actor, I *promise*. I wouldn't have let you hire him if he wasn't."

"True. And the table read went fine, so that's a start," Elle added, trying desperately to match Whitney's level of confidence and enthusiasm. She knew, however, it would be impossible. No one was as invested as she was in this show, and that would never change. America had to fall in love with David McKenzie *and* they had to want Molly to as well.

Elle watched as Gina, her hips swaying in a confident strut, strolled to Luke. She was dressed in a business suit with a skirt that rested a few inches above her knees. The tank beneath her blazer dipped into a low V, exposing a generous amount of cleavage. Normally, Gina's cleavage would have no impact on Elle, but this time said cleavage was uncomfortably close to Luke—and she didn't like that. Her teeth clenched and her hands balled into fists as she observed them.

Whitney leaned in close to Elle. "You have to get used to seeing them like this."

Elle's teeth remained clenched, but she opened her hands and placed them into her lap. "I know."

Whitney patted Elle's leg softly. "Chemistry is good. We want chemistry."

"You're right, I know. This is just . . . it's all new territory for me, that's all."

"I get it. But this too shall pass." Whitney stood and blocked Elle's view of her two leads. "I gotta run. Good luck today and let me know how it goes."

"Will do."

Elle glanced at her watch, knowing it was time for filming to begin. Rob returned to his chair; his feet bounced against the floor and his knees bobbed up and down. If Elle weren't consumed by her own anxiety, she would have attempted to quell his.

"You ready?" Rob asked.

"As ready as I'll ever be." Elle faked the most confident smile she could muster and patted Rob on the wrist, her signal to get filming started.

"Let's do this." Rob stood, walked next to camera one and gestured for his assistant, Tim, to bring out the marker. "Places, people. I need quiet on the set!"

Tim, a man in his early twenties, stood for a moment, allowing everyone to settle down and prepare for filming. Then he held the marker for camera one. "*Follow the Sun*, episode seven, take one."

"And action!" Rob yelled, and episode seven was on its way.

• • • • •

"How did I do?" Luke looked exhausted after ten hours of filming. He wasn't used to the grueling ten-hour days or the multiple takes every scene required. But to the naked eye, it didn't seem to faze him. He didn't hesitate when Rob or Elle requested he change his approach to a line, and he listened intently to all instructions given to him.

And best of all, his chemistry with Gina was off the charts. Although, that was the most difficult part of the day for Elle—but she was working on it. She couldn't let her jealousy of his obvious attraction to a Hollywood actress affect her desire for a successful show.

"You did great."

"So . . . we only got through about six pages today. Is that normal?"

"Of course. I know it's tedious, but it's the nature of the beast. It'll take us an entire week to film this episode. We've only just begun."

He placed his hands in his pockets, nodding along as Elle spoke. "I'm famished," he said. "How about you?"

"Yeah, I avoided the craft services table. I gained ten pounds the first season. They make it way too easy to eat junk."

Actually, Elle had gained *fifteen* pounds, but she thought ten sounded better when retelling the story. Craft services was a staple for any film or television shoot—a catering company provided all kinds of delectable treats . . . sandwiches, doughnuts, bagels and cream cheese. Almost everything but a salad was available for their ten- to twelve-hour shoots. Elle had grown accustomed to bringing her lunch in to avoid eating all of the tempting desserts and pastries.

Luke rubbed the back of his neck. "I was too nervous to eat."

The innocent expression on Luke's face made Elle's heart melt just slightly. His honesty and sweetness were endearing and she couldn't let another second go by without kissing him gently on the lips, not caring who might see the act of PDA.

Luke grinned. "What was that for?"

"Nothing, really. I just think you're pretty great."

"I think you're pretty great too, Ms. Riley. Shall we eat?"

Elle stopped dead in her tracks. "Oh, right. One minute, I just need to find Gina."

Luke's relaxed face contorted slightly. He looked confused. "Gina? How come?"

"She knows the name of the pizza place."

Luke relaxed. "Oh, that. She told me earlier. It's Anthony's Pub in Westwood."

Elle was puzzled. Why would Gina and Luke be discussing the restaurant? Did Elle mention Gina told her about the place? Her brain was fuzzy. After working ten hours, there was no sense in pushing the issue, so she simply asked Luke for the address.

"That I don't know. But maybe they have a website."

Elle retrieved her phone from her purse, typing in the name of the restaurant and town. Westwood was a college town surrounding the UCLA campus, so it didn't surprise her that a bar and pizza joint would be popular there. When she googled the place, however, no website was listed, only an address and phone number.

"Shall we?" she asked, leading Luke to her car on the studio lot.

• • • • •

Anthony's Pub was a tiny bar and restaurant tucked into a side street just minutes from campus. Elle felt right at home the moment they walked through the door. She was surrounded by Chicago. Chicago Bears banners hung from the ceiling, a framed Coach Ditka sweater-vest was in a glass case behind the bar, and the walls were painted in navy blue and pumpkin orange.

The place even smelled like home.

"Do you smell that?" she asked as they walked inside the cozy restaurant, greeted at once by the leather stools next to the thick oak bar. The aromas of oregano, basil, and melted butter saturated the air. Elle breathed in deeply to bask in the comfort the smells brought to her senses.

Luke placed his hand on the small of her back. "If it tastes half as good as it smells, I think I'll be in love with this place."

"I've had it. Trust me, it's to die for."

Despite the bar area buzzing with college students, they were able to find a small table near the back of the restaurant. Their waitress, a petite brunette with a dimply grin, took their drink orders while they pondered the pizza.

"You know I'll eat anything . . . and you're the expert. What do you recommend?"

"Italian sausage for sure. Very Chicago. Do you like mushrooms?"

Luke scrunched his nose. "They're not my favorite. But I'll take one for the team if you so desire."

Elle laughed, taking his outstretched hand in her own. "Nah, we'll skip it. What about pepperoni? It'll be a meat lover's pizza."

"Ah, now you're talking. That sounds awesome."

Their waitress arrived with a glass of cabernet and a stein of beer. Luke ordered the pizza and they sat back in their chairs, discussing their day.

"So you really think I did all right, huh?"

Elle wasn't sure if Luke was fishing for compliments or if he was really quite so uncertain about his performance, but she found it refreshing regardless. In her experience, he was an anomaly. Nolan and other actors like him were frequently overconfident about their abilities and their egos bruised easily when criticized. Luke, however, was a strong actor considering his lack of experience in front of a camera, and Elle was confident that once he got acclimated to the routine, he'd become a fine actor, perhaps even one worthy of an Emmy nod.

"You were great."

"Back to the grind tomorrow, huh?"

Elle nodded, taking a small sip of her wine, savoring the notes of blackberry and oak. "You'll get used to it."

"Oh, I don't mind," he said, looking as if he was trying to reassure her of his enthusiasm for the show. "I loved it. I think the entire process is fascinating."

"Me too."

And it was the truth. Since moving to California, she'd submerged herself in every aspect of television show creation. She wanted to know absolutely everything there was to know, and she hoped it showed in her series. She knew the ropes, the process, the *rules* of executing a quality television program and she was damn proud of it.

When the pizza arrived, Luke served Elle first before placing a steaming hot piece of deep-dish pie on his plate. Layers of thick melted cheese pooled on their plates and the marinara appeared to be filled with fresh crushed tomatoes and spices. The two moaned their approval of the meal with each bite.

"How have I never tried this place?" Luke asked.

Elle shrugged. "Outside, it just looks like a college bar. I'm shocked they don't advertise their pizza."

"I know," Luke replied. "Clearly it's the star of the show."

Elle chuckled before narrowing her eyes. "Did you just pun on purpose?"

"I'm sorry, I couldn't resist. I have television on the brain."

Luke reached for Elle's hand, taking it in his own and kissing the palm.

"Forgiven."

Luke's mouth fell open as Elle said that simple word he'd said only weeks before. He then kissed her palm again; this time his lips lingered against her sensitive skin. His eyes closed as his mouth seduced her hand. They'd made love dozens of times, but this small act was one of the most enticing things Luke had done in her presence. So intimate, so sensual. She was hooked. Arousal built inside of Elle and despite her fatigue after a long, tedious workday, and despite the fact they weren't yet finished with dinner, Elle was possessed by a different kind of hunger.

The hunger for Luke. She wanted him right then and there.

Her thoughts were interrupted by a deep, and oddly familiar, voice.

"Are you enjoying your meal, folks?"

She'd know that voice anywhere. It had been ten years, but it was the same. Exactly the same.

Elle gasped. Her heart sped out of control and a rush of adrenaline flooded her belly. As she mustered the energy to turn to face the man who had stolen her heart years ago, Luke looked at her with confusion in his eyes. When she did turn and look at the man, his mouth dropped and his eyes were wide. He was as shocked as Elle.

"Rigby?"

Troy Saladino hadn't aged much in the ten years they'd been apart. His muscular chest pulled at his crisp white shirt. His olive skin was just as she'd remembered it. His hair was still cut short, with just a touch of gel to create a purposely messed-up appearance near his forehead.

"Troy?"

Elle stood face-to-face with the only man she ever loved. But instead of hugging him or greeting him in any sort of amicable fashion, she could only stare at him in disbelief, not knowing what move on her part would be deemed acceptable. He took a small step back, running his fingers through his hair.

"I haven't seen you since . . . since—"

"Vegas." He finished her sentence for her, then cleared his throat. His cheeks turned a deep shade of crimson. His chest rose and fell and he turned away briefly, covering his mouth with his hand.

"Elle?"

Luke had risen from his chair and taken Elle's hand in his own.

"I'm sorry, what did you call her?" Troy looked down at the joined hands. Elle watched his eyes focus on the simple display of affection.

"Luke, can you give us a minute?" Elle asked, placing a hand on Luke's shoulder.

"Are you sure?" Luke stared at Troy as he asked the question.

"Yes. I, uh . . . I just need a minute, okay?"

"Fine. I'll be here."

Luke returned to the table, not taking his eyes off Troy. Elle turned back to Troy, eyeing the bar as if to ask him to talk with her away from the table.

"What are you doing here?" Troy asked when they reached the bar.

"I work in Los Angeles, I have a TV show. *Follow the Sun*. Didn't you know that?"

Troy crossed his arms in front of his chest. "No, I didn't."

Elle rolled her eyes, knowing in her gut he was saying that out of spite. There was no way he didn't know about her show—it was on every week, the characters were draped across billboards, they'd posed for *Entertainment Weekly*. It was everywhere in the pop culture subconscious.

"Fine, okay, I've heard of it. But I didn't know it was yours. You're like, what? An actress or something?"

Anger was building inside of Elle, an emotion she thought she'd never allow herself to feel when it came to him. Troy knew Elle had wanted to write. Even in college, she'd majored in English with a focus on creative writing. For him to assume she'd abandoned her love of writing to act was absurd. Didn't he know her better than that?

"No, I created the show. They're based on my novels."

Troy licked his lips, looking smug. And for a brief second, Elle wanted to punch him right in the face. But then she remembered what happened ten years ago and she reeled her emotions back in.

"Oh, that's right. You're a writer, I forgot."

"Whatever." Elle tapped her finger on the bar. "What are *you* doing here? I thought you still lived in Chicago."

"Ahh, keeping tabs on me, Rigby?"

"I stopped asking years ago, Troy. If I had, do you really think I'd be here?" Her brow raised, she tipped her chin. Troy flinched, receiving her unspoken message.

"How do I know this wasn't a ploy? You show up with Mr. Hot Shot over there and try to make me jealous or someth—"

"Are you out of your mind?" Elle's voice had turned to an agitated squeal. No one knew how to push her buttons like Troy Saladino. Absolutely nobody. When several patrons at the bar turned to glare at Elle, she lowered her voice. "You know that's not my style. When I hurt people, it's *not* intentional. Despite what they might think . . ."

Troy lowered his chin, pulling back against his neck. "Fine, whatever. So you're here."

"I'm here," Elle conceded. "And you, what . . . you work here?"

"Actually, it's mine. I own it."

Elle swallowed hard, remembering how quickly she fell in love with the pizza of Anthony's Pub. The pizza Troy had created.

"Why the name? If you own the place, why didn't you name it Troy's Pub?"

"It was my father's name, remember?"

"Was?" Elle asked, feeling terrible for a moment as she remembered Tony Saladino, one of the nicest men she'd ever encountered. And suddenly, it all made sense. The smells of home, the delectable homemade sauce and familiar spices. Mr. Saladino was a genius in the kitchen and prepared pizza for his family quite often.

"He passed away two years ago."

Elle lowered her voice, looking at the floor. "Oh God. I'm so sorry."

"Yeah, well . . ." Troy looked back toward Elle's table. And in that very moment, Elle realized she'd completely forgotten about Luke. She turned to see him sitting at the table, watching their heated discussion.

"I should really get back."

"To your boyfriend?" Troy asked, his voice low as he stared at Luke with contempt in his deep eyes. Elle used to crave the soulful, expressive nature of those eyes. Now, they held nothing for her but disdain. Her stomach flipped and she felt like she could vomit.

Wouldn't that just be the icing on the cake?

"Yeah," she said softly, not wanting to explain the nature of her relationship with Luke. The conversation was awkward enough already. "To my boyfriend."

"Lucky guy." His words were snide, as if he was trying to transfer his anger to its rightful owner. She knew who that owner was. They both did. He crossed his arms in front of his chest and tilted his head to the side. "Has anyone warned him yet?"

"What do you mean?"

"Not to get too attached, the poor sap."

His words were like a swift punch to the gut. And she knew if she didn't walk away that instant, she'd sob in front of him, exposing her pain to the world. There was no way she'd allow that. Not after ten years.

"Good-bye, Troy."

Elle returned to the table, leaving Troy standing at the bar. Luke had paid the bill and requested their pizza be boxed up to go. Elle was grateful for the gesture as she knew she couldn't stand being inside Troy's restaurant for even just a moment longer.

She needed to run far, far away from Anthony's Pub.

Chapter 8

"Wanna talk about it?"

Luke's question interrupted the hurricane inside Elle's head as they drove along the highway, headed back to Elle's home. Thoughts of Troy, both good and bad, flew with wild abandon around her brain. Despite the calm, tranquil breeze of the evening, she couldn't focus on anything, not even Luke's request. She shook her head. She knew it wasn't fair to shut down in such a manner but had no idea what to even say.

Luke reached to take her hand in his. Elle squeezed his fingertips while staring at the road ahead, attempting to process the events of that evening. Troy lived in California, not back in Chicago as she'd assumed. He owned a restaurant only half an hour from her place. And if his eyes were any indication, he still resented her just as much as the day he left her behind in their hotel room at the Bellagio. That final thought made a chill run down her spine.

Even though she was filled with resentment and lingering questions toward her ex, the thought of him hating her was just . . . too much.

Luke released her hand and turned off the radio. "Listen, I'm not gonna pretend to know what happened back there, but whatever it is, you can tell me."

Elle turned to face Luke. His wavy locks blew in the evening breeze. He was so handsome, with such a good heart, she knew he deserved to know the truth about Troy, the truth about her past. But their relationship was new and she was apprehensive.

"He's an ex."

Luke chuckled and patted her bare knee. "I figured that."

"A complicated one."

"Were you together long?"

Elle shook her head before resting it on her hand. Her elbow perched against the interior of Luke's SUV. "On and off. We couldn't seem to figure it out."

"What did he call you . . . back at the restaurant?"

Elle pressed her eyes shut before repeating her nickname. "Rigby."

Luke paused. "What does that mean?"

"It's from the Beatles song." Elle waited for Luke to make the connection to the song, but his brow remained knitted as his eyes remained on the road. "My real name is Eleanor. Elle is just a nickname."

"Sorry, I don't know the song. I'm not really a fan." He clenched his teeth, baring his pearly whites in a *please forgive me* manner.

Of course listening to the Beatles wasn't a prerequisite to date her, but she always found herself surprised when people weren't as wrapped up in the pop culture icons as she was. "Oh, I had no idea. Sorry, I just assumed—"

"I don't dislike them or anything. I just prefer the Stones."

Elle liked the Rolling Stones, but in her mind there was no comparison. She'd once read an editorial in which the writer claimed the 1960s were all about the Stones, not the Beatles. She'd vehemently disagreed.

Luke cleared his throat and continued. "So when did you go out?"

"Ten years ago."

"Wow. Long time." He paused, shifting in his seat. He looked uncomfortable and Elle could tell he was choosing his words carefully. "And you still . . . never mind." He shook his head.

Elle shifted in her seat, turning her body toward Luke. "No, what is it?"

"Nah." He patted her leg again, this time allowing it to linger on her knee. "It's way too soon for discussions like that. It's not like we're exclusive . . ."

Elle's brow formed a deep crease above her nose and uncertainty built within her. Luke's tone was confusing. He was either fishing for a declaration of exclusivity or relieving himself of any sort of commitment hovering in the SUV. Normally, she'd confront him and insist on knowing exactly what he meant by that. But Troy's reemergence was more than enough chaos for her to handle at the moment. She felt like she was walking through the surfing part of a fun house where you have to walk through the turning disk. Around and around it goes, as your feet attempt to walk across its constantly spinning axis. She was disoriented, confused, and felt as if she'd left her bearings back at Anthony's Pub.

The remainder of the car ride was silent. Elle stared out the window, breathing in the ocean air as they entered Santa Monica. She craved the comforts of home and wanted nothing more than to hide under the plush covers of her bed, allowing only Linus to puncture her solitude.

Luke walked Elle to her front door, his hands in his pockets and his lips pressed in a straight line. Elle fumbled with her keys, her hands trembled, and her concentration faltered. When she inserted the proper key, the door pushed open. She sighed with relief, turning back to Luke.

"I think we should call it a night."

Luke nodded. "I figured that."

"I'll see you tomorrow." She faked a smile. "Bright and early."

"You got it." Luke removed his hands from his pockets, placing them on Elle's waist, pulling her close. "Good night, Elle. I hope you have pleasant dreams."

Elle pressed her eyes tight, willing the tears that were forming to go the hell away. She had no time to cry over Troy or the burden he placed on her mind and she had no time to ponder what this meant for her budding relationship with Luke.

Elle pressed her lips to Luke's, softly at first, but when his fingers gripped into the skin of her back, she opened her mouth to deepen the kiss. She cupped his cheeks with her hands, pressing them tightly to his warm skin, hoping he could make everything better. Somehow.

With one outstretched arm, Luke opened the door, walking Elle backward into her house. His mouth drifted to her neck and the tickling sensation of his lips served as respite for her conflicted body and mind. Luke's touch was intoxicating and she wanted nothing more than to get lost in the beautiful man who was worshiping her body, awakening every cell with his expert touch.

In a swift motion, he'd taken her hands and lifted them above her head, pressing her back into the cold wood of the door. A small gasp left Elle's mouth and her eyes locked with his. Luke's voice was husky and deep. "I'll make you forget about him."

One simple tear, filled with the pain of the past and conflict of the present, fell from Elle's eye. Luke watched it as it drifted down her cheek. When the warm tear reached her jaw, he lunged slightly and

kissed it from her skin. Elle was tormented by guilt. She wanted to succumb to Luke, to indulge in the way he made her feel, but how could
she do that when her thoughts kept drifting back to someone else?

Elle freed herself from his grasp. She wiped her cheek with the
back of her hand, turning back toward the door. "We should really
call it a night."

Luke grabbed her hand, pulling her back. He nuzzled his nose
against the most sensitive part of her ear. "Be here now," he whispered. "Nowhere else. Just here."

Overwrought with both sadness and arousal, Elle pressed her
lips to Luke's; he reached to support her, hoisting her up against the
door, allowing her to wrap both legs around his waist. He rocked
into her again and again. The sensation of him, hard beneath his
jeans, sent Elle into a frenzy. She wanted to escape into Luke, to
forget about Troy and the burdensome conflict of her past.

With her legs still wrapped around his waist, Luke carried her
upstairs to the bedroom. They made love in the darkness and when
Luke drifted off to sleep, Elle stared up at the ceiling, once again
enveloped in the incident at Anthony's Pub. Despite her sated desires,
despite the slow rise and fall of the handsome man next to her in bed,
a man she'd done nothing but think about for the last few months,
she was back at the pub. She was standing next to the bar, looking
into Troy's soulful eyes, wanting to know more about him, despite
the resentment that stood within her like a hulking tower. She was
standing there, smelling the marinara, feeling the heavy weight of
the bar against her fingertips and staring at the man she couldn't
forget despite the rantings in her head and the tugging of her heart.

She tried.

She tried to forget about Troy.

But that just wasn't possible.

Chapter 9

The fourth season of *Follow the Sun* was well on its way. Six episodes had aired and the tabloids had received word of a new actor who would soon grace the screen of the television hit. Paparazzi stalked Luke like newly discovered prey in the wild. He was a fresh face and although he wasn't involved in any kind of personal controversy just yet, the photographers held on to any shred of a chance they could get at discovering just the tiniest bit of dirt on Luke Kingston.

Nicole had been fielding phone calls from the gossip rags for several weeks. Elle had given her assistant a script to follow. She was to acknowledge Luke's role on the show, but to answer nothing else. Of course, Nicole knew nothing of Elle's personal relationship with the new member of the cast. A very small circle of people was aware of that information and Elle intended to keep it that way.

Elle and Rob were discussing episode fifteen in her office when Nicole knocked on the door.

"Elle, sorry to bother you, but you have a delivery."

Elle was confused. Nicole knew that, aside from an emergency, she was not to be disturbed while meeting with a colleague, especially Rob or Whitney. Whatever it was, Nicole could place it on her desk when they'd finished their discussion.

"Okay, bring it in, whatever it is."

"Um, actually, it's a pizza."

"Pizza?" Elle glanced at her watch. It was barely 11:00 a.m.

A distinctive flutter spread throughout her abdomen and her heart rate increased within seconds when the deliveryman slid next to Nicole and revealed his face. A face she couldn't forget even after ten years of trying. A face she hadn't seen in weeks since their awkward confrontation at Anthony's Pub.

"Oh." Elle stood, staring at Troy, who with one hand was holding a small white, green, and red pizza box. His other arm was hidden from view. His dark hair was perfectly coifed and a set of dark sunglasses rested atop his head.

"Thought you might be hungry."

Rob stood, looking down at his cell. "That reminds me, I told Whitney I'd meet her for a bite. I'll check in later, Elle."

"Thanks."

Rob followed Nicole out of the office and Elle stood staring at Troy. The butterflies in her stomach started out tiny, but were now spreading their wings and bouncing around inside her. She attempted to appear stoic, to sound like her normally confident, collected self. But he knew her too well. He must have known how anxious she was to see him again.

"Rigby."

"Troy. What are you doing here?"

Troy extended his other arm, revealing a small, pale green branch with slim leaves. Two small olives hung from the sprig.

"You brought me an olive branch?" She resisted a smile as best she could, but the truth was, she was touched by the sentiment.

"It was either this or a jar of olives. I thought this was a little more symbolic."

"Most definitely." Elle crossed her arms in front of her chest but walked closer to Troy, taking the branch from his hand. His fingers brushed hers and an undeniable electricity traveled up her arm and down her spine.

"How on earth did you get in here?"

"I told the security guard I was delivering your lunch. You didn't get to finish eating when you came to my place, and I felt bad about that."

"Thanks. Come, sit."

Elle watched as Troy glanced around her office, taking in the photographs on the walls, the posters of previous seasons, and her framed Emmy nomination letter. Once he'd inspected every bit of memorabilia, he sat opposite her, placing the pizza box on her desk.

"Sausage and mushroom, your favorite."

Elle tilted her head, again touched by the gesture. This wasn't the same Troy who'd confronted her in the restaurant. This Troy was kinder, gentler, more in control of his emotions. This Troy reminded her of just how sweet he could be. He had a soft side, even though he did his best to conceal it.

"I asked around. The show's a big hit. Congratulations."

"You asked around?"

"You know, my staff. The waitresses are huge fans. I may be asking you for some autographs sometime in the near future." He chuckled, rubbing his thumb and forefinger against his chin. The slightest bit of stubble was coming through and Elle remembered how much she used to love running her fingers over his five o'clock shadow.

"Ah, I should've known you had an ulterior motive," Elle teased.

Troy shrugged. "What can I say? I'm full of 'em, I guess."

One of the butterflies in Elle's abdomen stretched its wings to full capacity and she grasped her desk to get her bearings. Being in such close quarters with Troy was unreal—a scenario she'd played out in her head dozens of times over the years. She'd practiced speeches, rehearsed scenes in her head. She'd confront him for leaving her alone in that hotel room. No plane ticket home. No clue as to where he had gone.

But now, she was finding it difficult to simply form a coherent thought while in his presence. She looked around her office as Troy opened the box of steaming deep-dish pizza.

"Plates. I, um," she stammered. "I don't have plates. Give me a minute, okay?"

"Sure."

Elle hurried out of her office, walking briskly down the hall to the kitchen to collect plates, napkins, forks, and knives for their lunch. She had no idea how it would even be possible for her to eat around him. There was no way her frayed nerves would allow it. She retrieved two cans of soda from the fridge and made her way back to the office.

Troy looked relaxed sitting in the office chair, his arm casually draped along the back. One ankle rested on his opposite knee and his hand rested on his thigh. His comfort and ease was sexy, yet disheartening. She didn't want to be alone in her anxiety. She wanted them to suffer together, to commiserate in their discomfort. But that didn't appear to be the case.

"I got you a Coke. Do you still—?"

"Yep. Haven't kicked my sugar habit."

Elle placed the can in front of Troy.

"And I see you haven't kicked your poison habit either." Troy always insisted Elle's addiction to diet soda was her unhealthiest habit. He was vehemently against all artificial sweeteners, referring to them as poison to the body.

"Yep, still addicted."

"I guess we haven't changed all that much, have we?"

Elle paused before popping the top of her can. Her eyes bored into Troy's. "That remains to be seen, doesn't it?"

Troy's lips pressed into a thin line and he nodded. The tension in the air was thicker than the deep-dish pizza he sliced open with the knife. He served Elle first, then himself before closing the box and pushing it to the side. The room was still as Elle and Troy stared at one another. They'd already spent entirely too much time dancing around the topic at hand. The elephant in the room was wearing a cowboy hat and a feather boa—it demanded to be seen, discussed, *felt*.

She stabbed her pizza with her fork, which stood straight up in the layers of cheese, sauce, and toppings. *"So* I hope you'll forgive me, but I'm terrible at small talk. I need to know why you're here."

"I was hoping we'd cut to the chase. I'm here because I can't stop thinking about you."

"Oh." A lump formed in Elle's throat as heat grew in her cheeks. She never thought she'd hear those words from Troy Saladino. But she liked them. She liked them a lot.

"The thing is, I gave up hope a long time ago. I never thought I'd see you again."

Elle crossed her arms in front of her chest, tilting her head. "And whose fault is that?"

Troy flinched. "I probably deserve that."

"Probably?"

Troy closed his eyes, shook his head, and continued. "We're in the same city. I *had* to see you."

"You *left*, and then you shut me out. I tried . . . so many times, I tried."

Troy closed his eyes and grimaced. If he thought she wouldn't bring that up, he was sorely mistaken. The years could soften some things, but his sudden departure from her life was not one of them.

"I know," he said.

"I know nothing about your life. Are you married? Divorced? Do you have kids?"

"Yes."

"Yes?" Her heartbeat kicked up a notch as she attempted to appear calm and collected. "To which question?"

"I have a daughter. She's the reason I live out here."

Troy was a father? Elle's stomach tied itself into knots. She hadn't expected that.

"And your wife?"

"I'm not married."

"Divorced, then?"

"No. I've only been married once."

Troy's eyebrows dipped as he peered into Elle's eyes. His face softened, and without meaning to, she mirrored his expression immediately. Even after ten years, their connection was as strong as ever.

"What's your daughter's name?"

"Payton."

Elle tilted her head. "You didn't."

Troy was obsessed with the Chicago Bears, as most Chicagoans were. He was especially enamored of Walter Payton, one of the most prolific running backs in the NFL. Elle would never forget Troy's drunken rendition of the Super Bowl Shuffle, especially when he'd place the sweatband around his head and proclaim himself Walter.

Troy threw his head back in laughter, then held his hands up in surrender.

"Her mother named her, I swear. But of course I didn't object."

"Well, it's a beautiful name. How old is she?"

"She'll be nine on Christmas Day."

Elle swallowed hard, and an ache developed in her gut. *Nine?* His daughter was going to be *nine years old,* which meant that as Elle spent months attempting to get over him and his disappearance from her world, Troy wasted no time in moving on. She could feel the blood draining from her cheeks.

"Nine?"

"Rigby, I—"

"Nine?" Her eyes widened as she glared at Troy, who looked up at the ceiling, guilt spreading across his face.

"I know what you're thinking, but it's *not* like that. It was a rebound, and her mother and I are still friends."

Elle shifted in her seat, but said nothing. Troy cleared his throat before filling the awkward silence that lingered between them.

"It works for us *and* I get to be in my daughter's life, which is all I want. She's my whole world."

"I see." Elle pushed the rejection she was feeling down below the surface and resolved to focus on the facts. She wanted more information; she wanted to know everything she could. Troy was a puzzle and she was determined to make the pieces come together, even if they would never quite fit.

"You said she's the reason you're here . . ."

"Yeah. Her mom moved here seven years ago. She married a guy in the recording industry and I couldn't be across the country from my kid. So I followed them here."

"Well, now I know why we never ran into each other when I was still in Chicago."

Troy nodded. "Yeah."

"But a restaurant? When we—I mean, you were an accountant—"

"I know." Troy stood and paced Elle's office. "I was. Even out here, I was. I worked at a talent agency for a long time. But when my dad got sick, things changed. I changed."

"I'm sorry about your dad. I had no idea. I would have been there." The guilt Elle felt for missing Tony Saladino's services was palpable. He'd always been good to her, even when things between her and his son were rocky.

"I know."

"What changed?"

"I was miserable, ya know? I went to work every day, crunching numbers, meeting with clients, and I hated it. I went back to Chicago to help out whenever I could. I'd take long weekends and take my dad to chemo. We'd sit and talk and he knew—he *knew* I was miserable. He told me life was short. And for the first time, I believed him."

"The restaurant's great," Elle said. "It felt like home, like being back in Chicago."

"I'm glad you think so. Aside from Payton, it's my pride and joy."

"You found your dream."

"And you obviously found yours." Troy gestured to the frames on the walls. "Seriously, Rigby, this is the big time. Your show is all the buzz, you have an Emmy nomination."

"I didn't win."

"Still. You're living the dream."

"Yeah." She paused, allowing her eyes to wander around her office in appreciation of the career she'd built. "I guess I am."

"How did this happen?" He gestured to their surroundings.

"Well, years ago I wrote a book. And then another . . . and another. They were picked up by a publisher and just over five years ago, I got this call. It was the head of the studio wanting a meeting."

"That must've been wild."

"It was. Wild and scary and just . . . crazy. They made me an offer I couldn't refuse, and before I knew it I was packing up my car and moving here. I rented for a while and then bought my place. It's not quite home yet, but it's getting there."

"Wow." Troy licked his lips and ran his fingers through his hair. "Would it be weird if I said I was proud of you?"

Elle smirked, appreciating Troy's honesty given the awkward situation they found themselves in. "A little bit, but thanks. Hey, let's eat before this delicious pizza gets cold."

"You're right. Dig in." Troy returned to his seat and dug into his pizza as Elle did the same. They ate, mostly in comfortable silence. Elle oohed and ahhed over the delicious pie.

"This was your dad's recipe, wasn't it?"

Troy nodded, wiping his mouth with a napkin and taking a sip of his Coke. "Mostly. I've been experimenting with the spice palette."

"Whatever you're doing, it's perfection." Elle took another large bite, closing her eyes as she relished the rustic Italian flavors of the pizza. "Does your mom ever visit? She must miss you."

"She lives in Long Beach, actually. I convinced her to buy this tiny cottage right on the water. Payton loves going to Nana's place."

"Nice." She hesitated to say her next statement, but blurted it out before her type A personality could reel it back in. "I'd love to meet her."

Troy's mouth opened, and his eyes met hers. For a sliver of a moment, Elle thought he looked hopeful, softer, and slightly vulnerable. Yes, their discussion was mostly surface—catching up with one another, glossing over the gritty details and covering the need-to-know basics. But Elle was genuinely interested in meeting his daughter. She surprised even herself with that realization. And if she wanted to meet Payton, that meant their story wasn't quite over, despite what the scripts in her desk drawer might say.

"I'm sure she'd love you," Troy said with a soft smile, tilting his head to the side. Elle's heart did a double take and the butterflies spread their wings. And they fluttered. It was a hopeful flutter. Her inner cynic wanted to scream her head off, shaming Elle for allowing the turn of this conversation to transpire. Troy deserved her resentment, her inner conflict, and her regrets. He didn't deserve her hope.

"Why are you here?" Her voice cracked with the words.

Troy wrinkled his nose and pursed his lips. "I told you, I couldn't stop thinking about you."

"Ten years, Troy. Ten ridiculously long years."

Silence swept over the room. Troy's nostrils flared as he gritted his teeth.

"You and I both know there was a damn good reason why I left."

There it was, the punch to the gut Elle was waiting for. She wondered if they'd ever be able to stand in a room together without him throwing her mistakes in her face. They sat in silence for several minutes, playing an awkward game of chicken. Troy was the first to jump.

"Listen, I've kept you long enough," Troy said. "And the lunch crowd should be starting soon."

Elle stood, reaching for the top of the pizza box. Troy's hand stopped her. "No, you keep that. Share it with . . . well, share it with whoever you want."

Elle walked Troy to the door. When he reached to pull her into a hug, she found herself relaxing into his embrace, breathing in the scent of him. Troy smelled like spearmint and fresh soap. And as she inhaled, years of memories surged through her brain. Some blissful, some unbearable. But many worth hanging on to. At least, she hoped they were.

Elle gritted her teeth, realizing she'd just given Troy Saladino her hope.

Dammit.

Chapter 10

"That's a wrap, people."

The bells sounded. Cast and crew members scattered from the soundstage. Elle sighed, knowing another episode was ready for editing and the final stages of production. Coincidentally, Luke's first episode, shot a few weeks prior, would air that evening. He'd officially be tabloid fodder, which was unsettling to Elle. She wasn't quite ready to share him with the American public.

From the corner of her eye she saw Luke and Gina huddled together. Surprised, she turned to give them her full attention. Gina was pressing her cheek to Luke's, her right arm outstretched, holding her phone until it flashed. Elle focused on the satisfied smile across Luke's face. And despite the irritation she felt toward Gina, she was genuinely happy for Luke. In just a few hours, America would be introduced to him. He'd made it. His career was on the rise and, professionally speaking, it was a gigantic milestone for the actor. Elle chose to focus on that, rather than the actress standing beside him.

Gina had been quite the diva since the altercation between her and Nolan during the table read. Elle knowing about their problems did nothing for her attitude, either. And frankly, Elle was tired of her entitled behavior. Yes, she was the star of the show, but she should respect those who wrote the lines she delivered.

Elle shrugged off her frustration, knowing the migraine taking up residence behind her eyes was probably the culprit. She needed to go home, turn off all the lights, slather peppermint oil on her forehead and temples, and call it a night. She reached for her bag, but a familiar hand grabbed it first, handing it to her.

Luke.

"The rest of the cast is going out for drinks. You up for it?"

Elle shook her head. "I have a killer headache. I need to go home."

"Do you care if I go?" Luke tilted his head, both eyebrows raised, and his cerulean eyes gleaming beneath the stage lights.

"Not at all. I'm going to bed as soon as I get home. My head's killing me."

"I'm sorry. I'll see you tomorrow. Table read at ten, right?"

Elle rubbed her thumb and forefinger against her forehead, attempting to remember her schedule. "Yeah, that sounds right."

"Do you need me to drive you? You don't look so good. Sorta pale." Luke placed his hand at the base of her chin as he inspected her face. Elle sloughed him off. Their relationship was still under wraps and she didn't need prying eyes attempting to dissect it.

"Sorry," he muttered.

"It's okay. And no, I can drive myself. Thank you, though." Elle pulled the corners of her mouth up in a weak smile. "Go, have fun. Watch yourself on screen."

"That's the plan." Luke winked at Elle as he walked away, joining Gina and the other cast members near the door of the soundstage.

"You won't be able to keep it a secret much longer."

Rob was standing by the craft services table, his arms crossed in front of his chest. Elle avoided the judgment she knew was lingering behind his gaze.

"I know."

She didn't have the energy to debate her relationship status right now, especially with the director. She gathered the rest of her things and made her way out of the studio, away from the stress and pressure of *Follow the Sun*.

•••••

The aroma of peppermint inundated Elle's bedroom. Her temples tingled as the oil permeated her pores, relieving the pain of her migraine. Despite her desire to fall asleep and wake up completely healed, her brain refused to wind down. Thoughts of Luke and Troy besieged her aching head.

Elle's mind drifted to the day, eleven years ago, when she and Troy had decided to be a couple—to finally give themselves a chance at a romantic relationship rather than a friendship riddled with sexual chemistry and tension.

Troy was twenty-four years old, and Elle was about to turn twenty-four as well. Elle was working as a journalist for the *Chicago Tribune*. Well, officially she was a journalist, but unofficially she worked in the classifieds department. She was a glorified data entry specialist, but she came to work each day, paying her dues in the hopes of being promoted within the company. She hoped to one day receive an actual assignment for an actual article that would be printed in the newspaper. In her spare time, she was crafting short stories. Ironically, the classifieds she read each day were useful for small bits of information. When someone expects four-hundred-and-fifty dollars for a ten-year-old birdcage, it can get the creative juices flowing.

Troy was working as an accountant for Wolf & Company and seemed to be passionate about helping companies grow and develop. He was always good with numbers, so organized and determined. That was something he and Elle had in common. He worked at least fifty hours per week, and at the end of the day he and Elle would meet for a drink at one of the bars in Wrigleyville. Elle had three roommates, as did Troy. Chicago real estate was tough business, and sharing was inevitable, no matter how well an entry-level position paid.

One summer evening, the night before her birthday, they were enjoying a couple of drinks at John Barleycorn, a local bar filled with sports fans and local twentysomethings alike. The Cubs were playing on the big screen. Troy and Elle nibbled on sliders as they drank their beer. Elle had just ended a relationship with one of Troy's roommates.

Ethan was all wrong for her. In many ways, she regretted that relationship the moment it began. They'd hooked up after a party at Troy's place. Ethan said all the right things and seduced Elle with compliments. And as she had in the past, even though she wasn't quite aware of it, Elle sought Troy's attention in all the wrong ways. She'd spent years regretting her behavior at the campsite, knowing Troy was all-in. He wanted her, and not just for a measly hookup in a tent. He wanted a relationship with her. Which is what she *thought* she wanted, too.

After five years, however, she and Troy were still just friends. Close ones, yes, but friends just the same, and Elle was getting restless. So she and Ethan dated casually for six weeks. She'd ended it over a cup of coffee that morning. Ethan was, as predicted, not the least bit upset. Neither of them had gone into it with any sort of grand expectation. But he'd said something that morning. Something Elle couldn't get off her mind. And after three beers, she was finally ready to talk about it.

"Ethan said something this morning." She placed her beer on the coaster, wiping the back of her mouth with her hand.

Troy sighed. "I thought you were fine. Why are you bringing him up again, Rigby? He's a douche."

"He's your friend."

"Yeah, but he's a douche. He doesn't deserve you." Troy's eyebrows pulled in tight and a little crease formed above his nose.

"You're cute when you do that," she slurred.

"Okay, *you're* cut off."

Elle slid from her barstool and stood next to Troy. "I'm serious. I love that you look out for me."

Troy's expression softened. "I always will, you know that."

"I do." She looked down; her ballet flats were sticking to the beer on the floor. "But he said something . . . and I want to know what *you* think about it."

"Okay, fine. Hit me." Troy took another swig of his beer, placing it back on the coaster before him, before turning to Elle, giving her his full attention.

"Ethan thinks . . ." She was losing her nerve. Without thinking, she grabbed her beer and chugged. She downed the amber liquid until her pint glass was empty but for a few lone suds at the bottom.

"Whoa, must be serious."

"He thinks I'm in love with you," she blurted out, swallowing hard as she stared at Troy. His eyes widened and his mouth dropped slightly. He stared at her lips, then looked to her nose, her cheeks, her eyes.

"And?"

Despite the look of surprise, Elle could also see his muscles tighten, as if he was bracing himself for disappointment. And she knew, she knew she'd been playing games with him for far too long. It was time to grow up—to face her feelings for him, to give herself a real chance at happiness with Troy Saladino.

"And I think he's right."

Troy nodded, swallowed hard, and lifted his glass to his lips, draining the beer just as Elle had done. He then turned his body and flagged down the bartender, tapping his glass to ask for a refill on his beer. Still, he said nothing as he angled himself back toward Elle. Tears formed in her eyes as she wondered if she was too late. If Troy had given up on her long ago, outside of that tent.

"And tomorrow?" Troy asked.

"What do you mean?"

"I mean, tomorrow, when your buzz is gone, what will your answer be? No more games, Rigby, I'm serious." His pupils widened as he glared at her.

Elle placed her fingers in Troy's short hair, running them through slowly as she gazed into his pained eyes. She knew that, yes, the beer had given her liquid courage. But she'd felt this way for years; she just hadn't been ready to face it.

"It's been years, Troy. Years. Tomorrow will be just another day on the calendar. Another day I've loved you. Buzz, no buzz. It doesn't matter. It's the truth and I'm *finally* ready for you to hear it." She grabbed her empty glass. "I just needed this to give me the guts."

Troy took her hand in his and she looked down at his fingertips stroking her skin. When she raised her attention back to his face, she couldn't read his expression. Relief? Love? Confusion?

"And you? How do you feel?"

Troy squeezed her hand. "You know how I feel."

"Show me." Elle tilted her chin up, challenging him to kiss her. Troy abandoned his barstool and stood, placing his hand behind her neck and pulling her in for a kiss. She smiled as their lips made contact and immediately Troy deepened the kiss, stroking her tongue with his. For just a moment, they were nothing but lips, tongues, and roaming hands, until Troy pulled back, breathing heavily and pressing his forehead to hers.

"Wanna get outta here?"

"Yes."

They'd walked arm in arm back to Troy's apartment, his hand resting protectively over hers as they made their way down the block.

They made love for the second time. And the next morning, Elle didn't run. She stayed, and for three hundred and sixty-four days, they were completely smitten. Until they went to Vegas. And everything fell apart.

Tears streamed down Elle's face as she lay in silence in her bedroom. Linus snuggled into her side, attempting to comfort her. But nothing could. Troy was the most significant regret of her life. She cried for their mistakes, for their separation, and for the time they'd lost. But mostly, she cried for the contented moments like the one they spent walking from John Barleycorn's to Troy's apartment. The night she was given a fresh start with the only guy who'd ever captured her heart. She cried for the hope that took up residence in her heart that evening, and for the hope that still remained after so much time.

Chapter 11

Elle crashed into Luke's dressing room with a ferocity she hadn't expected. Justine, the makeup artist, looked up from her canvas with a start, still clutching her bottle of concealer. Her eyes were wide and she stepped back from Luke, who turned his body to face Elle. It was seven fifteen in the morning, with less than an hour before he was needed on set. But for Elle, this couldn't wait. Not even a moment longer.

"Elle, what the hell is going on?"

Elle's nostrils flared as she stalked toward Luke. Her eyes never left his, even as she addressed the makeup artist. "Justine, will you excuse us, please?"

"Yes, of course. I'll be back in five minutes." Justine placed her concealer and sponges on Luke's dressing table and scurried from the room, closing the door softly behind her.

Luke stood, tearing the paper bib from his collar. "What's going on?"

"This." Elle shoved her iPad into Luke's hands.

"Perez Hilton? Who is that?"

"Gossip site, like TMZ. Explain the pictures, Luke."

Luke's eyes closed and his head tilted up toward the ceiling. "It was late, we'd had a few drinks. It was nothing."

Elle scrolled through her iPad, revealing a dozen shots of Luke with Gina at a local bar. Luke's arm was wrapped around her waist, his nose nuzzled into her ear. To Elle, they appeared awfully friendly. Too friendly.

"Listen, I *know* we aren't exclusive. That's not what this is about."

Luke crossed his arms in front of his chest. "Then what's it about?"

"Gina. With Gina comes drama, rumors, gossip rags. Everything I try to stay away from and you *know* that."

"I'm not seeing her."

"Coulda fooled me." Elle pursed her lips. "Listen, if you want to end this, just say so. Date Gina, date whomever you choose. Just leave me out of the bullshit."

"Says the woman who can't stop thinking about her ex."

"*Excuse* me?"

"You heard me."

Elle froze, uncertain of what she could say in rebuttal. Luke was right. Since their first encounter with Troy weeks earlier, she'd been different, distracted. Her heart and her mind were muddled and confused. And that was her fault, not Luke's. She was being unfair. She knew that, but she had enough confusion weighing her down; the idea of having to deal with Gina's dramatics was just too much to handle.

"Look, I'm sorry, I just—" She waved her iPad. "You know this stuff drives me crazy. It pulls my focus, and I can't have that."

Luke closed the gap between them, wrapping his arms around her waist. "I'm not interested in Gina. Yes, I was being friendly, and it was loud in the bar so when I talked to her, I leaned in. That's all these photos show."

Elle tilted her head, narrowing her eyes at Luke. "Do you think I'm stupid?"

"My lips never touched hers. If they had, don't you think Paris Hilton would have put that on her blog?"

Elle allowed a laugh to escape her lips. "*Perez.* Perez Hilton."

Luke chuckled, pulling his lips into a playful smirk. "What did I say?"

"Paris. As in the hotel magnate's daughter. The one who eats gigantic cheeseburgers while washing cars."

"Ah, that's right." Luke pulled Elle in close, tickling her ear with his lips. "C'mon. You know me. Nothing happened."

Elle wanted to believe Luke. She wanted to believe every word that left his mouth. But the truth was, she didn't know him. Not really. They'd known each other for a few months, and reality was setting in on their relationship. Reality that included both Troy and Gina. And she wasn't sure where that would leave them.

"Besides, stuff like this is good, right? I mean, for the show."

If Luke's eyes hadn't held such innocence and obvious good nature, she would've been tempted to slap him right across his beautiful square jaw. That type of statement was the *exact* reason why she didn't date actors—or get involved with anything that could be spread across gossip rags or websites.

"Maybe. There's a delicate balance between good and bad press."

"I thought all press was good press."

"And that's why *you* are an actor and I'm not."

Elle's posture stiffened and she pulled away from Luke's embrace, missing him the second they parted. He rubbed his chin as he peered into her eyes.

"I should go. Justine will be back any minute and I don't want to halt production."

"Fine, but . . . are we okay?"

Elle nodded, faking a smile, knowing there was nothing more to say. "Yes, we're fine. I'll see you out there."

• • • • •

"He has a point."

Whitney took a large sip of her lemon drop martini as the two ladies sat at the bar and waited for their dessert to arrive. Elle rolled her eyes, not wanting to hear it. Whitney should side with her, not Luke. Was it juvenile? Of course, but after two martinis of her own, it's exactly how she was feeling.

"Explain."

"Well." Whitney hesitated, biting her bottom lip. "You're not exclusive, you have no real commitment. He can see Gina and you can see Troy if you want to—see if there's still something there."

"Did you seriously just say that? Troy isn't someone I'd *see*. Troy is all or nothing. And there will *always* be something there."

"Who says?"

"Me. I say." Elle shook her head. "Our past is just . . . it's this sea of uncertainty, you know? When we were together, it was blissful—"

Whitney made a gagging sound into her martini glass. "Blissful? I don't think I've ever heard Elle Riley use that word."

Elle shrugged, shifting uncomfortably on the leather cushion of the barstool. "It's the truth. But then . . . things always go wrong. Always. They get convoluted and confusing and we end up screaming at each other. Or I get terrified and shut things down completely."

"Is that what happened in Vegas? You've never really told me."

Elle's eyes moistened. "I can't . . . I can't even articulate what happened in Vegas. I wish I could. Let's just say it was the worst day of my life."

Whitney placed her hand on Elle's shaky fingers. "It's okay. We don't have to talk about that. One day you'll tell me."

"Thanks." She wiped the moisture from her eyes. "So what do I do, Whit? I feel so lost."

"Well, you and Luke are okay now, right? I mean, you threw your tantrum, he calmed you down, and now you're just . . . I don't know, kinda dealing with the aftermath?"

Elle swirled her drink and nodded. "Yeah. In a nutshell."

"Ladies." The bartender slid a large plate toward them. A large slice of flourless chocolate cake sat atop the white plate, adorned with two forks. Chocolate and caramel drizzle decorated the dessert, making it almost too beautiful to eat. "Enjoy."

Whitney's eyes rolled to the back of her head as she tasted the cake. Elle giggled, watching her friend close her eyes tight, the fork still inside her closed mouth.

"That good, huh?" the bartender asked with a laugh.

"Honey, all we need is whipped cream and a curtain."

Elle rolled her eyes.

"I'm serious," Whitney insisted. "I need a moment alone with this cake."

Elle laughed into her hand, shaking her head at Whitney's candor. The bartender erupted into laughter, slapped the bar, and gazed at Whitney.

"We should put that on the specials board—it'd be the perfect slogan."

Whitney pointed her fork at the bartender. "You should! You'll have wall-to-wall women in this place."

"Sounds good to me." Dimples formed on the bartender's cheeks. "I'm Mac, by the way."

"Hey, Mac." Whitney flipped her long chocolate locks behind her shoulder before extending her hand. "I'm Whitney. This is Elle."

"Nice to meet you, ladies. I'll, um . . . leave you with your dessert. But I'll check on you later."

"You'd better."

Whitney watched the bartender as he walked away while Elle dug back into the cake.

"You're watching his ass, aren't you?"

"Yep. And I'm pretty sure I'm going home with him."

Whitney tipped her head when the bartender looked back in their direction before taking another bite of the delectable dessert. Elle watched her best friend in awe. Her confidence, her humor, her take-life-by-the-balls attitude were all things she admired. Elle had spent so many years living with her own imperfections and fears. Pushing people away in the name of saving herself from being hurt. She knew she could learn a thing or two from her best friend.

• • • • •

As predicted, after hours of flirting, Whitney left for the evening with Mac the dimple-cheeked bartender, but not before calling a cab for Elle. Once she finished her final martini, a more-than-just-a-little-buzzed Elle climbed into the taxi and, without even planning to, gave the driver the address for Anthony's Pub rather than her home.

Despite her pounding heart and mounting anxiety, a besotted Elle made her way into the bar, plopping herself onto the nearest empty barstool.

"We're closing in twenty minutes," a young bartender warned

her, a fake smile plastered to her face. Elle studied the plastic-like features of the bartender, disliking the malleable appearance of her nose and cheekbones. And for the slightest of seconds, Elle wondered if Troy was attracted to women like her. It had been a long time since she'd observed Troy's dating preferences and was no longer familiar with his "type." She could only hope that even though he now lived in Los Angeles, he wasn't falling under the spell of women addicted to plastic surgery.

"Can I get a martini?"

"Sure. What kind?"

"Surprise me." Elle craned her neck to look around the restaurant and bar. "Is Troy in?"

"Mr. Saladino?"

Relief spread through Elle's nerves with that simple clarification. Anyone who called him *that* was definitely not keeping his bed warm.

"Yeah. Mr. Saladino."

"He's in the kitchen. I can get him if you like."

"I like," Elle slurred before giggling. When she did, a small burp slipped out. "Ooh, excuse me."

"No problem, I'll get him in a sec." The bartender finished mixing Elle's drink, pouring a purple-infused martini into a glass and garnishing it with a maraschino cherry.

"Mmm." Elle pressed the glass to her inviting lips, but was interrupted when a rough hand swiped the glass from her grip.

"I think you're cut off. Mel, could you grab her some water?"

"Sure, Mr. Saladino."

Elle stared, mouth agape, at Troy, who was clutching the glass protectively, covering the glass with the top of his hand, and clearly out of her reach.

Elle attempted to stand, but lost her footing slightly and bumped into the wood of the bar. "You. I was looking for you, *Mr. Sal-a-dino.*"

"You smell like a bottle of vodka." Troy supported her elbow with his hand, easing her back onto her barstool. His hand lingered there until Elle, in a more-than-obvious fashion, stared down at his hand on her arm.

"I was out with Whitney."

"I don't know who that is." Troy furrowed his brow.

"There's a lot you don't know about me, isn't there, Mr. Saladino?"

"I guess so." Troy's voice was rough, but calm and collected despite the fact she made no qualms about her attempts to goad him. "Why do you keep calling me that?"

"Your bartender said it earlier. It's cute." She took her pinky finger and tapped the end of Troy's nose. He rolled his eyes, but couldn't suppress a grin.

"Why are you here, Eleanor?"

Elle stood, wrinkled her nose, and placed her hands on her hips. "I don't like when you call me that. You always call me Rigby."

Troy looked away briefly, before making eye contact. "I was attempting to show you my serious side. Apparently, that isn't working today."

"Not really." Elle giggled, then burped again. She covered her mouth up tight.

"You didn't answer my question, by the way."

"Oh." Elle bit her top lip and scrunched her nose up tight. "What was that again?"

"Oh lord, you really are tanked." Troy cleared his throat. "I asked you why you're here."

"I don't know. I mean, my boyfriend, you met him way over there actually." She pointed toward the back of the restaurant. "Well, he isn't actually my boyfriend, but he was on some website all snuggly with the star of my show. They weren't kissing or screwing or anything, but c'mon, it's probably happening. I mean, it's Gina and she does that sorta thing, and knowing her she's doing it to get to me because of Whitney sleeping with Nolan. Can you believe that? I mean, it's *my show*. And then I went out with Whitney and she went home with Mac and I just got a cab and here I am." Her words came out in rambles, and she had no idea if he even understood half of what she said. She took a large sip of water and waited for Troy to respond. After several seconds, he finally did.

"Ah, I see."

Troy took a large step back and his fingers pawed at the stubble on his chin. Even through her drunken haze, Elle knew what that meant. He was irritated with her. If only her brain would slow down enough for her to remember what she had just blurted out like a drunken maniac.

"Look, I don't know what's going on between us, if anything at all. And I know this is going to sound harsh, but I don't mean it that way—"

"What do you mean? What way?" Elle interrupted.

"I'm not interested in being your second choice or your drunken booty call. I don't want you coming here after fights with your boyfriend who's not really your boyfriend. If you come here, do it because there's nowhere else you'd rather be. Because you want *me*. And then, maybe there'll be something for us to figure out."

He placed the martini glass on the bar, far out of her reach, and walked in the other direction. Tears formed in Elle's eyes as rejection collected in her gut. Troy's rejection was the worst kind of rejection. She'd felt it before and the familiar sting was creeping through her body, pouring through her nervous system and paralyzing her heart.

"So that's it? I put myself out there, and that's all you have to say?"

"I'm not playing games with you. Not anymore. If this is your idea of putting yourself out there, then we don't stand a chance anyway." He hung his head and pursed his lips, rubbing the skin of his neck with his hand. "I'll call you a cab. Go home, sleep it off. Hopefully you'll have some clarity in the morning."

"You'll never forgive me, will you? This is all just . . . pointless, isn't it?"

Troy's chest rose and fell and Elle noticed moisture collecting in his eyes. "I don't know. I really don't. But this isn't the answer and I think you know that."

She nodded, tears streaming down her burning cheeks. "I'll never forgive *me* either. I wish I could go back . . . every single day, I wish."

Troy pulled her into his arms. Elle clutched the fabric of his polo shirt, sobbing into the tightly woven cotton. He smoothed her hair down to the tips, again and again until her breathing slowed, until her sobs lessened.

"C'mon, Rigby. I'll take you home."

Chapter 12

When Elle awoke, the ceiling was spinning out of control. Her forehead and temples pounded in agony and the back of her mouth was as dry as bone. Ever so slowly, she eased herself to a seated position and recognized the clothes on her body as the ones she wore to the bar with Whitney. Her memory was fuzzy, but the note on her nightstand cleared up any uncertainty in her brain.

E–
I slept on the couch to make sure you're okay.
Come down when you're ready for coffee.

–T

Troy brought her home the night before. She vaguely remembered their interaction at his restaurant, and was hazy on the specifics of their conversation. She could only hope she didn't embarrass herself terribly. There was only one way to find out.

After stopping in her bathroom to down two ibuprofen and a large glass of water, Elle washed her face, brushed her teeth, changed into fresh clothes, and walked downstairs. When she reached the bottom of the staircase, she could smell coffee brewing and could hear the familiar tunes of the Beatles.

This, despite her hangover, was how Elle had always imagined waking up with Troy. Coffee and the Beatles. She couldn't think of a better way to start the day. She took a deep breath before walking into her kitchen.

Troy was seated at the table, coffee cup in hand. He eyed Elle with caution as she approached the gurgling coffeepot. She reached into the cabinet, retrieved a mug, and poured herself a steaming cup.

"I hope it's okay I'm still here."

"Of course." Elle joined Troy at the table. She raised the mug to her mouth, the aroma of the beverage tickling her nose and stirring the hunger of her empty belly. "Thanks for bringing me home. And putting me to bed."

"Sure. I was worried you'd pass out in a cab. Plus, I just wanted to make sure, you know . . ."

"Yeah, I know. Thank you."

"Nice place."

"You like it?"

"I love it. Your island is the size of my entire kitchen. You've done well for yourself, Rigby." Troy took another swig from his mug, giving Elle a genuine smile.

"I know it's a little much, but it's growing on me."

"Don't do that. Don't downplay your success. You should be proud of this, of everything you've accomplished. I know I am."

"That means a lot to me."

"It's the truth."

An awkward silence hung over the knotted walnut table. Elle played with the corner of the lime green place mat below her mug. She wasn't sure of what to say to Troy. She hadn't expected him to be in her home quite so soon, but the situation had become unavoidable due to her behavior the night before.

"About last night," he began and anxiety spread throughout her body, unsure of what he might say. She didn't want to embarrass herself any more than she already had the night before.

"I know." Elle closed her eyes tight, clutching her mug. "It was wrong of me to show up like that."

Troy leaned back in his chair, scratching lightly at his forehead with the tips of his fingers. "How much do you even remember?"

"Honestly? Not much."

"That's to be expected, I guess."

"Did I humiliate myself? You can be honest."

"Not at all. I promise," Troy deadpanned. He was sparing her feelings; she could feel it in her gut. He always was a terrible liar, especially when it came to her and her ability to humiliate herself. Her eyes were sore; she had a strong feeling she'd cried.

Dammit, she thought, cursing the inventor of the martini and all bartenders who served them.

"I have to ask you something." She felt courage brewing inside her. She had to know. "Why'd you let so much time go by? I mean—would you ever have found me again if I hadn't stumbled into your restaurant by mistake?"

"Honestly?"

Elle shrugged, closed her eyes briefly, and shook her head, attempting to stay casual and add lightness to her voice. "Why not?"

He looked down at the floor, shaking his head slowly, ever so slowly. "I'm not sure. It never felt like the right time and it was easier to just avoid you. I was angry for so long."

"I know."

"There was a time when I never thought I'd *stop* being angry at you."

"And now?"

Troy shrugged. "Jury's still out, I guess. But it's no longer a unanimous vote."

"Hmm." That was the only thing Elle could manage to say.

"And you?"

"My jury?" Elle asked with a slight smile.

"Yeah."

"They've never been unanimous."

Troy said nothing, but nodded slowly, breaking eye contact.

What Elle didn't tell Troy was the jurors were forming a coup against the one cynical, judgmental juror who wanted Troy to walk out of her house and never return. The jurors in her mind were throwing chairs, punching walls, doing anything they could to make that one simple voice go silent. But that juror wouldn't budge and she reminded Elle that no matter how smooth this conversation was going, no matter how much she loved being in the same room as Troy, there was still so much to discuss before they could ever consider themselves healed. And Elle knew that bitch of a juror was right.

"Listen, I should go."

"Are you sure? I—"

"Yeah, I need to close out the registers from last night and get the kitchen prepped."

Elle hung her head, realizing Troy had skipped those things the night before to take care of her drunken self. "Of course. Thank you again . . . for everything."

Elle walked Troy to her front door. Feeling brave, she asked. "Will I see you again?"

"I certainly hope so. Just lay off the booze next time, okay?"

Elle laughed behind her hand. "I promise."

Troy opened his arms to her and she entered his embrace, savoring the familiar feel of his arms around her. When Troy pulled back, he looked into Elle's eyes and placed the tiniest of kisses on her lips, his lips gently grazing hers. Before she had the chance to choose whether or not to return the affection, he pulled away, his eyes still closed for a short moment as if he was savoring their gentle contact. Elle swallowed hard, wishing he'd press his lips to hers once again. But he didn't. He simply smiled and walked slowly to his car, pausing to wave before climbing into the vehicle.

Elle closed the door, pressing her back against it. Once again, her brain was inundated with thoughts of Troy—their past, their awkward encounters in the present. With his reemergence into her life, Elle wondered if she'd ever be able to stop thinking about him. If the jurors inside her head were any indication, it was going to be a struggle.

• • • • •

After a long hot shower, several cups of coffee, and a decent breakfast, Elle was feeling less stricken by the previous night's activities. To her relief, it was a Saturday. She took the opportunity to lose herself in a good story. She hadn't read a full-length novel in ages. It was time for her to rectify that.

Elle grabbed her iPad, tapped on her Kindle app, and scrolled through the latest titles she'd grabbed online. While scrolling, she reminisced as she eyed her own titles on the device.

She'd written four books, each one about her relationship with Troy. She'd transformed their complex love story into an ongoing saga between Desmond and Molly. She'd poured her heart into those novels, but each had a very clear message.

She was fine.

No matter what happened with Desmond, Molly was resilient, strong, stoic. She could take anything, handle anything, deal with anything. She was a clear projection of how Elle longed to be while carrying out her day-to-day life and while dealing with her and Troy's heartbreaking past.

She tapped on the first book in the series, reading the title page aloud to herself: I'll Follow the Sun *by Eleanor Riley*. The network had shortened it for the television series, in order to make it more succinct, more modern. She turned to the first page.

Chapter 1

Whoever said love was blind never met Desmond Fiore.

He owned any room he entered, his charisma bouncing from the walls of the casinos of Las Vegas, captivating the women around him.

And despite the fact that he was her greatest competition, Molly Lynch was drawn to him in a way she resented and despised.

Elle laughed at the first words of her book, immediately remembering the emotions she felt when constructing those first sentences. She turned the pages several at a time, skimming through Desmond and Molly's ups and downs, their fights and makeup sessions, their failed attempts at romance, and the moments that made her knees buckle with passion.

Their story was worthy of telling.

Unlike in years past, she wondered if perhaps Molly *didn't* have it all figured out. Maybe Molly had a lot to learn about Desmond. He wanted to protect her, keep her safe, take care of her. But more than that, despite everything, he was *proud* of her and everything she'd accomplished. Tears threatened to build in Elle's eyes as she was struck with that realization.

In the books she'd crafted, Desmond was never proud of Molly. Did he protect her? Yes. Did he care for her? In his own way. But this character she created from memory, from the longings of her heart, was jaded, flawed, and not quite accurate.

And for the first time in ten years, as she read through the passages in that first novel, she wondered if perhaps their story wasn't quite over.

Her reading was interrupted by the ping of her cell phone. She grabbed it, hoping to hear from Whitney. Her friend was smart. She took measures to maintain her safety when going home with men; however, Elle couldn't help feeling protective of her when Saturday mornings rolled around. Over the years, she'd requested a simple text to let her know all was well.

To her surprise, when she glanced at the screen, it wasn't a text from Whitney, but rather one from Luke.

I miss you. Any plans today?

Elle smiled as she stared at the simple words. Despite her unfinished business with Troy, she was still drawn to the handsome actor. Despite Luke's naivety about the world of Hollywood, or his possible flirtation with his leading actress, Elle was in no hurry to end their relationship.

Luke relaxed her like no other man had in the past. He fascinated her with his laid-back nature, and being near him satisfied her in a new and inexplicable way.

No plans. What'd you have in mind?

Elle placed the phone back down and moved her attention back to her book. Before she could even find her place in the story, her phone pinged once again.

You. Me. Whatever you want.

Excitement stirred in her belly as she thought about a day spent with Luke. She made a firm decision not to mention anything about Gina or the pictures of them at the bar. She was going to enjoy him, trust him, lose herself in him. She wanted to enjoy how he made her feel and nothing more.

Come over.

With a spring in her step, Elle jogged up her winding staircase and promptly changed into a hot-pink sundress with a plunging neckline. She placed a pair of strappy sandals on her feet and proceeded to fix her hair and makeup. By the time she'd finished applying, her doorbell rang. She smiled at her reflection before jogging downstairs to answer the door. She was so focused, she almost missed the text message from Whitney:

Home safe and sound. "Big Mac" was just that.

Elle rolled her eyes, but laughed as she tucked her cell back into her pocket and opened the door. "That was quick."

Luke removed his sunglasses and placed a kiss on her cheek before crossing the threshold to enter her home. Without knowing it, he'd worn an outfit that complemented hers perfectly. A faded navy blue t-shirt that pulled at his pec muscles and dark washed jeans that hugged his muscular thighs.

"I couldn't wait."

"Good." Elle drank him in with her eyes, willing herself to be strong enough not to simply drag him up to her bedroom immediately. She wanted to spend more time with him, learn what made Luke Kingston tick, discover if they had much in common. Their sexual chemistry was undeniable, but their intellectual chemistry was still undecided.

Closing the space between them, Luke wrapped an arm around her waist, nuzzling into her neck.

"You smell good. Are you hungry?"

"Famished."

"Great. I made a reservation at The Ivy."

The swirls of excitement in Elle's belly dropped to the floor. The Ivy was known for celebrity sightings. Not only that, it was littered with paparazzi. The Ivy was a place she'd avoided successfully since moving to California and she had no intention of ever eating there. Elle was a private person. Luke knew that, and despite the promise she'd made herself earlier not to mention Luke and the photos of him with Gina, she was not willing to compromise her desire for a private life.

"The Ivy? Why would you want to go there?" Elle didn't want to sound accusatory in her question, but she was feeling unsettled. Why would Luke want to take her there knowing how private she was? Especially after he'd already been photographed just a few days prior.

"What do you mean? They have this killer patio. I thought we could enjoy the sunshine."

"Luke, I thought you knew how I felt about places like that. If you don't, then I need to be more clear. I have no interest in participating in the Hollywood game. I don't want to spend my weekends looking for photo ops or avoiding paparazzi. It's not how I'm built. It's not how I want to live my life."

"Oh." Luke took a step back, running his fingers through his waves. "I hadn't really thought about that. My agent suggested it when I spoke to her yesterday."

"Your agent?"

"Yeah. But I mean, it's not a big deal. If you don't want to go there that's fine." Luke placed his hands loosely on his hips, waiting for Elle's answer.

She hesitated before speaking. "Let's go somewhere else."

"You pick." His behavior was nonchalant. Somehow with Luke, things never seemed to erupt into a full-blown altercation, which was not what Elle was used to. With Troy, things always seemed to become something worthy of discussion. Luke's lack of concern was confusing. Did he just not care enough to fight with her? Or could she stand to learn a thing or two from his relaxed demeanor?

Elle chose a quiet bistro in Santa Monica overlooking the sand and surf. They feasted on oysters, scallops, and shrimp scampi. The soothing sounds of the waves crashing against the sand calmed Elle's nerves and helped her relax. Luke held her hand as they ate. They talked about the show, which was holding its own in the Nielsen ratings. The network was pleased with Luke's role on the show and the new love story developing between his character and Gina's.

"You won't believe what's happening on Twitter."

Elle finished chewing before responding. "What do you mean?"

"I've gained thousands of new followers in just a few weeks. Two hundred new ones just this morning. It's crazy. I mean, crazy awesome, but crazy."

"I'm sure that'll continue. The viewers love you," Elle deadpanned.

"Geez, you say that like it's a bad thing."

"No." Elle shook her head, wiping her mouth with her napkin. "I'm sorry, I didn't mean it like that. I'm thrilled they're loving you on the show. I'm just—I don't know . . ."

"Talk to me. First the Ivy and now this. What's going on in that gorgeous head of yours?"

"It's nothing, I just . . . It's really easy for all of this to go to someone's head. In some ways, it's almost unavoidable. I'd just hate for that to happen . . ."

"It's not going to change my feelings for you, if that's what you're worried about."

"That's not it." She shook her head vehemently. "I just think it's important to avoid all of the craziness, stay on the perimeter. The Ivy, Twitter, Facebook fans, dodging the paparazzi—it's all very Hollywood."

"And you think I'm too Hollywood?"

"I'm not sure yet," she answered honestly.

"I've been a struggling actor for eight years. And now, I'm on the biggest show on television. Do you understand what a thrill that is for me? How it's changed my life?"

Elle nodded, attempting to put herself in Luke's shoes. He'd worked for years to achieve this—of course he was allowed to celebrate his newly earned success. She just didn't want it to consume him. She'd seen it happen so many times before. When Gina first auditioned for the role of Molly, she was one of the sweetest actresses Elle had met during the casting process. But now . . .

"Of course," she conceded, "I'm sorry. I really am happy for you."

"Try to relax. Everything has a way of working itself out."

She could only hope Luke was right. But her thoughts weighed heavily in her gut. As much as she loved spending time with him, having him in her life and exploring their sexual relationship, she worried they were on two very different paths. The path Luke was on led to fame, fortune, and women fawning at his feet while photographers sold pictures of him and said women to the highest bidder. The path she was on was pointed in the exact opposite direction. Only time would tell if those paths would merge or eventually split in two.

Chapter 13

"Elle, there's a call for you on line one."

Elle snapped her swollen eyes from her computer, wiping them with a tissue. She was in the process of writing Nolan's last lines on the show. It was an emotional scene. After all, she was, for all intents and purposes, saying good-bye to the character of Desmond to make way for David. She'd accepted this inevitable event on her show, but knowing what Desmond represented made her especially vulnerable to carrying it out.

"Elle Riley."

"Elle, Sebastian Crane."

Elle inhaled deeply at the squeaky voice of Gina's loathsome agent. Sebastian Crane was a hotshot agent who represented several big television stars. Infamous for his Napoleon complex, Sebastian had no problem hoisting his ego around town on behalf of his clients. Sebastian Crane represented everything Elle despised about the industry. He was ostentatious, pushy, and greedy as hell.

"Sebastian, what a pleasure." Elle did her best to hide her displeasure at receiving his call. "What can I do for you?" Elle hated the facade she was forced to hide behind when dealing with Hollywood players like Sebastian. But she'd learned it was a necessary evil for the sake of her career and the show she loved so much.

"We need to discuss Gina and her future on your show."

Elle's gut dropped, anxiety flooding her abdomen. First Nolan, now Gina?

"I don't understand."

"She's feeling a little frustrated, Elle. A little neglected. Catch my drift?"

"Umm, not at all. What seems to be the problem?" She shifted uncomfortably in her seat. In what way could Gina possibly be *neglected*?

"Her screen time. It's down twenty percent since last season. My assistant ran the numbers."

"We've only shot the first twelve episodes. I assure you she'll have plenty of screen time."

Irritation spread through every cell of her body. If Gina was feeling frustrated, why didn't she talk to Elle directly rather than sending her guard dog?

"I certainly hope so. If not, we may have a problem."

"Slow down, Sebastian. The thing is, we've introduced a new character."

"I understand that—"

"I don't think you do. There are three main characters right now. But by the end of the season, Nolan will be gone. It'll all work out fine. Tell your *client* to relax."

"We won't relax until after contract negotiations."

No he did not! He did not just threaten me.

Elle took a deep breath, popped open her candy stash drawer, and pulled out a bag of Twizzlers. She took a bite, closed her eyes, and prepared to let Sebastian's idle threat remain just that—idle.

"Gina is the star of the show. It will all work out fine, I assure you."

"Great. So we have an understanding."

"Yes, we do." Elle snarled silently at the receiver, wanting to claw Sebastian's little eyes out. Instead, she took a bite of the sweet strawberry candy. "You take care now."

She heard the click on the other end and placed the receiver in the cradle. Sebastian never said good-bye; it was his way of maintaining control. Elle nibbled on the candy, pondering their conversation and what to do next. Confronting Gina was probably not the best avenue to take, but she was tired of the actress and her attitude.

They had never been besties, but Gina had been especially distant with Elle since that first awkward table read with Nolan. She was embarrassed Elle knew about Nolan and her personal relationship, but in Elle's opinion, she had taken it too far. Their professional relationship was suffering because of it and she wasn't quite sure how to fix it if Gina was determined to remain prickly.

Ignoring her better judgment, Elle texted Gina, asking her to join her in her office for a chat.

When Gina didn't reply, Elle resumed writing Nolan's final scene. Just as her eyes were filling with fresh tears, Nicole buzzed in.

"Gina is here to see you."

Dammit.

The last thing she wanted was for Gina to think her tears had anything to do with Sebastian's call. She grabbed new tissues, dabbing her eyes gently so as not to cause splotchy skin. She waved her hands rapidly for fresh air to hit her cheeks, but it was no use. She couldn't stall any longer.

"Send her in."

Gina opened the door, daggers in her eyes, and sat opposite Elle, saying nothing. Her arms crossed defiantly across her chest set the tone perfectly for how the conversation would go.

"Nice to see you, Gina. Twizzler?"

"No, thanks. I'm off sugar."

One thing Elle did admire about Gina was her willpower. She was one of those actresses who could lose twenty pounds for a role with no difficulty, no matter the time constraints. Elle could never give up carbs. Ever. Her candy stash helped her get through any crisis, personal or professional, and she had accepted the extra five pounds because of it.

"Listen, I just spoke to Sebastian."

Gina looked at the floor, her chin dipping to her chest. Even though Gina liked to act tough, Elle knew she valued her role on the show and didn't want to jeopardize it by allowing Sebastian to go too far off the cuff.

When the actress said nothing, Elle continued. "I hope you know that balancing Luke and Nolan is the reason for the dip in your screen time, and that I'll do whatever I can to fix it when the story permits."

Gina pressed her hands to the arms of her chair, pushing up to her feet. "Is that all?"

"Whoa, hold on," Elle said, standing to confront the actress' abrupt behavior. "What's going on with you?"

Once again, Gina crossed her arms, her eyes boring into Elle's. "I know you're pissed. About the photos. You're punishing me because I went out with Luke."

"Went *out with*? We're not in middle school. You two went out for drinks, a photographer found you. It's not the end of the world and I'm *not* punishing you. You know me better than that. I'd never jeopardize my show over petty jealousy."

Gina shifted her weight back and forth, her jaw clenched. "Fine, whatever. Are we done?"

"Listen, I know things have been weird between us since the table read."

"You mean when I found out your *best friend* slept with Nolan?"

Elle cringed, took a deep breath, and continued. "Yes. But that has *nothing* to do with me, Gina. You and I—"

"Did you know?"

Elle had quite the poker face. She could keep it together in almost any given situation without tipping her hand. But she felt Gina deserved the truth.

"Yes. But *not* when it happened. I found out shortly before you did. And at the time, I had no idea you and Nolan were even involved."

"Seriously?" The daggers remained in Gina's eyes, but skepticism climbed onto her face as well. "I find that hard to believe."

"I'm dead serious, Gina. In fact, I feel pretty silly I couldn't tell. I just thought you had amazing chemistry. I still think you do."

"Well, we're over. So . . ." Her eyes moistened and Elle contemplated handing her the tissue box, but she decided against it, afraid Gina might storm off. Gina took a deep breath, raised an eyebrow, and flipped her hair behind her shoulder. "I'm on to bigger and *better* things."

Elle couldn't help but wonder if she was referring to Luke. She suppressed the suspicion brewing inside her, making an informed decision to trust Luke. But the pictures of them laughing and chatting at the bar crept back into her brain.

"Good for you." Elle returned to her seat, ready to finish the exchange and return to her script. "I'll see you tomorrow. Table read, nine o'clock."

Gina narrowed her eyes, and Elle suspected she was studying her for vulnerability. She'd let hell freeze over before allowing Gina Romano to see her emotions and conflict over Luke. Only those she trusted the most in the world were allowed to see her at her most exposed. And Gina would never be on that tiny list of people. Elle watched her as she left the office, leaving the door wide open so Elle would have to close it.

Such a pain in the ass.

Elle grabbed another Twizzler before closing the door. She placed the tissue box next to her monitor, took a deep breath, and returned to Desmond's final words.

• • • • •

"Whitney Bartolina."

Elle was so choked up as she clutched the phone to her ear, she almost couldn't get the words out. But she needed her best friend. She needed her support, her understanding, her love. She cleared her throat and attempted to speak without sobbing.

"Can you go to lunch?"

"Ellie." Whitney only used that name when Elle was upset or in a panic. It was her version of handling Elle with kid gloves. It was endearing and comforted Elle in an inexplicable way. "What's going on?"

"I need you."

"Gimme five."

"Okay."

Elle placed the phone back in the cradle and closed the finished document for Desmond's final script. She knew saying good-bye to his character would be emotional, but she didn't expect this. She didn't expect the devastation that consumed her. She wasn't ready— the script was beautiful and she had every confidence it would play out well on-screen, but she wasn't ready to let go.

Whitney arrived, rushing into the office and placing her hands on Elle's shoulders, peering into her eyes.

"I'm here. What's happening?"

"Desmond, I—I wrote his last words. It's over."

"Oh," Whitney said with a deliberate nod. Elle knew she understood, at least to some degree, the gravity of the situation. She knew how haunted Elle had been the past ten years, and that Desmond was Elle's connection to Troy. Despite the fact the real Troy had resurfaced, the character of Desmond was a lifeline for Elle. A connection to their past and the love they had shared.

"Want to get out of here? Go somewhere quiet?"

"I don't care." Elle dabbed at her face with more tissue. The box was almost empty.

"Tell you what. Let's order in."

"No pizza!" Elle said quickly, before covering her mouth with her hand. "Sorry, just . . . no pizza."

"I get it. I'll take care of it. Give me two minutes."

Whitney walked outside and spoke briefly to Nicole. Elle opened the candy drawer, pouring every bit of sugary comfort onto her desk. When Whitney returned, she tilted her head, eyed the desk and the brightly colored packages covering it, and took a seat, opening a fresh package of Swedish Fish.

"Nicole's placing an order with the deli down the block. And she's clearing your schedule for the rest of the day. Now, talk to me, honey."

Elle nodded, feeling a knot form in the back of her throat. "I didn't think—" She paused. "I didn't think I'd be like this, ya know? I mean, I knew it'd be hard. I knew that, but . . . still, I just . . ."

"Ellie, you're spinning. Take a second, okay? I'm not going any-where."

"This character . . . he's more than a character . . . to me."

"I know he is."

Elle stopped, took a deep breath. "I'm ready to tell you about Vegas. About what happened there. None of this will make sense if I don't."

"I'm all ears."

Chapter 14

B right sunlight streamed through Troy's bedroom window. Elle rolled over to avoid starting the day, but was soon quite aware of the time when Troy opened the bedroom door.

"Rise and shine, sleepy."

"Coffee, I smell coffee." Her voice was deep and raspy from a restful night's sleep. Troy entered the room, carrying a small tray. A tiny vase with one simple pink rose grabbed her attention immediately.

"Breakfast in bed. But you have to sit up."

"You cooked? I love when you cook." Elle eased up to a seated position and Troy placed the tray above her legs and a small kiss on her lips. "What did I do to deserve this?"

"Happy anniversary. We started dating a year ago today."

Troy always was the romantic in their relationship. Elle couldn't believe they'd been dating for an entire year. Where had the time gone? She was the happiest she'd ever been in almost twenty-five years. Which reminded her . . .

"And my birthday's tomorrow."

"I know." He kissed her again, this time on the forehead. "It's a big weekend. In fact, I thought we could talk about that."

Elle took a large sip of coffee, savoring Troy's ability to mix her favorite hazelnut roast with the perfect amount of cream and sugar. "Heaven in a cup" is what she called it, and no one made it as perfectly as he did. Not even she could duplicate his recipe.

"Talk about what? I'll be twenty-five, no big deal. Let's just go to dinner or something."

"I had a better idea."

Elle narrowed her eyes at Troy, whose expression had changed in an instant. He looked anxious as his fingers tapped quickly on his thigh.

"How about a trip?"

"Like a getaway?" Elle brightened at the idea, then bit her bottom lip, wondering where they might go.

"Something like that," Troy replied. His fingers continued to tap anxiously as Elle pondered the possibilities. Where would they go? Perhaps a road trip up to Door County for wine sampling. Perhaps a trip down to Champaign to visit their alma mater. No matter the location, she could think of no better way to spend the weekend. Until she saw it.

Troy reached into his pocket, placing a velvet box on the tray.

"Oh my God," Elle said, her voice deadpan and her eyes wide as she looked down at the unexpected gift. "Is that—?"

"Look, I know we've never talked about this, but . . . it's all I can think about. You, me, a future together. I want to marry you, Rigby."

Elle's palms were sweating and adrenaline coursed through her veins.

Marriage? Really?

"Troy, I—"

"I remember back in college, you said you hated fancy weddings . . . you wanted to get married on a whim. You said it was 'the epitome of romance.'"

Elle remembered saying that, but was astounded Troy remembered as well. He'd paid attention.

"Let's do it, Rigby. Let's get married today. I'm so in love with you."

"Today?" Elle's heart pounded and her belly flipped. She scrunched her nose as she pondered something she knew she wasn't quite ready for. "I mean, I—"

Troy's eyes were wide and bright, sparkling in the morning sunshine. Elle's mouth went dry, overwhelmed by the proposal. They'd spent an entire year together, and unlike the past when all they could do was argue, they'd had three hundred and sixty-four days of absolute joy. Picnics in the park, museums on the weekends, nights on the couch with Chinese takeout or a Chicago-style pizza. Troy was thoughtful, protective, and romantic. And she loved him . . . more than she could ever imagine loving another person.

"Do you love me, Rigby?"

"Of course I do. You know that."

"Please marry me. Please make me the happiest man alive." A crease formed above his nose. To deny him happiness would kill her. And she loved Troy Saladino. She really did.

"Yes." The word flew from her mouth. All she could think of was pleasing the man she loved so very much. "But where?"

"Where else? Vegas, baby."

"Oh my God," Elle whispered, struggling to catch her breath. "I've never been to Vegas."

Everything Elle knew about Las Vegas she'd learned from movies and commercials. All she could picture was a dirty chapel with a pastor dressed up like Elvis Presley. Her stomach churned at the thought.

"Well, that's about to change."

Troy opened the box, revealing a simple princess-cut diamond on a white gold band. Elle sighed as she took in its beauty and simplicity. Troy knew her so well. They'd never looked at rings together, but if they had, this was the exact ring she would have selected. Simple, classy, and gorgeous. Troy eased it onto her shaky finger. A tear slid down her cheek as she looked into his eager eyes.

"It fits you perfectly." Troy raised her fingertips to his lips, placing a gentle kiss on her pale skin.

"Are you sure about this?" Elle blurted out, again without considering the consequences of her words. Troy grimaced, but nodded firmly.

"I've never been more sure. But you . . . I want you to be sure. If this is too much, you can think about it, take some time, we can wait—"

Part of her wanted to take advantage of that offer. To ponder the idea of their future together. Hell, she'd only been awake for less than five minutes. And there was part of her that wasn't even certain she was awake. What if this was all a dream? But her heart had other plans.

"No." She shook her head decisively. "Eleanor Saladino. I like the sound of that."

"Eleanor Rigby Saladino," he corrected her.

"Right," she said with a laugh. She took a bite of her buttery rye toast and another sip of coffee.

"You've seriously made me the happiest man alive."

Troy leaned in, pushed her hair behind her shoulders, and placed soft kisses on the delicate skin of her neck. She shuddered with pleasure as his lips continued to explore her skin.

"So . . . when do we leave?"

Troy pulled back, running his fingers through his short dark hair. "Our flight leaves in three hours."

"Holy crap." Elle covered her mouth with her hand.

He'd already booked the flight?

Her brain was running a mile a minute, wondering just how long this plan had been in the works. How he'd been certain she'd say yes. She couldn't let Troy see a look of consternation on her face. She did her best to focus on the present. "I guess we'd better get ready then." Elle scarfed down her toast and downed her coffee.

"I borrowed luggage from my folks and I'm already packed. We just have to swing by your place on the way to the airport."

Adrenaline coursed through Elle's body as she took the fastest shower of her life. As she scrubbed down her skin, she avoided the little voice in her head questioning whether this was the best choice. After all, she still had her apartment and Troy had his and they each had roommates. The logistics were complicated and it overwhelmed her to think about it, so she pushed the thoughts from her mind, focusing instead on the romantic gesture Troy had made. If it was possible, she was falling even more in love with him with each passing minute, knowing the preparation he'd put into making this weekend romantic and special.

• • • • •

Elle couldn't stop her knees from bobbing up and down as they sat in the limousine. Troy's hand rested in her lap.

"You okay?"

Elle's throat was dry as the limousine approached their hotel. Desperately, she attempted to quell the apprehension that mounted in her chest. Troy wrapped an arm around her and leaned in close.

"You seem nervous."

"I'm just excited," Elle lied. "It's a big day, right?"

"The biggest." Troy grinned from ear to ear as he peered out the window. Elle watched the man she loved, conflict overflowing within her. She loved him—there was no doubt about that. But, she couldn't silence the voice in her head that screamed she was making a mistake. A big one.

When they arrived at the Bellagio Hotel, Elle and Troy checked in to their room. They'd discussed their plans. First, they would retrieve their marriage license, followed by a romantic dinner at Vic & Anthony's Steakhouse. And finally, they would marry under the stars of Las Vegas. Troy had arranged for a gazebo ceremony at Mon Bel Ami Wedding Chapel at midnight. Elle was again blown away by his thoughtfulness. When he'd shown her the website for Mon Bel Ami, she knew it was completely her taste. Pictures of a rustic gazebo with hanging greenery and twinkling lights made her swoon.

The only thing missing was a dress.

Elle had packed several cocktail dresses, but none of them seemed proper to marry in. She wasn't sure if there was time to purchase one, but she knew she wanted to feel like a bride. And no cocktail dress would help her feel that way.

"Is there time . . . to get a dress?" Elle asked when she emerged from the enormous bathroom in their suite. The fluffy robe was soft against her skin, and she snuggled up to Troy, who was sitting on the bed.

Troy grinned.

"You didn't."

"Check the closet."

Elle opened the closet doors and gasped. Five different dresses, sheathed in clear garment bags, were hanging from the bar of the closet.

"They're rentals. So unfortunately, you won't be able to keep the one you choose."

Tears brewed in her eyes as she stared at Troy, who'd joined her by the closet entrance. "I can't believe it. You thought of everything, didn't you?"

"I wanted it to be special." He shrugged.

"It is. It *so* is." Elle wrapped her arms around Troy, pulling him close. Then, she turned her attention back to the five garment bags. "Now, which one should I wear?"

She opened the first dress. An ivory, strapless lace gown with a black satin sash, elegant, modern and formfitting. She slipped herself into the exquisite frock. Troy zipped the dress and Elle walked to the full-length mirror on the bathroom door. She sighed, gazing at her reflection. She looked like a bride. A beautiful bride.

"It's perfect."

"There are four more. You don't have to settle—" Troy had moved to the bar and was pouring himself a glass of Johnnie Walker Platinum, his favorite scotch. Elle had ordered it from the hotel to surprise him and she was happy to see him indulging in his favorite drink since he'd gone to such great lengths to make the weekend so special for her.

"I'm not settling. It's elegant, timeless. I'm in love with it." She spun gently to and fro, eyeing the dress from all angles. She loved the way it accentuated her curves and hugged her hips. It was as if the dress had been made specifically for her.

Troy truly knows me. He knows me so well.

"And," she said, giddily, walking quickly to her suitcase, "I can even wear my favorite black heels."

She slipped the shoes on her feet and walked back to the mirror, enveloped in the happiness surrounding her in that hotel room. Troy's reflection could be seen with her own as he leaned down to kiss her exposed neck, her hair still up in a fluffy white towel.

"I'll take my shower now, and we'll begin our night, Mrs. Almost Saladino."

Elle giggled. Troy polished off his glass of scotch and walked into the bathroom, closing the door behind him. Elle ignored the anxious flipping of her stomach at the mention of her future last name. Everyone had jitters just before tying the knot, and she was no different from any of the millions of brides before her who were overwhelmed by their nerves. She took a deep breath, carefully removed the dress, and began to groom herself for their evening.

Her hair was curled, tumbling in loose waves down her back. Her makeup was finally complete as she closed her cosmetics bag. Elle slipped off her cozy robe and stepped back into the lace gown. She emerged from the bathroom, feeling beautiful and excited. She lost her breath when she saw him.

Troy looked ridiculously handsome in his tuxedo, the color of midnight. He was fixing the collar of his crisp white shirt when their eyes locked.

"Wow," Elle sighed. She walked to him, smoothing down the lapels of the suit. "You're so dapper."

"You'd better believe it, baby." Troy winked. Then he took a small step back, holding Elle's hands in his own, gazing at her from head to toe.

"You're stunning. The most beautiful bride ever."

"Thank you." She blushed, pressing her lips together, feeling overwhelmed by the emotions in the room. They were doing this . . . really doing this. It wasn't just a fantasy anymore. It was a reality. The anxious flip returned to her belly, and she pressed her hand into her abdomen, trying to calm herself.

"You okay?"

"Mmm-hmm," she answered, swallowing hard. Troy narrowed his eyes; his hand grazed her cheek softly as he studied her, making her feel uneasy. She didn't want him to know about her jitters. It was clear to Elle he had none to match hers. No, Troy wasn't anxious—he was elated, enamored, and excited.

"Listen, Rigby, if you need more time—"

Again, Elle interrupted Troy's offer of more time. She was dressed head to toe in wedding garb. The love of her life was standing before her in a tuxedo, looking as handsome as humanly possible.

She was getting married. She'd be absolutely insane to walk away.

"No. I'm ready. Let's do this."

•••••

Elle stood in her beautiful gown, her hands trembling as she studied her surroundings. Midnight was approaching, and the scorching heat of Las Vegas had cooled. A faint breeze blew against her clammy skin as she focused on her groom-to-be. Troy was standing beneath the gazebo, hands clasped in front of him, an expression of ease on his face. She wished she could will herself to be so confident, so at ease with this life-changing event. That voice had returned, telling her she was too young to get married, that their relationship wasn't quite there yet, that she was swept up in the romance of it all. That she'd regret it and soon. But the idea of disappointing Troy, of ruining their picture-perfect romance, was more terrifying than going through with it. She loved him more than she thought she loved herself. And so, as a sign of her love, she took a leap, knowing she might take a terrible fall.

The small bouquet in her hands shook in response to her trembling fingers. Sweat formed on her neck as she walked down the white runner leading to the gazebo. "Here, There and Everywhere," the Beatles' song Troy always said reminded him of her, played as she joined him in front of the judge, a tall man with a kind face. She took a deep breath, looked him in the eye, and made a choice. She chose to marry the man she loved.

Their vows were simple. They would love, honor, and cherish for as long as they both should live. They were pronounced man and wife and they kissed under the stars.

"We did it, Rigby," Troy murmured into her ear. Elle swallowed hard, wrapping her arms around his neck, seeking comfort and solace.

They returned to their suite, where they toasted with two sparkling glasses of champagne. The sweet intoxicating liquid helped ease Elle's anxiety and she and Troy made love for hours. Troy fell asleep with his arms wrapped around Elle. But she couldn't sleep. She simply stared at the wall, hoping for answers. Hoping for an epiphany. Hoping she did the right thing.

The next morning, Elle awoke before Troy, and a stiff pain formed in her chest. She slid out of his embrace and eased herself out of the warm bed. When she walked toward the bathroom, she saw it.

The dress. Her beautiful lace dress was draped across the chest at the foot of the bed. But instead of reminiscing in the blissful memories of the night before, she looked at the gorgeous garment with regret.

Regret and an overwhelming sense of panic. Sheer panic. That voice she'd suppressed before walking down the aisle was back. And it was dominating her psyche.

Her lungs felt as if they might collapse within her chest as she stroked the lace of the gown. She closed her eyes tight, withdrawing her hand from the fabric. Her eyes moistened as she dashed to the safety of the bathroom.

She locked the door behind her before grasping her hair with her hand. She lifted the seat of the toilet and waited for sickness to arrive. Her stomach was doing backflips over and over, so much so that nausea pervaded her body. She heaved again and again into the bowl, needing this horrible feeling to flee her. But it only grew worse with each passing minute. She clutched the ceramic bowl, hanging her head as sweat poured from her skin.

A knock at the door startled her. "Rigby, you okay?"

Troy sounded worried. No, more than worried. He sounded terrified.

"Just a minute," she managed to squeak out. She wiped her slick forehead, attempting to calm herself down. But her stomach continued to tumble within her belly and sweat continued to bead on her forehead, neck, and arms.

"You're scaring me, Rigby. Are you sick?"

"I don't know. Just—I need a minute."

"Okay. I'm here."

With shaking arms and legs, Elle managed to climb to her feet and pull her robe to the floor. She crumpled herself on top of the fluffy robe, clutching the fabric in her fist. Tears streamed down her cheeks and landed on the soft terry.

It was a mistake. All of it.

She knew it in her gut. The self-saboteur in her was alive and well, and confident she wasn't ready to be someone's wife. She was lying on the bathroom floor, suffering from a panic attack because deep within her soul, she knew she was not capable of being joined to someone for the rest of her life. At least not yet. Not at the new age of twenty-five.

I'm too young. Too immature. Not ready. Not settled.

The thoughts swirled in her head, combined with an overwhelming amount of pure guilt.

On the other side of the door was a man who loved her. Who *was* ready, mature, settled. A man who would do just about anything for her. And she knew that, by day's end, she would break his heart. That thought killed her, paralyzed her, and left her lying helpless on a bathrobe in the middle of their bathroom.

When her pulse returned to normal and the sweat had stopped forming on her brow, she was able to catch her breath.

You love him. You want this. You love him. Pull it together.

One hour after she first collapsed onto the bathroom floor, Elle emerged with combed hair, a clean face, and a relaxed demeanor. She was determined to see this through—to push her feelings of regret to the side and enjoy her birthday with Troy.

You love him. He can't see you this way. You'll break his heart.

Troy was sitting on the edge of the bed in a white cotton t-shirt and boxer shorts. His elbows dug into his thighs and his hands joined together, his knuckles squeezed tightly, making his skin turn a ghastly shade of white. He jumped to his feet as she left the sanctuary of the bathroom.

"Baby, what's going on?"

"My stomach," she lied. "I think it was the champagne. I'm okay now."

She placed a kiss on his cheek, her hands tucked into the robe, still trembling. He smoothed her hair down, pressing his lips to hers.

"You had me so worried."

"I'm fine, I promise."

"I, uh, I'm guessing you're not hungry?" His eyes were cautious, his shoulders stiff.

"I could eat," she said with a shrug. Another lie. She wanted nothing to do with food, but was determined to function normally. They had two days left in Las Vegas before leaving Tuesday morning. She had two days to adjust to her new status as a married woman. Two days to push the nagging anguish from her mind and body.

• • • • •

She managed to keep up the facade for one full day. Until it all came tumbling down the following morning. Once again, she found herself crumpled in a ball on the bathroom floor, clutching her abdomen. Only this time, she had forgotten to lock the door behind her.

Troy barreled into the bathroom after his first knock went unanswered. Elle jumped to her knees as he crashed into the room. His face was red, his eyes wide.

"Enough is enough. What the hell is going on with you? Are you sick? You have to tell me."

The guilt Elle had felt for the past twenty-four hours multiplied in that brief moment. Knowing Troy, he was probably terrified she had some terminal illness or secret disease she'd managed to hide. If only it was something so innocent, so benign. If that were her reality, he would still love her at the end of the conversation. But she knew, despite her every desire to remain with him as an unmarried couple, that Troy was an all-or-nothing man. He'd given her opportunities to say no, to ask for more time, and she hadn't taken them.

He'd never forgive her for this.

"I . . . I'm just thinking. I can't stop thinking."

Troy's look of concern changed in an instant. It was now a look of suspicion.

"About what?"

Elle's forehead wrinkled as she held back tears. Her nose scrunched and her lips pursed tightly together. She had no idea what to say.

"About what, Eleanor?"

Eleanor. He never called her Eleanor. Panic rose once again in her chest.

She closed her eyes tight and answered. "Us. About us."

"I don't understand. I thought—" He paused, his mouth agape, his hands on his hips. "I thought you wanted this. I thought we were happy, that *you* were happy."

"I was."

"Was? Then what the hell changed?"

"Please don't yell at me." Elle walked past him, heading for the bedroom. She needed more air, needed to breathe.

"Don't walk away from this!" Troy followed behind her. "Eleanor!"

"I—I'm sorry. You told me I could have more time. I should have taken it. I should have thought things through. But you were so . . . so . . ."

"I didn't pressure you," he said, his voice low, his features sunken, defeated.

"I know that." Elle wrapped her arms around her abdomen, clutching hard, attempting to comfort herself.

"I thought you wanted me, wanted this. I can't *believe* how stupid I am." Troy walked to the corner, pressing his fists against the wall, his head lowered.

"I *do* want you."

"Stop it. Stop it right now."

"I'm sorry, I'll do anything to make it up to you. Anything."

"How can you possibly do that? The thought of being my wife is making you sick—*physically sick*. Do you know how humiliating that is?" Troy's scarlet cheeks deepened as rage consumed his features. Elle dug her fingernails into her skin as she watched his anger grow.

"I didn't know . . . I didn't know I'd feel this way. I was trying! Trying to pull it together . . . for you."

"For me? How considerate of you."

Elle walked to Troy, placing her hand on the side of his face. He flinched at her touch. "I mean it. I love you, Troy. I do."

He averted his eyes, avoiding hers. "Love doesn't feel like this."

"I'm sorry. So very sorry."

"We took vows, Eleanor. And now, what? They're over? They meant nothing? I meant every word. Every fucking word."

Tears streamed down Elle's cheeks. She knew what she wanted was repressible, but she was hanging on by a thread, unsure of how long she could continue a charade with such life-changing consequences. She wanted to convince Troy they could still be happy together, despite their current spiral. Despite the way he looked at her, as if she were a stranger.

"We can fix this and still be together."

"And how would we do that?" Troy scoffed.

"An annulment. We could get one, and just—just go back to the way things were. To being Troy and Rigby, a happy couple who live in separate apartments but spend every weekend together. Who take walks in Grant Park and order moo shoo pork from China Garden—"

"An annulment? Are you serious?"

Elle nodded, knowing that dissolving the marriage was the only way she could survive.

I'm too young. Too immature. Not ready. Not settled.

"I can't believe this. I can't fucking believe—I gave you so many chances to say no, to say you weren't ready, that you needed more time. But you didn't take them. You let me look like a goddamn fool!"

Elle sat on the bed, taking in his wrath, hoping he'd eventually calm down. That they'd be able to speak calmly to one another. She watched as Troy returned to the edge of the bed, his elbows once again digging into his thighs. His head hanging in despair.

"I'm so sorry." Her cheeks were covered in tears; her voice cracked in anguish. She was hanging on for dear life, terrified of losing Troy forever. She joined him on the bed, running her fingers through his hair as her other arm wrapped around his torso. "This is my fault, *all my fault*. But please, please don't give up on me, Troy. Please. I need you."

"I don't know what to say," he whispered, his voice guarded, lifeless. "Why can't you just . . . try? You know, give it a few days—see if your cold feet go away?"

Elle swallowed hard. She knew this was Troy's final act of forgiveness—the only opportunity he would give her to save the relationship. But she couldn't do it. She'd drown if she did. And she'd resent him for the rest of her life.

"No. I can't be married, Troy. I'm sorry. This was . . . it was a mistake."

And for the first time in the many years she'd known Troy Saladino, she watched as he cried. She watched as his eyes grew misty. And she watched as tears streamed down his blood-red cheeks. His hand clutched his forehead as he sobbed. Elle wrapped her arms around him, clutching him tight, and wishing they could go back to the morning in his apartment when everything was sunshine and roses. When their relationship was euphoric and heavenly. Instead, she clung to the man whose heart she'd destroyed. Her fingertips dug into his skin as her sobs matched his.

• • • • •

Elle awoke, alone on the bed.

Troy was gone.

She searched the closets, the bathroom, the drawers.

His bags, his clothes, everything was gone.

He'd left her.

Her heart thumped wildly in her chest as she pinned her hair up, wrapped herself in a fluffy white robe, and grabbed her key card. With reckless abandon, she ran to the elevator, pressing the button again and again. "C'mon, dammit. C'mon."

Finally, the elevator arrived. A young couple stood, mouths agape at her disheveled appearance as Elle entered the car, pressing the "L" button, despite the fact that it was already glowing. Her pulse raced as she pondered what to ask the front desk. Somehow no question would hide her mortification. When the elevator reached the lobby, Elle sprinted to the expansive front desk. A woman with short, white hair and wide eyes waved Elle to her station. Her name badge said "Geraldine."

"Young lady, are you all right? Do you need an ambulance?"

Elle looked down at her disheveled appearance, realizing that a bathrobe and bare feet was not the appropriate dress for the Bellagio Hotel lobby.

"No, I . . ." she began, taking in the onlookers around her. "My boyf—I mean, my husband seems to have left. I need to know if he checked out."

The crease above Geraldine's nose deepened as she listened to Elle's request. "Room number, dear?"

"307," Elle answered. "The reservation should be under Saladino."

"Oh, yes." Geraldine studied the screen and sighed. "He checked out about an hour ago. The room is paid through Tuesday. So, you're free to stay until then, dear."

"He's *gone*?" Her voice cracked as tears formed in her already sore, red eyes. Her lungs tightened and her hands trembled.

This can't be happening, she thought, her mind racing. *How could he leave me like this?*

"Did he get another room?"

"I can check, just one moment." Geraldine tapped at her keyboard, scrunched her nose, and shook her head. "No, I'm afraid not. We have only one reservation under that name, and it's for the room you're staying in."

"Right," Elle muttered, her fingers tapping the desk at a frantic pace. "Thank you for your help."

Mortified and forlorn, Elle pulled her robe tight to her chest and walked past the elevators to the stairwell. Slowly, she made her way up the stairs, her mind blank and defeated. When she reached her room, she stripped herself down and entered the shower, turning the water as hot as she could handle. She stood in the scorching hot stream and sobbed, her hands pressed against the glass of the shower. She knew he wouldn't return. She knew it was over.

Her skin was red and splotchy when she emerged from the bathroom, wrapped in a towel. Her sopping wet hair dripped down her back as she curled up in a ball on the bed. When she grew cold, she spotted his bathrobe draped over a chair. She wrapped the soft terry cloth around her shaky body and inhaled the residue of his cologne. She sobbed while watching the door, hoping he'd walk through it, until finally she drifted into a dreamless sleep.

The next morning, alone and defeated, Elle boarded the plane to Chicago, staring at the empty seat for the duration of the flight. Her eyes were bone dry, unable to cry anymore.

When she arrived at O'Hare Airport, she climbed into a cab, directing the driver to Troy's apartment. She had to see him.

She climbed the stairs of his building, leaned her luggage against the wall, and knocked on the door. She held her breath as the sound of footsteps approaching grew louder. She could see his feet through the crack of light at the bottom of the door. Just as she pondered what to say, those feet moved out of sight, and once again Elle could hear footsteps.

He was walking away.

Elle pounded on the door. "Troy! Troy, please open the door."

Silence.

Tears sprang from her eyes as she pounded relentlessly against the harsh wood, but no one answered. Embarrassed and exhausted, Elle slid to sit on the floor, her head tapping against the wood.

"Troy, I'm sorry. Please don't do this."

After an hour of sitting in Troy's dirty hallway, Elle pulled herself to her feet and gripped her luggage, dragging it down the stairs and into a cab.

• • • • •

Later that week, Elle arrived home after an exhausting day at work to find an unmarked envelope lying in the entryway.

A certificate of annulment signed by Troy.

It was over. She got what she thought she wanted.

But all she wanted was to go back. To go back to the woman who lay in a heap on the bathroom floor. She'd tell that woman to snap out of it, to embrace her new life with her new husband. To embrace the possibilities of their life as a married couple. She'd tell that miserable, terrified girl to grow up, to appreciate what she had before it was gone.

But she couldn't go back.

And now, just like Troy's, her heart was ripped to shreds. And she'd never be the same.

Chapter 15

W hoa."

Whitney leaned forward in her chair and clutched a Twizzler with both hands. She stared at Elle in disbelief and Elle wanted to hide her head in shame from her best friend. She couldn't imagine what Whitney must have been thinking about her behavior in Vegas.

"I tried, Whit. I tried to get him back."

Whitney sat up straight and wiped her cheek with the back of her hand. "You did?"

Elle nodded and tears formed in her eyes all over again. "After I went to his place, I sent him e-mails, left voice mail messages, wrote letters, and taped notes to his door. It never mattered. He changed his phone number, his e-mail address, *everything*. There was nothing I could do."

"It was too late." Whitney's voice was a sharp whisper.

"He was done." She'd hear the shuffling of feet, and someone would stand, look through the peephole, and then walk away. And her heart broke more and more each time until finally she couldn't even bear the thought of crossing the threshold of his building.

"So you filed the annulment papers?"

Elle sniffed, then wiped her eyes and nose with a tissue. "I had to, Whit. I had this idea the first time I went there. I was going to bring them with me, tear them up, beg his forgiveness. But he didn't answer the door. And eventually, I stopped putting them in my purse whenever I went there. There was no use."

"Oh, honey." Whitney placed her hand over her heart and tilted her head. "My heart is breaking. I can't believe you held on to this for ten years."

Elle was quiet for a moment. "Wouldn't you?"

Whitney closed her eyes and nodded. "Yeah, I guess I would. But I still don't understand. Why didn't you tell him you needed more time? Why did you walk down that aisle?"

"I've thought about this for years. *Literally* years. The honest answer is, I didn't want to disappoint him. The year we dated, I'm not kidding, was blissful. Perfect. If I'd said no that morning, everything would have changed. I loved him, Whit. I always wanted *him*."

"But not enough."

Elle cringed. "I guess not."

"But now he's back."

"Yeah, he's back and my life's in a tailspin. I have no idea what to do."

"Do you still have feelings for him?"

"I don't think I ever *stopped* having feelings for him."

"So maybe this is your chance. People come into our lives for a reason. Maybe this is your second chance at happiness, Ellie."

"I don't know. Part of me wants to think so, but I just—"

"Is it Luke? Is that the problem?"

Elle thought about the handsome actor, the one who calmed her but challenged her as well. The one who made her knees buckle and her toes tingle. Of course, he was a factor in her hesitation.

"Yeah. I mean, we're not exclusive, but the thought of him being with Gina . . . or anyone else really, it makes me want to punch something. Hard." A knot formed in Elle's belly just at the thought of Gina and Luke together.

"So tell him. Tell him you want to be monogamous."

"I don't know . . ." Her voice trailed off as she stared down at her desk.

"Because of Troy. You want to see what might happen."

"Maybe, yeah. I just feel—unsettled. My head is in a daze, and not in a good way. The idea of betraying either of them makes me sick to my stomach."

"You listen to me, you're a grown woman. There is *nothing* wrong with exploring this. You owe it to yourself to see what you want. Not what Troy wants or what Luke wants. But what *you* want."

"What if Troy's right about me? What if I can never commit to anyone else? Am I gonna end up some crazy old maid who writes about romance, but who has absolutely no idea what she's talking about?"

"Okay, bite your tongue. No one even says 'old maid' anymore. And have you ever thought maybe you just can't commit yourself to *him*?"

"I've considered it."

"But . . . ?"

"But I felt guilty. Troy's wonderful. I mean seriously, there's no one better."

"Honey, he could be the most perfect person on the planet, but if he's not the guy for you, that's all that matters. Stop. Feeling. Guilty."

Elle leaned her elbows on the desk, hanging her head in her hands. "If only . . ."

Elle heard Whitney rise to her feet to stand behind her. She stroked Elle's back gently with her hand. "What am I gonna do with you?"

"Put me to sleep," Elle joked. "Put me out of my misery."

"Nah. You're stronger than that. You're the strongest person I know."

"Me?" Elle's eyebrows pinched together. "You need to get out more."

"I'm serious, Ellie. You're a strong, intelligent, creative woman. Yes, you've made mistakes. Yes, you hurt someone you never intended to hurt. You're human, irrevocably human."

Elle stood, wiped her face, and sank into Whitney's arms. "Thank you for being you."

"I love you, honey. You'll figure this out."

"And if I don't?"

"You will."

Elle's moment of comfort in Whitney's arms was short-lived when Nicole buzzed.

"Elle, Luke Kingston is here to see you."

"Oh God," Elle murmured into Whitney's shoulder.

"He doesn't know any of this, does he?" Whitney handed her the box of tissue; Elle eagerly grabbed a tissue and dabbed her face. She didn't want Luke to see her like this.

"No."

Elle pressed against the intercom button. "Please send him in."

"No time like the present," Whitney said, walking to the door. "Text me later. Let me know how you're doing, all right?"

Luke opened the door, giving Elle a conflicted expression the moment he saw her tears. She knew it was time to be completely honest with him, even if it meant he ran as far away from her as possible. He and Whitney exchanged pleasantries before Whitney vacated the office. As soon as the door clicked behind her, Luke crossed the room to Elle, wrapping an arm around her.

"Baby, what's going on? You've been crying."

"I know. And I know I should tell you—"

"So tell me."

"It's . . . it's difficult."

"Listen to me, I can handle it. I promise." He pulled away, his hands still holding her arms. "Things have been different with you. Tell me what's going on. I feel like you're slipping through my fingers."

"I don't mean to, I just—I'm not sure where to start."

Elle sat in her chair and Luke eased himself against her desk, placing his hands in his pockets. "Have I done something? I know you think I've gone Hollywood, but I—"

"No, no." Elle shook her head decisively. "This isn't about that. It's about me. About what I did, a long time ago."

Luke flinched, but then his expression relaxed. "Knowing you, you're being too hard on yourself."

"Maybe you should wait until after you hear what I did. You might change your mind."

"Fine. Hit me." Luke smiled his boyish grin, and Elle knew right then and there she was safe with him. She could tell him anything, even what she did in Vegas.

"The owner of the restaurant . . ."

"Your ex-boyfriend."

"Actually, he was my husband."

Luke's eyes widened.

"It was brief," she added quickly, "but . . . it happened."

Luke rubbed his chin with his fingertips. "Didn't expect that, but okay. I don't care that you were married—is that what you were worried about?"

"It's more complicated than that. We did it on a whim, after dating for a while. And I broke it off almost immediately, like less than two days later. We were in Vegas and it was a mess. I hurt him so badly, Luke. More than I've ever hurt anyone."

"Why did you marry him? You know, if you didn't really want to?"

"I got all wrapped up in it, I guess. I didn't want the relationship to end, but that's exactly what happened. He couldn't forgive me and cut off contact for ten years."

"Ten years? Ouch."

"I thought he was still in Chicago. The last place in the world I expected him to be was here."

"Maybe he followed you." Luke raised his eyebrows and leaned his head forward, his lips pressed into a thin line. Was he being protective of her? If so, despite the fact she knew he was way off base in his assumption, she liked it. She liked him being protective of her. It was sexy, yet subtle.

"No, he didn't. He was just as shocked as I was." Elle studied Luke's expression. He didn't seem convinced. "If you knew Troy, you'd know he had no intention of *ever* seeing me again. He has a child and her mother relocated. That's the only reason he's here."

Luke pulled Elle from the chair, wrapping his arms around her and nuzzling into her neck. A delicious shiver ran down her spine. Luke in protective mode was possibly the sexiest Luke she'd yet to encounter. She wanted to lose herself in his embrace as she always did.

"There's more. The show you're working on is, for all intents and purposes, our story. He's Desmond and I'm Molly."

Luke pulled back, running his hand through his hair and glancing around Elle's office. "Wait, so you're telling me this . . . *all* of this is about *him*?"

Elle looked down at the carpet. "Yes."

"Are you still in love with the guy?"

"What?" Elle asked, taken aback. She had no idea how to answer that question tactfully. She'd never stopped having feelings for Troy. And part of her wondered if she ever would. "Are you seriously asking me that?"

"Yes."

"This is ridiculous." Elle returned to her chair and swiveled to open her desk drawer, retrieving a pen and paper, doing whatever she could to avoid the question. Luke grabbed the arm of her chair and brought her back to center. Once again, they locked eyes. The air in Elle's lungs seemed to fly from her chest.

"You didn't answer my question," Luke said, gritting his teeth.

"Are you . . . jealous?" The corner of Elle's mouth pulled up into a curious smile. She wanted to savor this moment with Luke, to forget the pain and anguish she'd caused herself and Troy.

Luke cocked his head to the side. "And what if I am?"

Elle scrunched her lips, enjoying this side of the carefree actor. Jealous Luke was even sexier than Protective Luke. She was never one to make men jealous, but she'd be lying if she said she didn't savor Luke's reaction. It made her ridiculously happy. As much as she fought it, a large grin crossed her face as they stared into each other's eyes.

"Look," Luke continued, his expression still serious, "I don't trust him. He left you behind and never looked back. He's a moron."

"Didn't you hear my story? I'm the moron. *Me*. I'm the one who destroyed him, not the other way around."

Luke pulled her gently from the chair and placed soft kisses on each of her cheeks. "Anyone who could walk away from you is an idiot. End of story. I don't care what mistakes you made. If he knew you, *really* knew you, he wouldn't have pushed. You have to do things on your own time."

Elle's breath caught. She disagreed with Luke. She didn't think Troy had pushed her. But she was astonished at how well Luke knew her—really knew her. He was right. Elle not only liked being in control, but doing things on her own time, her own schedule, was absolutely imperative for her comfort and happiness. It was her way, and the fact Luke understood that, that he respected it, was something to appreciate. Perhaps she wasn't giving the handsome actor enough credit. Obviously, he understood her more than she'd ever anticipated.

"You're right. I don't like to be pushed."

Luke licked his lips; his fingers ran south to Elle's ass. Without warning, he reached down and hoisted her up. She gasped and wrapped her legs around his waist. He shifted his weight to turn them, perching Elle atop her desk. And for the first time that day, she allowed Troy to leave her mind completely. She was completely and utterly wrapped up in Luke Kingston.

"Most of the time." She raised a devious eyebrow before taking his mouth with her own. Luke's hands roamed through her curly hair as his tongue pressed to hers. Her toes curled at the sensations overtaking her body. The touch, the feel of Luke was intoxicating and Elle couldn't get enough of him. Eagerly, her tongue caressed his and her hands ran up and down his back, pulling him as close to her as possible.

"Wanna get outta here?" he asked between kisses, his voice husky and deep. Elle could feel his length pressed against her pelvis, and she wanted to lose herself in him, to forget all of her mistakes, to take a break from reality.

"Lock the door," she whispered.

A satisfied grin crossed Luke's lips. "You never stop surprising me, Elle Riley."

"I hope that's a good thing."

Luke nodded before kissing her lips, her chin, her neck. "The best."

Chapter 16

Elle's heart thumped uncontrollably and shots of adrenaline zoomed through her abdomen. No matter how much positive self-talk she gave herself, the idea of seeing Troy was feeling like more than she could handle. After her drunken visit to his restaurant, they'd exchanged several text messages and agreed to meet for dinner on a Monday evening. Troy's restaurant was closed on Mondays and it was the only time he could get away during the dinner hour. When he asked if he could pick the place, Elle agreed immediately. Troy always had such impeccable taste when it came to food and restaurants. She'd only been in the Los Angeles area for a few years, and aside from the takeout places near her home and the studio, she was still pretty clueless about local cuisine.

Troy had chosen a tiny hole-in-the-wall Indian place. When she walked in, she inhaled the familiar scents. The smoky trace of cumin and the aromatic cardamom were the first she recognized. Next came the earthy tone of turmeric and the spicy smell of red pepper. She and Troy had eaten so much Indian food while living in Chicago since her apartment was above an Indian restaurant. Secretly, she wondered if that was the reason for his choice in restaurant. A walk down memory lane, perhaps? Regardless of the reason, Elle's mind was swimming in memories of Troy and Indian food. Of laughter and samosas. Of romantic sentiments and tikka masala.

Troy was waiting at a small table when she arrived. She glanced down at her watch, hoping she wasn't late. Troy chuckled as she approached, standing to greet her with a kiss on the cheek.

"You're right on time."

"How do you do that?"

"What?" Troy pulled the chair out for her.

She smiled as she sat. "Read my mind."

"You looked at your watch the second you saw me."

"Oh." Elle shook off her thoughts of kismet and serendipity. He had read her body language; that was all. "Of course. So you like this place?"

"Yeah. It's not as good as back home, but it's close." He gestured to the full wineglass in front of her place setting. "I ordered you a California rosé."

"Ah, perfect." Elle took a large sip of the slightly sweet wine, which in her opinion paired beautifully with Indian cuisine. "How are the samosas?"

"Ah yes, you and your samosas. You've always been an appetizer girl."

Elle liked how playful Troy was being. Their other interactions had been so tense, despite their efforts to keep things friendly. Today, he seemed more at ease, which in turn helped her to relax as well.

"Nobody gets between me and a mozzarella stick." Elle felt herself flirting and embraced it. After all their years apart, it felt good to be playful with Troy again.

"Or an order of nachos . . . or Wisconsin cheese curds . . . should I go on?" Troy winked and handed Elle her menu.

"Nah, I think we both know my affinity for snack food."

"Are you still keeping candy at your desk?"

"Of course, but only the fruity stuff. I gave up chocolate. Too fattening."

Troy shook his head and closed his eyes, chuckling under his breath. "I don't think you've ever had to worry about that."

"What? My weight?"

"Mm hmm, you've always had a great body." Troy's eyes roamed her as he spoke, centering on her chest. Elle wondered what had come over him—when did he have this sudden change of heart? He looked at her with appreciation rather than contempt, and it filled her heart with hope.

"Says the man with the permanent six-pack."

"Not anymore, I'm afraid. Too much pizza, it's gone to my gut." Troy smacked his stomach lightly with his palm. Elle rolled her eyes. His chest and abs still looked as firm as they did when they were a couple, at least with his clothes *on*.

"Sure," she murmured. "I *almost* believe that." Troy was never one to fish for a compliment, so she decided he was just being hard on himself. Seeing as he was a perfectionist like herself, that was the obvious conclusion.

Troy laughed again and finished his glass of scotch. Troy always ordered two fingers of scotch on the rocks before any dinner out, especially Indian food. When he received his first job offer after college, Elle had purchased a bottle of Johnnie Walker Platinum to celebrate. She'd purchased another for herself when the pilot of *Follow the Sun* first aired. Even though they'd enjoyed scotch together more times than she could count, she didn't know why she did it, since it was Troy's drink, not hers. But now guilt swarmed her belly as she remembered that she and Luke opened that bottle. Quickly, she pushed the guilt from her mind. She was determined to enjoy this meal, this evening, this time with Troy.

Their waitress took their order, and they quickly fell back into old patterns. Ordering two dishes to split as well as a large order of samosas to snack on prior to the entrees. The wine was doing its job. As she indulged in the second glass, tingles ran down her arms, and her muscles relaxed. Troy had finished his scotch and both were able to ease back into old banter.

Elle's teeth pierced the first samosa. Steam escaped the small puffy triangle and she relished the savory taste of peas, potatoes, and lentils.

"Mmm, why have I gone so long without having Indian food?" Elle shook her head in amazement as she savored the flavors in her mouth.

"How long?"

A small chunk of potato dropped to her plate and she hoped Troy hadn't noticed. "Hmm?"

"How long since you've had Indian food?"

Elle froze and looked down at her plate, avoiding eye contact. "A long time."

"I see." Troy nodded. "Since Chicago?"

Elle nodded, feeling foolish.

"Seriously?" Troy's voice dropped an octave.

When Elle first entered the restaurant, she had no idea just how long it'd been. She didn't realize just how many things were tied to her past with this man, just how stunted she'd allowed the past ten years to be without him. It went beyond her love life, beyond her fear of getting hurt. It was permeating her habits, her tastes, everything. She was thirty-five years old. It was time to figure out, finally, who she was.

Troy cleared his throat. "Rigby?"

Elle looked up with a confused expression, unaware of how long she'd been lost in thought.

"Where'd you go?"

"I was just thinking. I've been doing that a lot lately." She dabbed her mouth with her napkin and quickly gulped down the remainder of her wine.

Troy reached across the table. Elle hesitated briefly, looking at his outstretched arm, before grasping his fingertips with her own. "Maybe we both need to stop thinking so damn much."

Elle's teeth dug into her bottom lip as his words set in. "Maybe." They ate in silence for several minutes before Elle changed the subject. "Tell me about Payton."

Troy sat up tall in his chair, a gleam developing in his eyes. "She's awesome, such a great kid. I get to see her every other weekend and every Thursday."

"That must be hard."

"We make it work. I miss her a lot, though." He scratched the skin of his forehead, looking down at the table. "She's a lot like me."

Elle eased her elbows onto the table, perching her chin on her linked hands. "Like how? Is she stubborn?"

"Oh yeah, big-time. She's a pistol. Can't get much by that kid, she keeps me on my toes for sure."

"And her mother?"

"I guess you could say we're friends. If it wasn't for Payton, we wouldn't be, but we get along just fine. We've made the best out of a difficult situation."

"That's really admirable. Obviously, I'm not a parent, but I think it would be hard to raise a child with someone else, especially if you're not . . . you know, together."

Troy shifted in his seat, took another drink, then asked, "How about you? Do you think you'll ever want kids?"

Elle didn't expect that question; even though he delivered it casually, she knew it was loaded. Troy wanted to know how she felt about motherhood seeing as she was thirty-five, single, and without children. She was also married to her job, and worked at least fifty to sixty hours per week.

"Honestly? I'm not sure."

"Really? Did something change your mind? You always said—"

"I know, it's just . . . the show is so consuming. I'm not sure I could focus on a baby until it goes off the air. And I'm hoping that won't be for a long time." Elle picked at her food, unsure of how Troy would feel about her lack of drive toward motherhood. He was right, though. In her twenties, Elle always assumed she'd have a family. Hell, at that age, she expected to have at least two children by her midthirties. But she also never expected to be the creator of the biggest television drama on any network. Things change.

"Makes sense. You'd be good at it, though."

"You really think so?" She let out a sardonic laugh. "I think I'd be a nightmare. So anal-retentive, so structured and demanding." She laughed into her napkin.

"Nah." Troy studied her face, before licking his lips and smiling. "I think you'd do just fine."

For the first time since she entered the restaurant, a shot of adrenaline made its way through her body, making her quite aware of the effect Troy still had on her. His opinion mattered, as it always had. The fact he thought she'd be a good mom was endearing, special. It meant something.

"Thank you."

This time Elle extended her arm across the table, opening her hand in invitation. Troy's lips formed a soft smile before he placed his hand in hers. They sat in the middle of the restaurant, hands interlocked, and said nothing. They simply smiled at one another, appreciating the common ground they'd managed to find after so many years, and Elle was so grateful.

"I have to ask you something, and I hope it won't spoil the night because, so far, it's been really nice."

Tension hung over the table. Elle wrinkled her nose, but squeezed Troy's hand, waiting for his question.

"Are you still seeing that guy? The one you brought to my place?"

There was no way Elle would lie. She had to be honest. Instinctively, she pulled her hand from Troy's. He stared down at the empty space between them. "Yes. We're dating, but we're not a couple or anything just yet."

Troy's forehead relaxed and he scratched the back of his neck. His cheeks turned pink as he grinned. "Okay, cool."

"Cool?" Elle was amused. She'd expected tension, a possible ultimatum or a warning from Troy that he wouldn't get involved with her if she was seeing someone else. But instead he wore a boyish grin on his handsome face and she wished she could read his mind, if only for a brief moment, to know what was going on in his head.

"Yeah."

"I wish I could read your mind right now."

Troy leaned in across the table, his eyes boring into hers. "I don't think you're ready for that."

Elle felt bold, as if she had nothing to lose. Her breath was quickening as her eyes remained fixed on Troy's. "Try me."

Troy lowered his voice to a whisper. "Right now, I'm thinking about how good your lips would taste. I'm thinking about how much I want to pay the check, walk out of here, and press you up against the bricks of the building." He paused for a minute. "Should I go on?"

Elle had a sudden awareness of her own heartbeat; her fingers tingled with the need to touch and be touched by the gorgeous man on the other side of the table. Those eyes, those soulful brown eyes, focused on hers as if she were the most beautiful creature on the planet.

"Yes," she whispered.

He glanced around briefly before continuing. "I'm thinking about pressing you against that brick wall, and unbuttoning your blouse. I'd take my time, savoring the look and feel of you as I opened each one."

Elle swallowed hard, her palms began to sweat, and her nerve endings stirred beneath her skin. Their hands were still enmeshed on the table, and she realized Troy was now stroking her palm with his fingertips. That simple touch left her craving him, as much of him as she could possibly obtain. She wanted to make the table vanish, to push it all aside, eliminating all distance between her and the man who was making her heart pound out of control.

"What else?" She parted her legs slightly, feeling completely enveloped in her need for Troy.

"I'll pay the check and then I'll tell you. How does that sound?"

"Good."

Troy released her hand and rose from the table. He walked to the other side of the restaurant, where their waiter happened to be standing. He pulled him aside, opened his wallet, and handed him a bundle of cash. Then, with a cocky grin, he joined Elle, who managed to stand despite her wobbly and weakened knees.

When he took her hand and led her outside, Troy did exactly what he had described inside. The brick felt harsh against her back, but it didn't matter. All she wanted was to touch and explore every inch of Troy's body. His lips crashed against hers. One hand cupped her ass as the other toyed with the collar of her blouse.

"God, I've missed you," she murmured between kisses as Troy unbuttoned the first button of her blouse. "I've missed this."

"Shhh," Troy whispered, popping the next button, exposing the lace of her bra. His fingertips danced over the exposed fabric, tickling her sensitive skin, creating a delectable shiver down her spine. His lips pressed again to hers, and immediately Elle opened her mouth, inviting him in. He deepened the kiss, stroking her tongue with his own in determined yet gentle strokes. Arousal built within her as her hands roamed his back, his neck, his hair.

"Should we go somewhere . . . somewhere more private?" Elle asked, suddenly aware they were in public when she heard the voices of people walking past the restaurant. "Your place, maybe?"

"No," Troy answered.

Elle pressed her hands against his shoulders, pushing him away from her. "No?"

"I think we should say good night."

"You can't be serious." Elle's vision became clouded, and her throat ran dry.

"I think we should take things slow."

"You call this slow?" She could feel her pulse pounding in her ears. She planted her feet in a wide stance, crossing her arms in front of her chest. "What's going on, Troy? Are you still pissed off? Is this all a game to you?"

Troy ran his fingers through his hair. "No, of course not. You know me better than that."

"Maybe not." Her fingers fumbled to button her blouse. She felt ridiculous, foolish, like Troy was playing with her emotions. Turning her on only to walk away from her. She'd felt that ten years ago; she didn't want to feel it again.

Troy pushed her bangs from her eyes. "Don't say that. I promise you, I'm *not* playing games. I'm just trying to be respectful . . . and I want to be sure before anything . . . happens."

They locked eyes and Elle knew exactly what Troy was trying to say. He didn't want to sleep with her only to realize he could never truly forgive what happened in Las Vegas. He didn't want to lead her on.

"But I want to see you again." He pressed his forehead to hers and sighed. "God, I want to see you again."

Troy's lips pressed gently to hers and she relaxed, hoping to God he wasn't leading her on. She wanted to trust him so badly, yet wanted to run far, far away from the utter confusion only Troy could bring.

"When?" she asked, glaring at him with daggers in her eyes, still questioning his intentions.

"Saturday night."

"What about the restaurant?"

"I'll make it work."

"Okay, fine. Saturday."

They walked in silence to Elle's car. The only sounds were the cars whizzing by and the clicking of her heels against the pavement. With a chaste kiss, they said good night, and Elle drove home more confused than ever.

Why did things have to be so damn complicated?

Chapter 17

E lle was running late. She was needed on set, but was having trouble getting her things together. Her mind was jumbled—a mess. She couldn't focus and she was pretty sure she knew why.

Today was the day they would shoot Luke and Gina's first love scene. Their characters had shared a couple of kisses, enticing the audience with their chemistry and banter. But now, it was time for the story to take their relationship to the next level. Elle had written the scene, but hadn't thought about how it would feel to shoot it. She contemplated skipping the shoot. After all, Rob was the director and could handle it. But she'd never missed a shoot. Not ever. And she wasn't about to begin now. Yes, her feelings for Luke were strong—stronger than she expected when they first got involved. But her show . . . her show had always been, and would continue to be, her first priority. She was needed on set, and so that was where she'd be.

Her cell phone buzzed as she parked her car in the studio lot.

Troy.

His voice was soft when she answered the phone. "I hate to do this, but I have to postpone our dinner."

Although Elle was disappointed, she didn't want to convey it. "Everything okay?"

"Yeah, it's just . . . Payton's mom needs to switch weekends, so I have her Saturday."

A smile crossed her face and for just a moment she allowed herself to get excited about the potential for meeting Troy's daughter. "No need to cancel, I'd love to meet her. We can go to dinner, or maybe a movie? They're adapting another YA book into a movie, maybe we could—"

"I don't think that's the best idea, Rigby."

"Oh."

"I don't introduce Payton until I'm involved in something serious. In almost nine years, she's met only two women." When Elle said nothing, Troy sighed. "It's just . . . it's too soon. I hope you understand."

Elle knew it was too soon, and she knew Troy was being logical and protective over his daughter, but she couldn't help feeling disappointed and rejected. It seemed that, more and more, she could hear the distrust in his voice. He could deny his anger to her, but part of her wasn't sure he could ever really forgive her. She brushed that feeling off, knowing she was not a parent, and that an entirely new set of rules appeared when one took on that role.

"Of course." Her stomach clenched. "We'll reschedule for another time."

"I'm really sorry," he added. "I was looking forward to it."

"I was too." Elle cleared her throat, ignoring the tightening in her chest. "Well, you have a good weekend with Payton and we'll connect sometime next week."

"Thanks for being cool with this. I was nervous to call."

"Don't be silly. You're a dad first—I get that. We'll reschedule, it's no problem."

She hung up the phone, placed it in her purse, and entered the studio, determined to push Troy from her mind. The moment she saw Gina, she was reminded of the scene they were about to shoot. Gina was dressed in nothing but a strapless bra and panties, a sheet wrapped around her as she strutted across the set. The makeup team had done a hell of a job, bringing out the best in her features. Her dark eyes were doe-like, giving her a soft yet sexy appearance that would translate to viewers at home. A knot formed in Elle's stomach as Gina approached.

"Have you seen Luke?"

Elle clenched her jaw at the question, not wanting to think about them lying together on the set, going through the motions of an intimate encounter. Yes, there were half a dozen cameras taping their every move, their every embrace, their every kiss to make sure the lighting was perfect and that the feel of the scene was appropriate. It was far from romantic. But that didn't make it any less concerning to Elle.

"No, sorry. I just got in."

"Well, if you see him, tell him I'm looking for him. I want to show him my outfit." Gina flipped her hair and gave Elle a devious wink before walking away. Just before she was out of earshot, Gina yelled back to her, "Oh, and tell him it's time to decide. My publicist needs an answer."

Elle stared back at Gina with confusion, but rather than chase after the actress (which was exactly what Gina wanted) she pulled herself together, smoothed down her clothing, and joined Rob at the craft services table. Knowing she had no candy in her purse, she grabbed a doughnut and a napkin and plopped down in her chair.

"Morning." Rob tipped his baseball cap to Elle before taking a bite of his cherry Danish. "Rough day? You look—"

"—like *hell*." Elle heard the unmistakably blunt voice of Whitney.

"Well, good morning to you, too." Elle took a bite of the buttermilk doughnut, allowing the ridiculously sweet pastry to soothe her distressed mind. She took another, and then another, oblivious to the crumbs accumulating on her chest.

"With the way you're going to town on that doughnut, I'd say *something* is definitely wrong."

Elle polished off the doughnut, brushing the crumbs from her top before hopping from her chair to grab another. Whitney's mouth was agape when Elle returned to her chair.

"This must be serious."

The slightly acerbic tone of Whitney's observations annoyed Elle. She didn't need sarcasm. She needed to be left alone to do her job. If she needed to run on her treadmill that night to make up for the pastries, she would. She didn't need Whitney giving her a hard time.

"I don't wanna talk about it."

"Fine, okay. Whatever." Whitney grabbed a fruit cup from the table. "If you want to get drinks tonight, I'm free."

"Thanks. I just need to get through the day. I'll be fine."

It was a blatant lie, but Elle was tired of talking about her problems all the time. She was torn between two men, dealing with the guilt and actions of her past, and attempting to go about her life as if nothing had ever happened. For just one day, she wanted to give 100 percent of her energy to her job without all of those other emotions creeping in and ruining her composure.

"Message received," Whitney muttered. "We'll chat later."

"You two having trouble?" Rob was once again meddling. Perched in his seat, he leaned on the arm of his chair, his chin in his hands, waiting to hear the dirt. Elle grimaced in irritation. As much as she liked Rob, she was in no mood to deal with his prying nature.

"No, we're fine. Everything's fine." She glanced down at her watch and sighed. "Shouldn't we have started already?"

"I was waiting for you. Luke should be out in a minute and Gina's ready to go."

"Oh, believe me, I'm fully aware of *that*." Elle ran her hand through her hair while her foot tapped against the linoleum floor.

"Alrighty then. Let's get started." Rob stood, walked next to camera one, and gestured for Tim to bring out the marker. "Places, people. I need quiet on the set!"

Luke emerged from the hallway, wrapped in nothing but a towel. His hair was wet, as the character of David was supposed to be fresh from a morning shower. Elle swallowed hard as they locked eyes. He winked at her before joining Gina on set. Gina lay on the bed, wrapped in her sheet, and Luke positioned himself under the door frame to the bathroom. Steam billowed behind him as one of the makeup artists touched up a spot on his chin. He lifted his chin to accommodate her, still locking eyes with Elle. She shifted in her seat as she observed him. The way he looked at her, no matter where they were, was exhilarating. She felt naked and exposed, yet sexy and sensual just from one look from that man.

And now she had to watch that deliciously sexy man look at another woman that way. She was used to the banter, the kisses and the exchange of smoldering looks between her characters, but seeing them in such an intimate position was grating on her, and they hadn't even started to film!

Tim waited until the makeup artist had retreated from the set, then he held the marker for camera one. "*Follow the Sun*, episode fourteen, take one."

"And action!" Rob yelled. Elle sat back in her chair and braced herself for the agonizing set of takes that would make up her entire morning. Maybe it wouldn't be so bad . . .

• • • • •

It was worse than she could have ever imagined. Take after take of kisses, arms stroking skin, moans and murmurs between their lines—the lines Elle had written. She cursed herself as she watched them. Gina was in rare form and Elle was convinced several of her "mistakes" were planned, only to grate further on Elle's nerves.

"Cut!" Rob yelled after Gina said the wrong line yet again. The third time in less than ten minutes.

"Oh, damn." Gina giggled before glaring across the soundstage at Elle. "Looks like I messed it up again."

"No big deal." Luke shook his head, allowing his makeup artist to wipe the smudged lipstick from his face.

The makeup artist then leaned in to reapply Gina's crimson lipstick before they began another take.

Elle leaned toward Rob. "She's doing it on purpose. You know that, right?"

Rob brushed her off. "She's probably nervous. These scenes are difficult."

If Luke was annoyed by it all, he certainly wasn't exhibiting any signs of it. That, in and of itself, made Elle squirm in her seat. She wanted him to sigh, to roll his eyes, *something—anything*— to exhibit frustration in doing multiple takes of each kiss, each embrace, each line delivered between moments of physical contact. It was grating on her nerves, and yet she was berating herself for caring so much. He was doing his job. And she needed to get her head on straight and do hers. But first, she desperately needed a reprieve from a morning of watching him touch, stroke, and kiss someone other than herself.

"We should break for lunch."

"You got it."

When the scene reached a decent breaking spot, Rob stood and dismissed everyone for an hour-long lunch break. Elle breathed deeply as she watched Gina saunter from the soundstage. Feeling a new sense of purpose, Elle strode toward Luke.

"Hey, babe."

With no worries as to who might see them, Elle took Luke's hand. "Come with me."

He chuckled, but followed behind her, his hand linked with hers as they made their way down the hallway leading to his dressing room. She held her head high as they walked, undeterred in her desire for time alone with Luke. She was tired of sharing him with Gina.

They entered the room and Elle slammed the door, locking it behind them. She pressed Luke into the cold wood, stripping him of his towel and boxer shorts. A cocky grin crossed his face as he lifted her blouse over her head, pressing his lips to her collarbone. His tongue felt hot against her skin as it traveled up to her neck, over the curve of her chin and finally to her lips. Meanwhile his agile fingers unzipped her pencil skirt, dropping it to the floor.

Elle stood in her bra and panties, lust growing inside her. She needed him inside her, needed to feel him, to join him in the exquisite agony of mounting pleasure. She hoisted one of her arms around his waist and moved her pelvis toward his. He moaned into her mouth before pulling back.

"Come with me."

He led her to his makeup chair, where he sat down, his hands on her bare waist. Slowly, he tugged her panties until they dropped to the floor. Elle removed her bra, her eyes locked with his.

"You're in charge, remember?" Luke said. "Show me what you want."

"You," she murmured. "I want you."

"Show me," he whispered, digging his fingers into her hips. Elle straddled him, her knees bent against the smooth leather, her arms wrapped around his muscular neck. She eased herself onto him, and watched as he closed his eyes and dipped his head back as she took every inch of him into her body.

Ever so slowly, Elle rocked above him. Luke's fingers dug into the skin of her hips, and she welcomed the sensation as the arousal within her built steadily. Luke pulled her close, taking one nipple into his mouth, grazing it with his teeth.

"Oh God."

Elle quickened her pace, thrusting again and again.

"Come for me, baby," Luke whispered.

Elle cried out as her orgasm consumed her entire body. Sweet and satisfying electricity spread through her nerve endings and a feeling of euphoria consumed her as her body remained wrapped around Luke's. She could tell he was close to his own release. His hands, still digging into her hips, were urging her movements faster and faster until he threw his head back in ecstasy, groaning into the thick air of the dressing room.

Elle collapsed onto him, her heart pounding out of control, sweat running down her back. Luke wrapped his arms around her, pulling her into a tight embrace. After a quiet moment spent in one another's arms, Elle slid from the chair. She attempted to stand, but found herself clutching the counter. Her legs felt like jelly, and she was having trouble getting her bearings. She'd never had orgasms like the ones she had with Luke. Their intensity was simply incomparable to anything else she experienced with any other lover.

"Well, that was hot." Luke sat in his makeup chair, looking spent. Elle handed him his boxer shorts, after she found them draped over a lamp in front of the expansive mirror on the wall. "We should do that more often. I don't know what came over you, but I like it."

His tone of voice was playful. He was teasing her. Clearly, her intentions were more than obvious.

"Don't be a smartass. You know what came over me." An image of Gina popped back into Elle's head and she remembered the insinuation about a publicist. "By the way, she said you have to make a decision? Something about her publicist and needing an answer . . ."

"Oh." Luke ran his fingers through his mussed-up hair, and his nose wrinkled slightly as he licked his lips. "*That*. I wanted to talk to you about that, but we haven't seen much of each other lately."

"What is it?" Elle hoped it was nothing serious, nothing that would jeopardize their budding relationship.

"There was such a great reaction to that Perez Hilton thing that her publicist thinks we should have a showmance."

Elle's jaw dropped. She had no idea what to say. Luke sighed. "It's this thing where we pretend to be a couple—"

"I know what it is, Luke. I'm in the business, remember?"

"So what do you think? It wouldn't be real. Just like two or three months of being seen in public or whatever to get the tongues wagging."

"Is this really what you want for yourself? Fake romance to boost your career?"

"Well, when you put it that way—"

"And where is the line drawn? Will you be kissing in public? Making out in restaurant booths, what?" Aggressively, Elle slid her panties up her legs as aggravation threatened to change the tone of their discussion. Gina's lips on Luke in the studio was difficult enough; the last thing she needed was to see them on gossip rags and websites.

He rose from his seat, stood before her, and ran his hands down her arms still beading with sweat. "I like when you're jealous."

"I'm not jealous." Elle slid her bra back on her thin frame. Luke tipped his chin and raised his eyebrows. "I'm *not*!"

"Okay, okay, whatever you say. But for the record, it's hot as hell. And I like this side of you."

She crossed her arms in front of her chest, widening her stance. "And what side is that?"

Luke wrapped his arms around her waist and pulled her close, nuzzling her neck with his nose. "The side of you that reacts. Instead of being all stoic and strong, you took what you wanted. And I was more than happy to give it to you."

"You're changing the subject."

"That's because I'm trying to keep you on your toes."

"And what does that mean?"

"I'm telling her no, Elle. I was *always* going to tell her no. I just wanted to see how you feel about me . . . how you really feel about me."

Elle's lips parted. "Seriously? You have no intention of going along with it?"

"Absolutely none. I want to make a name for myself the right way—with my work. But you have to admit you've been pulling away from me. One minute, we're having a great time, the next you're somewhere else completely. I had to know how you really feel."

Elle's voice came out in a whisper. "I'm crazy about you . . . obviously."

"It's good to hear." He shrugged, his eyes sincere and vulnerable. "I know you're seeing him, I can feel it."

"W-what? How did you . . . I mean—" Elle rambled, taking several steps back. How did he read her so well?

"Look, I get it, all right? I know you need to figure this out." Luke paused and looked up at the ceiling, avoiding Elle's eyes. His tone had changed. There was a bite to his words, a tick in his jaw. "And I *also* know you won't be able to move on until you do. But the thought of you with him . . ."

"What? Tell me."

Luke clenched his fists and pursed his lips. "Let's just say I'd rather you didn't. But this isn't about me. It's about you."

"What do you mean, it's not about you? Of course it is."

"Not all of it."

Elle glanced down at the floor. Right then and there, she knew Luke was falling for her just as much as she was falling for him. Gina wasn't the issue, *she* was. A tremendous amount of guilt was going to swallow her whole. Part of her heart still belonged to Troy. Was she a terrible person for seeing them both at the same time? Despite any titles or proclamations of exclusivity, she was fully aware of the negative impact she could have on either or both of the men in her life. The thought of hurting either of them made her chest ache.

Luke walked to her, wrapping his arms back around her waist.

"But as much as it pisses me off, knowing you're still seeing him, I'm willing to wait. You, Elle Riley, are *worth* the wait."

"That may be the sweetest thing anyone has ever said to me."

He shrugged. "It's the truth."

She ran her fingers through his wavy hair, feeling choked up. "Why do you always say the right thing? I mean, seriously, how did you get to be so damn wonderful?"

Luke shrugged, his cheeks scarlet. "I've never felt this way before."

"Never?"

"Nope." He kissed the tip of her nose. "Not ever."

Elle's eyes moistened and a lump formed in her throat as she processed what Luke had said. *Not ever?* She was overwhelmed, but, she was surprised to realize, not scared. Reluctantly, she glanced at her watch. More than anything, she wanted to stay and finish their conversation, but the lunch hour was almost over and she needed to clear things up with Whitney. "You must be starving. You should grab a sandwich back on set."

"Good idea, that *was* quite a bit of exertion." He laughed, kissing her gently on her ear. Her muscles relaxed beneath his lips, until she remembered what she had to do.

"I have to see Whitney, I was pretty rude to her earlier and I want to apologize."

Elle finished dressing, smoothed down the chaotic curls on her head, and kissed Luke one last time. She was dreading a blowup with her best friend. It was only noon and she was already processing more emotion than she usually did all day.

"Hey," he murmured with his arms wrapped around her back. "Are we okay? Your muscles are tense all of a sudden."

"I'm not thrilled with your little trick . . . but yeah, we're just fine. *More* than fine. Just promise me you'll tell Gina."

"I'll tell her the minute I see her. I meant what I said, Elle. It's not something I'm even remotely interested in."

"I know."

Elle smiled and kissed him softly on the cheek before walking to Whitney's office with her tail between her legs. When she knocked on the door, there was no response, which was odd since Whitney typically worked through the lunch hour. From the other side of the door, she heard a moan. And then another, and another. First a man, then a woman.

Elle laughed silently to herself, realizing she wasn't the only one who used the lunch hour for a quickie. Curious as to who might be on the other side of the door, she mentally gave Whitney a high five before digging through her purse for a notepad. When she found it, she scribbled a short apology and slipped it under the door, hoping she and Whitney would be just fine as soon as Whit read the message. There was no way in hell she would interrupt what was happening on the other side of that door.

In haste, so as not to draw attention to herself, she slipped back down the hallway and returned to the set, bracing herself for several more hours of torture. Only this time, she could watch Luke with satisfaction, knowing she, not Gina, was the one he desired when the director said, "Cut."

Chapter 18

The shrill sound of her house phone woke Elle from a deep sleep. An unexpected deep sleep. It was the morning of the Golden Globe award nominations. In years past she had trouble sleeping longer than a few hours. Perhaps it was the fact the fall season of *Follow the Sun* was dominating the number-one spot in the Nielsen ratings, or Elle's confidence in her show's role within the network, but for whatever reason she had slept in, only to be woken by the excited voice of Whitney.

"Oh my God, did I seriously just wake you?"

"Yes," she grumbled into the receiver, unable to focus her hazy eyes.

"Hurry up! Best Drama is next!"

Elle reached out her arm, still heavy with sleep, to grab the remote. Her nerves got the best of her and her fingers fumbled with the numbers.

"Oh my God," Whitney grumbled on the other end of the line. "You're going to miss it."

Elle struggled to focus her eyes. "I'm doing the best I can. Don't be a pain in the ass."

Finally, Elle turned to the proper channel just as *Follow the Sun* was read from the list of nominees. She and Whitney sat in silence for a moment. She'd done it. *They'd* done it. Elle's eyes filled with tears and she bit down on her bottom lip to prevent her emotions from spilling over.

"You did it," Whitney whispered.

Elle took a deep breath to calm her pounding heartbeat, and swiped a tear from her cheek. She had to remember to keep things in perspective and not to get her hopes up. "It's just a nomination."

"Stop it. Don't do that. Don't you *dare* do that. You freaking did it! This is something to celebrate!"

"I know, I just—I'm overwhelmed." Elle stared at the screen in awe.

"Just soak it in, my friend," Whitney said. Elle could hear Whitney's smile in her voice. "Soak it in."

"I will, I promise." Elle ran her fingers through her hair, finally allowing a satisfied smile to pull at the corners of her mouth.

"By the way, sleeping through the award nominations? So unlike you. I thought you'd be up hours ago, cleaning out your cabinets or something." Whitney chuckled into the phone. Whenever Elle was nervous, she had to keep her mind busy. Cleaning, rearranging, organizing were some of the things she ran to when anxious. Because of this, her cabinets were extremely well organized.

"I know, I'm shocked myself. So what did I miss?"

"Nolan and Gina are up for Best Actor and Actress. And now Best Drama. Maybe we'll grab it this year."

Elle released a sigh, not even realizing she was holding her breath. This was their second nomination for the award given by the Hollywood Foreign Press Association. They'd lost the previous year to a stellar drama in its final season. They hadn't stood a chance. But this year . . . well, this year they had a shot.

"This is . . . wow, this is phenomenal. Any tough contenders for the spot? I missed the other nominations."

"Yeah, a couple. But I think we can take 'em, especially after last week's Nielsens. Maybe Nolan will win this year, too. God, he'd be *so* happy."

"Gina would, too."

An uncomfortable pause passed over the phone. "Well, yeah."

"Things still weird between you two?" Elle asked.

"She's just a bitch on a mission to erase my existence from the planet. Seriously, she hasn't made eye contact with me in months . . . even when I apologized. Whatever, I'm over it. But speaking of her crazy ass—do you mean to tell me she's been nice to *you*?"

Elle chose not to share Gina's antics regarding a proposed show-mance with Luke. If she did, she knew how Whitney would react, and she wanted to hold on to her good feelings regarding the nominations. "Well, no, but she's the star of my show. I have to try, no matter how much she pisses me off. The show comes first, you know that. We're losing Nolan, there's no way I'm losing her, too."

"You're a better person than I am, my dear." Whitney laughed. "Enough about her. We should celebrate tonight. Drinks? Dinner? Dancing? All of the above?"

"I wish I could. But I'm actually seeing Troy tonight. He's taking me to see a Beatles cover band at Levitt Pavilion."

"Ah, Vegas is stepping it up, huh?"

Whitney didn't sound impressed. Elle knew her best friend's

claws came out when it involved Troy. Yes, she finally understood his reasons for leaving Elle the way he did, but as time had gone by, she reminded Elle of his decade-long absence from her life, and that if she hadn't walked into his restaurant, who knows how long that absence would have continued? Whitney didn't trust him, but Elle felt she was simply showing her preference for Luke.

"Wearing your Team Luke shirt this early in the morning, huh?" Elle teased.

"You better believe it. Speaking of that sexy man, how does he feel about this date with your ex-husband?"

Elle sat up in her bed, wiping the sleep from her eyes. "He's fine with it. In fact, he's been so great about this whole thing—so patient."

"Just don't push it. He's still a *man*."

"What's that supposed to mean?" Elle grimaced. She didn't want to think about Luke growing tired of her or walking away from what they were building. The idea sent uncomfortable adrenaline into her empty belly.

"Men don't share. He's crazy about you and I know that's the *only* reason he's putting up with all of this."

"I can't help it, Whit. I have to know if something's still there after all this time."

"I know, I get it—closure, unfinished business, yada yada yada. Just . . . be careful, okay? I don't want you to lose out on Kingston. I have a good feeling about him."

If only things were that simple. She wished she could echo Whitney's sentiment, but something in the pit of her stomach said the opposite. She knew the Hollywood bug had bitten him slightly, and she was hesitant to relax completely, not knowing what could be thrown their way. No matter her intense feelings toward the actor, her guard was still up, keeping him at a slight distance. Whitney made her wonder if, even without the complication of Troy, that distance could be their undoing. She pushed that thought down in her subconscious and quickly changed the subject.

"Speaking of *good feelings*, I keep meaning to ask you about last Wednesday."

"What about it?" Whitney's voice was unexpectedly sharp, defensive, very un-Whitney.

"Um"—Elle paused—"nothing, I just . . . it sounded like you were having a good time in your office and I . . ."

"Oh, that? That was nothing."

Whitney was never one to hold back when it came to her dalliances. In fact, Whitney was never one to hold back in any aspect of her personal or professional life. Elle was taken aback, and unsure of what to say. So she let it go. If and when Whitney was ready to talk about it, Elle was confident she would. They said their awkward goodbyes, and when they hung up, Elle turned on the television, hoping to catch the commentary from the anchors on the *Today Show*.

"A big day for Elle Riley and the cast of *Follow the Sun*, garnering three Golden Globe nominations," the smiling male anchor with deep-set dimples said to his coanchor.

"I'm crazy about that show," his coanchor said, her eyes wide. "The tension is insane."

"My wife loves it too." The handsome anchor smirked. "She takes complete control of the television every week. If I make a noise I'm in trouble."

The female anchor laughed with exuberance. "Looks like it's the one to beat."

Elle sat on the edge of the bed, smiling from ear to ear. She could only hope their predictions were correct.

• • • • •

"What a perfect night for this."

The sun had already set when they arrived at MacArthur Park. In his hands, Troy carried a steaming hot pizza fresh from the oven of Anthony's Pub. Over her shoulder, Elle carried a tote bag with two bottles of merlot, a blanket, and everything else they needed for their dinner. At Troy's suggestion, they arrived early. The cover band was gaining in popularity, and since all shows at Levitt Pavilion were free of charge, it would be a crowded Thursday evening. As they approached the pavilion, couples, families, and other large groups of people seemed to have the same idea. The show wouldn't start for an hour, and it was already crowded. By the time the band took the stage, it would be packed.

"I think you'll love these guys. They've been at it for years."

"Kinda like that band in Chicago—I'm blanking on the name. Remember them? We saw them the summer after junior year. God, I can't believe I can't remember their name."

"American English."

Elle tapped Troy's shoulder playfully. "Yes, that's it. They were so good."

"These guys are just as good. Although they don't have the mop tops."

Elle scrunched her nose. "I loved the mop tops—it made them authentic."

"These guys have more of a Sergeant Pepper look." He gestured to his chin. "Long hair, beards, goatees."

"Got it."

When they reached an unclaimed area of grass about twenty yards from the stage, Troy stopped. "Does this work?"

Elle nodded and removed the blanket from her tote. Together, they spread the blanket over the warm grass. Elle was dressed in the most 1960s-chic outfit she could assemble. Cropped pants with a sweater set the color of pink lemonade. Large sunglasses à la Audrey Hepburn in *Breakfast at Tiffany's* rested on the bridge of her nose. Her hair was pulled up into a modern beehive as she embraced the time period and music she adored.

"You know, you're looking pretty hip this evening. I forgot you like to dress the part for these things." Troy's smile appeared genuine, as if he was reminiscing over Elle's small quirk. She loved that she could evoke pleasant memories for Troy, not just painful ones.

They finished their pizza as the band took the stage. Elle sipped her wine as she sat cross-legged on the blanket. Troy was seated with his legs out in front of him, leaning back on his elbows. They drank and chatted through the show. When the unique chords were struck for "I'll Follow the Sun," they were quiet. Troy narrowed his eyes at her; he opened his mouth to speak but said nothing. Elle looked down at the blanket, recognizing that look in his eyes. He was holding something back. Troy didn't know why she had selected this song as the basis for the books and the show, since he was unaware of his role in the creation of the plot. Or that he had been her muse for ten years. But still, tension lingered between them, and Elle wondered what Troy was thinking.

When the song ended, the band took a short intermission, and the two sat in silence on the blanket. Mothers escorted their children to the bathroom; some couples were packing up their belongings to avoid the traffic after the show. But Elle and Troy said nothing to one another. They simply stared ahead in silence.

"So," Troy began, clearing his throat. "Why that song?"

"What do you mean?"

"The title of the show . . . *and* your first book."

Elle removed her sunglasses and raised an eyebrow. A nervous chuckle escaped Troy's lips. "You got me. I looked it up on Amazon."

"Do you really want to know?" Elle's brow was knitted. She hated that every evening spent with Troy seemed to go back to their heart-break. Would they ever be able to move forward?

"Yeah, tell me." Troy was trying to appear nonchalant about the entire thing, but Elle knew better. He wanted to know.

"It's what I imagined you would say to me . . . after Vegas."

"Oh."

Troy knew the lyrics, of that Elle was certain, but she was nervous and felt the need to elaborate. "It's about this guy, right? And he's angry, he's really pissed at this girl who wouldn't commit to him. So he leaves and he's not coming back. And he wants her to know it."

"I know the song, Elle." Troy's voice was deep, strained.

"Sorry. Of course you do. It's just . . . of all the songs we both love, that one is how I imagined you felt about me."

"Like I wanted nothing to do with you?"

"Yes."

Troy pressed his fingertips to his forehead. "We should go. Are you ready?"

"But it's only intermission."

"I think we should go somewhere private." Troy paused. "To talk."

And there it was. She knew what was coming next. They'd go back to his place, where he'd officially break things off between them. He'd cite the lyrics, and thank her for reminding him of the pain he'd felt for years. He'd tell her he never wanted to see her again—that being near her was just too much. He was too angry, and always would be.

The drive back to his house was maddening for Elle. She wanted to scream, to beg, to cry, to do anything to slice the tension in two. But she was too afraid. And deep down, she knew Troy had something to say to her. She needed to give him the opportunity to be heard.

When they entered his apartment, Troy offered her another glass of wine. She walked around his home, wondering if this would be the first and last time she was welcome there. It was the epitome of a bachelor pad. The walls were bare, save for an eight-by-ten school portrait of Payton. Elle walked to the photograph and studied it. She was a beautiful girl with a smile that was the mirror image of her father's. Her eyes were just as deep in color, and her hair was the color of cinnamon, tucked into an adorable shoulder-length bob.

"Payton goes to private school?" Elle remarked, observing the girl was dressed in a uniform for her photo.

"Yeah." He handed her a fresh glass of merlot. "Have a seat, okay?"

"Sure."

Troy walked to his iPod, which sat on a side table next to the couch. Within seconds, the Beatles were singing into the small apartment. He then joined her on the couch.

Elle glanced down at Troy's hands, wrapped around a glass of scotch. His fingertips were trembling against the glass. She braced herself for the end of whatever this was.

Troy took a deep breath and placed the glass on the table. "I have to tell you something."

Elle, preparing to become emotional, set her glass next to his on the coffee table. "All right."

"I should have said this sooner, I should . . . but tonight, when you told me about the song, I just . . . I knew it. I knew it was time."

"I understand . . ." Elle began. Troy looked at her with confusion, tilting his head slightly. "I should go."

He reached for her, grabbing her arm. "No, please. Let me say this."

"Look, I get it, okay? It's too painful, you can't be around me because it reminds you of what I put you through. I was hoping we could . . . God, I don't know what I was hoping for." Tears formed in her eyes, and she felt like that girl on the other side of the door all over again. The feet were about to shuffle away and she would be left alone with her pain and regret.

"I've seen every episode."

Shock traveled from her brain to her toes. "What?"

"Your books, your show—I lied to you when I said I didn't know anything about them. I read every book. Twice. Years ago when they were first published." His eyes were glassy but determined as his hand traveled from her forearm to her wrist. "And I've seen every episode of your show. It's us, Rigby. It's about *us*."

Elle was stunned. Her brain fought to find the right response, but nothing seemed quite right. She was elated, yet confused. He cared enough to read her novels, enough to watch the show. Troy still *cared*. He didn't hate her. He didn't bring her there to cut off ties. He was confessing . . . to caring about her.

Without allowing another thought to creep through her already muddled brain, she lunged at Troy, her mouth crashing into his. His arms wrapped around her back, pulling her to his chest. Her fingers ran greedily through his silky hair. He opened his mouth, deepening the kiss. Elle moaned as his hands moved from her back to her chest, pulling at her sweater, stripping it from her body. His mouth moved to her exposed shoulders, the heat of his tongue waking her cool skin. A shudder ran down her spine and instinctively, she dropped her hands to clutch at the hem of his shirt, lifting it over his head, exposing his tan skin. Her eyes gazed down at his firm chest and abdomen.

"I knew you still had a six-pack," Elle whispered with a smirk, her fingers grazing the rock-hard muscles of his midsection. Troy eased Elle onto the couch, her legs wrapped around his waist and her pelvis tilted up toward his hips. She was losing herself in him. With every kiss, every touch, every moan, lick, and nibble, she was completely lost in Troy Saladino.

"God, I want you," Troy murmured into her ear, his hand cupping her breast, the tips of his fingers squeezing her supple skin. "I didn't realize how much I'd missed you."

She'd missed him, too. Far too many years had gone by, too many moments without one another, too many soured memories filled with heartache and remorse. As much as his touch made her body come alive, her brain was turning on her as she processed his words.

He didn't realize?

Elle had spent *ten years* missing Troy. She was so fully aware of her heartbreak that she created an outlet in which to deal with her grief. And he was just now realizing how much he missed her in return? Elle broke their kiss, pushing her hand into his chest.

"Wait, what? You didn't realize? But you said you watched the show, you read the books . . . I don't get it—"

"I just meant . . . you know." Troy eased himself to a seated position on the couch. The expression on his face turned from lustful to guilt-ridden. "I was bitter and I didn't want to admit it to myself. I walked away, I made a choice. If I admitted to myself I missed you, then where would I have been?"

"Miserable." Elle sniffed, holding back tears. "Just like me."

"I never wanted that—for you to be miserable. You have to believe me. I thought I needed a fresh start." Troy tucked some crazy, loose hair behind Elle's ear. His touch was comforting yet perplexing.

"And now?" she asked, her heart completely exposed with that question. She was giving Troy control, allowing him to squash her heart once and for all.

"I'm not sure."

Elle bit her lip and closed her eyes, accepting the honesty of his answer. After all, she could relate to his response. She herself was torn between two men. If Troy asked her to choose right then and there between him and Luke, she wouldn't be able to make that choice.

Troy continued before she could respond. "I have to be honest. Part of me wants to steal you away from the rest of the world. Make a new home, start over together, leave everything behind, ya know?"

"And the other part?" Elle deadpanned, bracing herself for the brutally honest answer she knew would leave his lips. She knew it was coming.

"The other part wishes you'd never showed up at my restaurant."

"But you *knew* I lived here. You watched the show, you read the books. You knew I was here."

"I was here first." He swallowed hard, his eyebrows arched. Elle knew he wasn't trying to be cruel; he was just stating the facts. He moved here with Payton long before her show was picked up by the network.

"Doesn't part of you wonder if it was all serendipitous? I mean, what are the chances of us both being here . . . in California?"

"Is that why you're here? Because you think this is fate or something?" Troy looked annoyed with her, like she was foolish or silly for believing such things. Yes, it went against her nature. Normally, she believed strongly in having control whenever possible. Leaving her heart and future to fate was completely out of her comfort zone. But when it came to Troy, most things were. He pushed her, challenged her like no one else.

"Would that be so terrible? To think all of this was somehow meant to happen? That we weren't ready for each other in our twenties? That maybe we just needed more time?"

"No," he answered, his voice impassive. "No, it's not terrible. But I don't think you can absolve yourself like that."

"Absolve myself?" Elle said, her voice rising. She stood, grabbed her sweater from the floor and returned it to her body. She paced the room as she struggled to find the right retort. But her mind was blank. "I'm not trying to absolve myself of anything!"

Troy pushed his palms into his knees, rising to his feet to stand opposite Elle. "I didn't mean it like that. God, I just—" He looked up at the ceiling, running his fingers through his hair. "How did we get here, Rigby? How did we go from that chapel in Vegas to this? I can't wrap my mind around it. Still . . . after all this time."

"I ask myself that same question every single day." She pressed her eyes tight. "The answer is . . . I have no idea."

Troy pulled her to him, wrapping his arms around her as she pressed her forehead to his chest.

"I'm not ready to give up," Troy said, his voice gravelly and deep. Elle knew he was holding back tears. "Not yet."

"Good." She wiped the tears from her cheeks. "I'm not either."

"Maybe you're right. Maybe it is fate."

"Don't patronize me," Elle said.

"I mean it. Neither of us had any intention of letting our guard down, of taking that leap. Maybe fate had to intervene, to bring us together again."

"Maybe."

They stood for several minutes, locked in a comforting embrace. Just as Elle was about to excuse herself, call it a night, and escape the confusion of his apartment, a familiar song came through the small iPod speaker.

"Here, There and Everywhere."

The song that always reminded Troy of her. The song to which she'd walked down the aisle. Her eyes locked with his.

"You still listen to this song? I thought you'd have banished it from your playlists a long time ago."

Troy brushed her bangs from her eyes. "Never."

A weak smile of relief crossed her lips. Troy cupped her face with his hands and kissed her. It was a gentle, soft kiss, but one filled with the depths of emotion they were both feeling. Without realizing it, they began to dance to the music. Their feet took small steps back and forth on the carpeting below, their hips swaying ever so slightly to the song. As confused as Elle was in Troy's arms, she was eager to know what fate had in store for them.

While they danced, Troy's phone rang. Instinctively, Elle pulled away, allowing him to answer it. Instead, Troy pulled her closer. "Let the machine get it."

Elle eased herself back into Troy's embrace, until a familiar voice came through.

"Hey, Troy, it's Amanda. Listen, I have a doctor's appointment on Wednesday afternoon, so I need to bring Payton a little early. Let me know if I should bring her to the restaurant or to your place."

Elle's jaw dropped and her hands stiffened around Troy's forearms. She couldn't believe her ears. Her mind was racing. No, Payton's mother couldn't possibly be . . .

"Amanda?" Her name was like venom on her lips.

"Rigby, I—"

"Amanda Bauer? From college? Are you kidding me right now?"

Troy pursed his lips and nodded. "I've been meaning to tell you, it's just—"

"You knew I'd be pissed."

"Yeah." Troy rubbed his neck and shrugged.

Elle paced the length of Troy's living room. Her muscles tightened and her hands balled into tight fists. "So, after Vegas, you went back to her? Again?"

"I told you, it was a rebound. It meant *nothing*."

Elle returned to the couch, pressing her forehead into her hands. Sweat grew on her forehead, her arms, her neck, and the room began to spin. "I can't believe this."

"It's not a big deal, seriously." Troy's tone changed to defensive, which stirred Elle's anger even more.

"Not a big deal? Are you kidding me? Every time I screwed up, you went back to her, Troy. You did it to hurt me, didn't you? Just like in college!"

Troy threw his arms up in the air, glaring at Elle. "So?"

"So, while I was writing you love letters and begging you to take me back, she was with you, sleeping with you, easing your pain?"

Troy stood in the middle of the room, hands on his hips. His jaw was clenched as he broke eye contact.

"The feet behind the door—how do I know they weren't hers?"

"What are you talking about?"

"I came to your door so many times . . . and every single time, someone would look through the peephole and walk away. Did Amanda see me through the peephole?"

"I don't remember, Rigby, it was a long time ago." The guilt on Troy's face betrayed him. Even if those feet never belonged to Amanda, the possibility was clear. While her heart was consumed with guilt, Troy was sleeping with Amanda. The thought made bile rise in Elle's throat.

"I think I'm gonna be sick." She jumped to her feet and ran to Troy's bathroom, slamming the door behind her. She held her hair with one hand and lifted the toilet seat with the other, hovering over the commode until her nausea settled and her nerves calmed.

Knock, knock, knock.

A chill ran down Elle's spine as the entire scenario took her right back to Las Vegas. Her, emotional and sick in the bathroom, with Troy knocking on the other side. Only this time, she wasn't worried about Troy's state of mind. It was time for self-preservation.

"Rigby, please . . . I didn't mean to hurt you, and I'm sorry you found out this way, but I'm never going to regret my daughter. She's my world—my entire world."

Elle's heart sank. She didn't want Troy to regret becoming a father, but the pain he caused her by rebounding with the one person he knew would upset her was like a nail through her already wounded heart. She climbed to her feet, splashed cold water on her face, and opened the bathroom door.

Troy leaned against the door frame, his brow furrowed in frustration.

"You're linked to her forever, Troy. No matter what happens with us, Amanda will always be in your life. When Payton graduates high school and college, when she gets married, has kids—you'll always be linked to her. Forever and always."

Troy sighed, leaning closer to Elle, his feet crossing the threshold of the bathroom. "Yes, that's true. But we're friends, Rigby, nothing more. I need you to believe me."

Elle wanted to brush it off, to believe that, outside of Payton, Amanda would have no role in their possible future together, but she couldn't do it.

"Please tell me you can get past this, Rigby, please."

"I don't know."

It was the truth. Yes, she'd hurt Troy deeply and hadn't forgiven herself for the mistakes she'd made. But, they were just that: mistakes. The pain that Troy caused her was deliberate. He fought dirty, and having a child with Amanda was one way to continue Elle's pain for years to come.

"I'll try," she said. "I promise I'll try."

Elle wondered if she and Troy would ever be able to stop making things more difficult for themselves. For each other. Would they ever be able to simply be happy together? Was it even possible?

Chapter 19

This place is gorgeous, Luke."

Elle ran her fingers across the granite countertops of the rental house Luke was considering in the Pacific Palisades. He asked her to visit the house with him on their lunch hour. The Pacific Palisades, a district on the west side of Los Angeles, was notorious for two things: being right on the ocean and being the chosen neighborhood for several Hollywood A-listers. He would be close to work, a short drive from Elle's place, and he would be on the water, but he would also be surrounded by big names. She could only hope he was more interested in the beautiful view than the hope of rubbing shoulders with big-name directors, actors, and actresses.

The ocean view caught Elle's eye and she quickly walked outside to the wooden deck, taking in the sea breeze. Luke followed, wrapping his arms around her, linking them across her midriff. All that stood between them and the ocean was a flight of stairs and a hundred yards of sandy beach. The waves crashed against the shore as they took in the majestic view.

"What do you think? Do you love it?"

"It's . . ." Elle turned to face Luke. "It's wonderful."

"The house is okay, nothing too impressive, a little small. But you can't beat this view. Look, there's even a hammock over here." He gestured to a cozy-looking hammock in the corner of the deck before nuzzling his nose into her neck. "You. Me. Naps in the sunshine with the sound of the waves crashing in the background. I should sign the rental agreement this second."

That thought delighted Elle. It was serene, calm, and sexy— every word she could use to describe Luke himself. When she was with him, life was fresh, new, and filled with possibilities. His calm demeanor and relaxed approach to life was contagious—she'd spent so many years entrenched in anxiety. Yes, it had led to success in her life, success she wouldn't trade for the world. But Luke was successful in his own right, and he wasn't bogged down with worry the way she was. Or the way Troy was, for that matter.

"Seriously, though, are you going to take it?"

"I have to see the rest of the place, but yeah, I think so. It's a year lease, which is perfect. It'll carry me into next season, and then I can figure out what to do next. Gotta wait to see if my contract is extended."

Elle placed a chaste kiss on his cheek. "I don't think you need to worry about that. Viewers *love* you. Our ratings are the best they've ever been."

"Ahh, but the creator of the show . . . I'm not so sure about her." His words were playful, impish, and so Elle decided to play along.

"Yeah, I hear she's a real hard-ass."

The wind blew and Elle's hair swished to the side, rising in the air like the flames of a fire. Luke took the ends of her hair gently in his hand, pressing it to her shoulder. "I wouldn't say that. But she may get sick of me."

"That seems *highly* unlikely." Elle giggled as Luke's hands drifted down to her waist. The tips of his fingertips stroked her skin gently under her blouse. She squirmed as he tickled her skin and Luke grinned from ear to ear, proud of his ability to keep her on her toes.

"I love that laugh. It's so beautiful."

"I didn't realize a laugh could be beautiful."

"Yours is."

Luke pulled Elle in for a kiss just as the leasing agent opened the screen door and cleared his throat.

"Mr. Kingston, I have another client arriving shortly. I need to know if you're interested—"

"I'll take it," Luke said with confidence, his eyes never leaving Elle's.

"Excellent." The agent stepped outside to join them. "The paperwork is on the kitchen counter. Deposit of first and last month's rent is due today, and you can move in on the first."

"Sounds great." Luke extended his arm to the agent, who then smiled and shook his hand.

"Excuse me, please. I need to make a phone call." He retreated back into the house, and Elle turned to Luke, a smile of excitement crossing her lips.

"Congratulations! I'm so excited for you!"

"Thank you." Luke grinned, then lifted Elle off her feet and spun her around the deck, his hands clutching her rib cage. For a split second, Elle wanted to slap his arm and demand to be put down. But then she forced herself to let go, to enjoy the moment. And within seconds, she was laughing with Luke, her hair blowing in the ocean breeze. When her toes touched the wood of the deck, she gazed into his carefree eyes, enveloped in his lively, seize-life-whenever-you-can outlook. And she liked it. She liked it a lot.

"We should get back. I've kept you away too long."

"Don't be silly, it's okay. We have plenty of time." Elle smoothed down her clothes, still trying to adjust to the brisk breeze of the deck. "Although, if I'm even a few minutes late, I'll have daggers from Gina."

Luke chuckled. "And how is that different from any other day? She always has daggers for you."

"Ugh, I know. It's exhausting."

"You could kill her off," Luke joked. Elle allowed herself to savor that thought for a quick moment, before shaking her head and returning to reality.

"Nah. We're losing Desmond. If I take Molly out of the equation, it won't even be the same show anymore."

"Would that be so awful? It could be a fresh start."

There was that term again. Troy had used it the previous week in his living room, and now Luke was using it in reference to the show.

"Or career suicide . . . for both of us. Molly is the heart and soul of the show. Even if the actress who plays her is a total pill."

"Don't let her get to you. She's not worth your time." Luke took Elle's hand in his and they walked into the kitchen, where he signed the contracts and handed a check to the leasing agent.

As he handed the pen to the leasing agent, Elle smiled. "Welcome home."

• • • • •

Even though Elle and Luke were five minutes late, the lead actors were nowhere to be found in the conference room. Their table read wasn't nearly finished and they were scheduled to run until at least 4:00 p.m., if not longer. The supporting cast was seated, ready to begin, but Gina and Nolan were absent. Elle wondered where they could be.

"Um . . . that's odd."

"Should I go look for them? See what's holding them up?" Luke offered, placing his hand on the knob.

"No, I'll do it. You can look over your script and I'll be right back. Text me if they show up, okay?"

Perplexed, Elle walked down the hallway, hoping she wouldn't interrupt a lovers' quarrel of some kind. She braced herself as she walked in the direction of the executive offices. When she turned a corner into the atrium, she heard shouting.

Oh boy.

She followed the screeching voice of Gina, who was standing in the doorway to Whitney's office.

"I can't believe this! You said it was over!"

"Baby, listen to me." Nolan could be heard from inside the office.

"Baby?" Whitney yelled, sounding appalled. "Since when is she your *baby*? Did you get back together with her?"

"I'm sorry, Whit. I can exp—"

"Don't apologize to her!" Gina shrieked, stomping her foot against the linoleum floor. "I am *so* done. You begged me, pleaded with me for another chance. And being the idiot I am, I gave it to you. But now I'm done. You can fuck off, Nolan Rivera. And take your little whore with you!"

Gina wiped her cheeks and stormed toward Elle, whose feet were frozen to the floor. Gina's cheeks were the color of a blasting fire engine. Elle felt terrible for her, unable to comprehend how it must feel to be the victim of infidelity. It was one of her biggest fears, and seeing it transpire right in front of her eyes was gut-wrenching.

"You knew about this, didn't you?" Gina's eyes were bulging from their sockets. Outrage poured from her skin.

"No! No, I promise you, I had no clue."

"I don't believe you." Tears streamed down Gina's cheeks as she yelled. "I gotta get outta here."

"Listen, take the day. We have the table read, but it's okay, just go home."

"I don't give a shit about the table read, Elle! Just leave me the hell alone."

Gina stormed away and Elle pulled herself together to approach the wreckage. Nolan was half-dressed, seated in a chair with his head in his hands. Whitney, her lipstick smeared, her hair disheveled, was standing behind her desk, her hand covering her mouth. She was just as shocked as Gina, just as betrayed.

"Nolan, will you give us a minute?"

Nolan stood, his tan skin flushed, his dark hair mussed. He looked to Whitney. "I never meant for any of this—"

"Stop." She put her hand up in front of her, her eyes closed tight. "Just stop. I don't wanna hear it. Clean yourself up and meet me in the conference room in ten minutes."

"Yes, ma'am." Nolan had never, not once in the years they'd worked together, called Elle *ma'am*. If she weren't so upset for Whitney, she would have chuckled at his sheepish behavior. But her loyalty to Whitney and her sympathy for Gina kept her features cold as stone.

Nolan left the office, closing the door behind him. Elle and Whitney stood in silence for a moment before Elle broke the tension. "You didn't know they were still together, did you?"

Whitney shook her head.

"Then why the secrecy? You told me it was a one-time thing. Why didn't you tell me you were sleeping with him?"

"We were keeping it to ourselves. He said he didn't want to hurt her and being the idiot I am, I believed him. God, I'm so stupid, Elle. So stupid!" Whitney smacked the wall with her palm, turned, and leaned down against her desk.

"You're not an idiot. You were trying to be sensitive and not make waves."

"I know, but now it's a freaking mess. I'm so sorry. I never meant to mess with your show."

"Don't worry about that. Nolan has only seven episodes to shoot, and then he's done. It'll work itself out." Elle walked to Whitney, rubbing her back with her hand. "But I'm worried about you. Were you two . . . serious?"

A sardonic laugh left Whitney's throat as she looked up to the ceiling. "Obviously not."

"I mean before what happened today. Were you . . . falling for him?"

In their four years of friendship, Elle had never witnessed Whitney have serious feelings about a man. She bounced from man to man without getting attached. But everything about this scenario felt different. The secrecy, the pained look on Whitney's face, and her reaction to Gina spoke volumes.

"Yes. Can you believe it? I'm such a fool."

"No, *he* is. You deserve so much more."

Elle's phone pinged with a text from Luke:

Nolan's here. Gina went home, but not sure why.

"I'm so sorry to do this, but I have to go. It's the table read."

"Of course, I get it." Whitney faked a smile.

"Dinner tonight? Just you and me?"

"Yes, thank you."

Elle placed a kiss on the top of Whitney's head. "It's gonna be okay."

But deep in the pit of her stomach she knew the repercussions from Gina's discovery would be just around the corner. It was just a matter of time before they reared their ugly heads.

• • • • •

"Start from the beginning."

Elle and Whitney were tucked into a quiet corner of a local French bistro, their favorite place to talk over delectable food and cocktails. Sipping martinis and nibbling on a favorite appetizer, black mussels poulette, Whitney was ready to discuss her relationship with Nolan.

"You know it happened once this spring and it was seriously no big deal, but this time it was different. He was pursuing me, like really working at it. So we started seeing each other a few times a week."

"Mostly in your office?" Elle gritted her teeth as she asked the question. She had no intention of being snarky, but she herself knew of two occasions when they'd been inappropriate in Whitney's office.

Whitney polished off her martini, wiping her lips with the back of her hand. "I'm sure it must seem that way, but there was more to it."

Elle gestured for the waiter, pointing at Whitney's empty glass. He nodded and stepped behind the bar to prepare another martini. Elle leaned in. "When did things start up again?"

"A month ago, I think . . . it was right after Mac the bartender."

"Gotcha. So did he take you out?"

"Not really. We met up at his place and mine, usually. I thought nothing of it—I thought we were just being careful. Gina's already a pain in the ass, we didn't want to poke the bear. The last thing I wanted was for her to take things out on you."

"I appreciate that, but I'm a big girl. I can handle her."

The waiter arrived with two fresh drinks. Elle quickly downed the rest of her martini and placed it on his empty tray. "Keep 'em coming."

"Not that it matters, anyway. He's just another cheating asshole." Whitney's fingers pressed against the rim of the glass. She stared down at the white tablecloth, so forlorn that Elle, for the first time, was worried about Whitney's heart. The heart she'd always admired—the one that was impervious to men and their antics. But watching her stare down at the cloth, her eyes red and puffy, her lips trembling, Elle realized she and her best friend had more in common than she'd once thought.

"How long do you think he was seeing her?"

"Who the hell knows? He's never getting into my pants again, that's for freaking sure." Whitney cleared her throat, took a large sip of her martini, and dug her elbow into the table, perching her chin on her palm. "Please change the subject. I need a distraction like immediately."

"Okay," Elle said with a laugh, searching her brain for something, other than men, to discuss. "The table read went well, despite Gina not being there."

Whitney rolled her eyes in exasperation. "I don't want to talk about her. Tell me about Luke . . . or Vegas. Distract me, I'm begging you."

Elle put her hands up in surrender. "Okay, okay. I'm at a loss when it comes to them. Luke is renting a place in the Palisades and—"

"Oh wow, that's exciting for him."

Elle nodded, looking down at her drink. "It is."

"You're still worried about him, huh? Afraid his head'll get too big or something?"

"Can you blame me? God, look at Nolan. Can you honestly say stardom hasn't gone to his head? When we first met him, he was an unknown, now he's leaving for movie roles, he's cheating on you, he's a freaking mess."

"Luke and Nolan are totally different people and you know it."

"For now." Elle shook her head. "Who's to say Luke won't change the longer he's in the limelight?"

"True, there's no way of knowing."

"Besides, it's not all about that. Troy has a lot to do with my current state of mind."

"I'm sure." Whitney nodded. "You two have so much baggage, it's intimidating."

"I know, and it seems like every time we try to leave it all in the past, it comes creeping forward and we get into some stupid fight."

"Do you think you can get past it?"

"I thought so . . . until he told me that Amanda Bauer is Payton's mother. Now that's all I can think about."

"Who's Amanda?"

"A girl he dated in college. I couldn't stand her. Every time I screwed up, he went back to her. And I think he did it to hurt me."

Whitney recoiled. "Well, that's odd."

"It's a pattern. His pattern, and it's awful." Elle sighed. "If there was ever something that would hurt me, it was this. He went back to her after Vegas. He went back to her again."

"And you don't think you can get past it?"

"In time, maybe. But I'm not sure about him. That's the problem."

"Forgive me for saying this, but . . . who's to say he won't walk away again?"

"What do you mean?"

"He didn't fight for you—you tried, you tried to get him back.

You practically begged, and he shut you out. Who's to say he won't do that all over again?"

"Whit, I asked for an annulment. I devastated him, wrecked him completely."

"I know, but the fact he wouldn't see you, wouldn't talk to you . . . nothing. It pisses me off. If you truly love someone, you have to forgive them, not run off and have sex and a child with your ex."

Elle shook her head, gritting her teeth. "He said it was just a rebound. She's married now and they're just friends. What *I* did was unforgivable, Whit."

"To him, yes. But the right guy would fight for you, forgive you for your mistakes, and try to move past everything. Not disappear for ten years. And I think you know it."

A distinct pain developed in Elle's gut. "I miss him. God, I've missed having him in my life. Before we were together, we were friends—the best of friends. And then, nothing. It was like he wiped away his existence from my life. This may sound silly, but I had to mourn him . . . almost as if he died."

"That's not silly at all. It's the truth."

"And now, I have this opportunity to fix things, to start again. It's exhilarating . . . and terrifying."

"Because you're afraid he'll disappear again, that he'll shut you out."

Elle chugged the rest of her martini. "Yeah, I guess. I can't lose him again, Whit. A part of me died the day I lost him. If another part of me goes, I don't know where I'll be. I really don't."

"You can't be with him just because you're afraid."

"That's not all, there's still something there. When I'm near him, my heart skips a beat, my stomach flutters."

"Forgive my honesty, Ellie, but I'm not sure he deserves you. I'll support whatever you choose, you *know* that. But your happiness . . .

and I mean actual, honest-to-goodness happiness: the loving-life, batshit-crazy-in-love kinda happiness—that's what I want for you. And I'm not sure that exists with him . . . or if it ever did."

"Stop. Please, just . . . I can't." Tears were threatening to spill from her eyes and she felt herself building a wall between herself and Whitney. She didn't want to hear it—any of it. "You don't know him. You only know my pain."

"That's true. I'm sorry, I'll stop."

"Thank you," Elle whispered, wiping her eyes with her cloth napkin. "Listen, I'll take care of the check, but I should get home. Big day tomorrow."

"Ellie, honey, don't go."

Elle stood, placed her purse on her shoulder. "I'm sorry, but I have to. Should I call you a cab?"

"No." Whitney leaned back in the booth. "I'll be fine."

"Great. I'll see you tomorrow."

"Yep." Whitney wouldn't make eye contact, but Elle was fine with that. She couldn't handle Whitney's skepticism regarding Troy and she needed the solitude of her home to calm her down. Maybe the morning would bring clarity, but until then, she needed to be alone and far away from Whitney's judgment.

Chapter 20

I can't believe you know how to do this," Elle remarked, leaning against the granite countertop of Luke's new kitchen. She sipped from her glass of white wine as the Rolling Stones played quietly from Luke's iPod.

"You've never made your own sushi before?"

Elle shook her head. "I've always left it to the professionals. But you're looking pretty skilled there."

Luke smiled and wiped his forehead with the back of his hand before returning his hands to the bamboo mat. "I had this part in a pilot, they taught us there."

"What was the role?"

"The whole show was set in a sushi bar. I played this buffoon whose dream was to be a sushi chef. I know it's shocking the show didn't get picked up, huh?" Luke shook his head with a laugh as he scooped a ball of rice with his hands, placing it in the center of the nori square. "Wanna try?"

"I don't know. You seem to be doing a great job and—"

"C'mon, I'll teach you. We'll do it together."

Elle lifted an eyebrow, placed her glass on the counter, and nestled herself between him and the kitchen island. Luke encircled her with his arms, his chin resting on her shoulder as he guided her hands.

"First, we have to press the rice down so it covers the nori." Together, they pressed the rice into the thin square of seaweed. Luke hummed into her ear as they worked. Elle couldn't make out the song, but the contented tone of the melody made her smile with satisfaction.

"Next, we need our fish. I already cut the salmon into strips. So take one of the strips and lay it horizontally."

She placed a long piece of fish atop the rice. "Like this?"

"Yep, you're a natural. Now add some cucumber strips, only two or three."

"Got it." Elle placed the vegetables next to the salmon. "Can we roll it now?"

"Okay, we're gonna use the closer edge of the rolling mat. We have to close on the filling with the nori making a rectangular-shaped hill, then we tighten it from above."

Luke's already deep voice dropped an octave as he instructed Elle on how to construct the sushi. "Keep it tight, with every move."

Elle giggled, removing her hand from the sushi and placing it against her mouth.

"What's so funny?" Luke kept his grip on the partially rolled sushi, but tilted his head to peer into Elle's eyes.

"Sorry, it just . . . it was starting to sound a little naughty."

"Elle Riley has a dirty mind, huh? I can certainly use *that* to my advantage."

"I'm sure you can. Seriously, though, you have this effect on me every time I'm with you . . ."

"And what's that?"

"I can't explain it—it's like, when I'm with you, I'm light-hearted, almost free-spirited. I've never been like that before."

"I don't believe that."

"It's true, unfortunately. Not even as a kid. But you . . . you're changing me." Elle returned her hand to the maki, assisting Luke as they finished pulling the bamboo mat tight, rolling one last time. When the roll was secure, she lifted her hands and turned to face him. "Like right now, I have this urge to just . . ." She bit down on her lip, narrowing her eyes.

"This should be interesting." Luke smirked, but there was more to that expression. His eyes darkened and his fingers gripped her hips, as if he knew exactly what she was thinking. That thought caused a chill to run down her spine. Luke licked his lips and tipped his chin toward her. "Finish your sentence."

"To jump up on the counter and seduce you right here, right now. Sushi be damned."

Luke's eyes widened and his mouth was agape. Without another word, he pushed the cutting board and fresh rolled sushi to the side. His hands gripped Elle's ass, hoisting her up on the island. She gasped as the cool countertop caused goose bumps to rise on her thighs. Luke's eyes darkened and his hands gripped her ponytail, pulling slightly as he took her mouth with his own.

Immediately Elle deepened the kiss, her tongue stroking his as her arms wrapped around his muscular back, pulling him closer. His woodsy scent tickled her senses and turned her on. She loved that smell. The soothing and intoxicating smell of Luke.

Luke pulled away slightly, a low growl escaping his lips as he pressed his forehead to Elle's shoulder.

"Listen, I have an idea . . ." he said.

Elle snickered, repeating the words he used earlier. "This should be interesting."

"Let's enjoy our meal, and then I'll surprise you."

Elle removed the already-prepared sushi rolls from the fridge as Luke ran his knife under the tap and cut the final maki roll into bite-sized pieces. Together, they sat at Luke's new dining room table, sharing the rolls and sipping wine.

"You know, as much as you're affecting me, I think I'm doing the same to you," Elle said.

"Why do you say that?" Luke poured Elle another glass, then ran his fingers through his hair, sitting back in his chair.

Elle tilted her head back toward the kitchen island. "You chose sushi over sex. That was a very type A personality thing to do, ya know."

Luke brushed her insinuation off with a shrug. "That's because I have *other* plans for you."

"Oh, really? I can't wait to hear this."

Luke popped a piece of sushi into his mouth, and wiggled his eyebrows. "You'll just have to wait and see. C'mon, let's eat."

Both grinning from ear to ear, they sat next to one another at the table, Luke's hand affixed to Elle's thigh while his other hand mastered the chopsticks. With each passing minute, his fingers traveled further and further up her skirt. The strokes of his fingers against her skin drove her wild, and despite the delicious fresh taste of the sushi, she wished the meal would end. She had to know what his *plans* were. The suspense was killing her in the most delectable way as his fingers reached the lace of her panties.

"What are you doing?" Elle whispered, arousal filling her from head to toe.

"Just giving you a taste of what's to come."

With determination and purpose, Elle placed her chopsticks across her porcelain plate. "I'm not hungry anymore."

Luke chuckled, looking down at Elle's plate. Several pieces of sushi remained, but Elle didn't care. She was no longer hungry for sushi, no matter how delicious it was. She wanted Luke, only Luke.

"Are you sure?"

"Absolutely certain."

Luke dabbed his mouth with the end of his napkin before dropping it on the hard wood of the table. "All right. Come with me."

Elle rose to her feet, placing her hand in his. They walked outside to the deck. The sky was dark and stars shone brightly over the crashing waves of the ocean. Luke tipped his head toward the shore.

"Care for a swim?"

"Are you kidding? We'll freeze! Plus, isn't it a little late for swimming?"

"Baby, we're in California . . . it's never too late for a swim. I'll keep you warm. What do you say?"

Elle kissed Luke's chiseled jaw. "Let's do it."

But then she remembered. Her nose wrinkled. "I didn't bring a suit."

Luke leaned in, his warm lips brushing against her ear. "You don't need one."

"Are you serious?"

"Yes."

"I don't know . . ." Elle glanced around the deck, searching for any innocent bystanders. She wasn't sure she had the guts to walk across the beach as naked as the day she was born. She was proud of her body—she ate right and worked out several times a week. But still . . . skinny-dipping was nothing she ever considered doing, even with Luke.

Elle could feel Luke's fingers pulling her blouse from underneath the waistline of her pencil skirt. The tips of his fingers tickled her belly as he dragged them against her bare skin.

"I can't imagine anything more beautiful than you naked in the moonlight."

Normally, Elle would overanalyze this situation. She'd grill Luke about the presence of his neighbors: their ages, their evening activities. She'd request a towel to cover herself while walking down to the water. But there was something about Luke that silenced her questioning, hesitant nature. Something stirred within her, and she realized she wanted nothing more than to jump in the ocean with Luke, to feel the crashing of the waves against her skin, and to feel the heat of Luke's body against her as they immersed themselves in the brisk water.

"You convinced me."

Elle kissed Luke as her hands joined his at removing her blouse. Without hesitation, she pulled it over her head and tossed it to the side. Luke stripped himself of his clothes while Elle removed her skirt, panties, and finally her bra. Together, they stood naked below the moonlight.

"I knew it." Luke pulled her close. Her nipples rose to meet the muscles of his chest. "Nothing more beautiful."

"Race ya!" Elle whooped into the night air, her palm smacking the taut muscles of his right butt cheek. Luke laughed and she could hear him following close behind her as her feet met the sand. The grainy texture dug at the bottoms of her feet until she reached the base of the shore. The sand turned cool, wet, and thick and her toes dug into the ever-stretching expanse of gritty earth.

Rather than simply dip her toes into the frosty water, Elle crashed into it with force, submerging herself in the invigorating waves spilling against the shore. Luke dove into the next wave. He rose from the water, his chest glistening as he ran his fingers through his drenched hair.

"Wow, it's cold."

"It feels amazing, don't you think?"

Elle dunked her hair into the water, taming the crazy strands pasted to her forehead. The water soothed her tresses, making them silky smooth against her fingertips.

"Now that you have me here," she said with a smile, "and no one's around . . ."

Luke wrapped his hands around Elle's waist, pulling her further away from shore. She felt weightless in the water as she wrapped her legs tightly around his waist. She could feel him hard beneath her. Her hand reached down to clutch him.

"I'm impressed . . ."

"Why's that?" Luke tipped his head to the side, looking confused.

"The cold water. I was prepared for shrinkage."

"Well, I'm no George Costanza," Luke said with a laugh, his hands stroking her thighs. Elle threw her head back in laughter, realizing no statement had ever been more accurate. Luke, with his chiseled abs, firm ass, and contented nature, was about as far away from the neurotic, stocky character from *Seinfeld* as possible.

"That's for damn sure."

Supporting her weight with one arm, Luke cradled her breast with the other, squeezing gently as he massaged her sensitive skin. Her nipples rose further just before Luke took one into his mouth. She gasped at the electric sensation traveling from her breast to her sex as his teeth grazed the nipple's tightly drawn peak.

"Oh my God," Elle murmured, pushing her hands against his shoulders and easing herself onto him. Slowly, she lowered herself down until he was completely inside her. She moaned at the feel of him, the way her muscles accepted his length. Again and again, she pressed her hips to his, thrusting beneath the soothing water. Luke continued to stroke her nipples with his tongue, first one then the other. The sensation of his lips, his tongue, his teeth was almost more than she could handle as she plunged in and out of the water with each of Luke's thrusts. She felt herself approaching climax and quickened her pace. A wave doused them with more water, but they were so immersed in one another, they didn't notice. Luke wiped the water from Elle's eyes, his fingers delicate against her drenched eyelids. He took her mouth in his, his tongue stroking hers as he moved her hips against his.

"You're so close. Let go, baby."

Elle threw her head back in ecstasy as her orgasm took over her entire body. Pulses of pleasure consumed her and she felt her muscles clench against Luke. Knowing how close he was as well, she didn't allow herself to slump into his shoulder, weak from her orgasm. Instead, she quickened her pace, lowering her hands to grip the muscles of his back, thrusting harder and harder until Luke growled into her ear, finding his own release.

With a sigh, Elle collapsed into his chest, satisfied and exhausted. Luke smoothed her hair and kissed the top of her head.

"Worth the wait?"

"It was." She breathed heavily against his cool, wet skin. "It most definitely was."

"Come on. Let's go back and get warm."

As if she weighed no more than a feather, Luke lifted Elle and placed her on her feet. With one last gentle kiss, they joined hands and ran into the cool evening air. Elle gasped as a chill collected on her skin. By the time they climbed the steps of his deck, her teeth were chattering and her chin was quivering in the cold.

"Here, put this on." Luke pulled her to the hammock, which held several towels and two white terrycloth robes. He wrapped one robe around her, and she pushed her shaking arms into the sleeves. Before dressing himself, he handed her a towel. She promptly flipped her hair toward the deck and wrapped her soaked tresses in the towel. Luke wrapped himself in the other robe, before pulling Elle into his chest. Her heart raced as he eased her into the hammock, his hands stroking her back to warm her.

"You planned this, huh? Towels and robes at the ready." Her chattering teeth were coming to a halt as Luke's body heat engulfed her. The hammock rocked back and forth as Elle eased her hand into Luke's open robe, running her fingers through the silky hair of his chest.

"I guess you *are* rubbing off on me." Luke kissed her forehead and lay back into the hammock.

"We're rubbing off on each other. I like it."

"I do, too. I can't believe you went skinny-dipping. I'm so impressed, it's ridiculous." Luke laughed, running his fingers through her hair. Elle joined him in laughter.

"You have that effect on me, I guess." Elle deepened their embrace, pulling his midsection in for a tight squeeze. Somehow, when she was wrapped in Luke's arms, the rest of the world just fell away. She was safe, protected, cared for.

"Good." Luke's hand stroked the soft cotton of Elle's robe, pulling her close. "We're yin and yang, huh?"

"In some ways, yeah." Elle took a deep breath, exhaling the brisk evening air. "But I think at our core, we're more similar than we think. You have such a good heart, Luke."

"I like to think so."

"Tell me something," Elle began. "Where do you see yourself in five years?"

"That sounds like a pretty loaded question."

"It's not, I promise. I'm just curious. I want to know your goals, your dreams. I want to know more about *you*."

"Hmm, five years. Well, I'll be . . . geez, I'll be almost forty. I'd like to think I'll be acting. Maybe television, or movies."

"I could see you in movies. Especially an action movie or a thriller."

"Not a chick flick? I'm disappointed in you, Ms. Riley. I think I could play one of those swoon-worthy guys."

"Oh, of course. I mean, you make the ladies swoon already. But I think you'd shine in other genres, too."

"Well, thank you. I did receive a film offer, actually. But I'm not sure if I should do it. Wanted to get your opinion on it."

Elle couldn't help cringing at the idea of a film offer—at the idea of Luke's path turning into Nolan's before her very eyes. She swallowed hard and did her very best not to lump him in with her contempt for Nolan. "A film offer? Seriously? Why didn't you tell me earlier? This is a huge deal."

"You distracted me." Luke let out another laugh. "Actually, it's an indie film. Ben Stevenson is directing and—"

"Are you serious? Ben Stevenson is incredible. You should do it."

"You haven't even heard anything about it yet."

"I don't care—he's brilliant. You should do it."

"I don't know . . . I mean, the timing is good. I'd be filming while we're on hiatus for the show, so there's no conflict."

"So what's the problem?"

"It's filming in Vancouver . . . for six weeks. I'm not sure I can be away from you that long."

"That's so sweet. But I can visit. We'll make it work if it's something you want."

"Or you could come with me . . ."

"To Vancouver? For six weeks?" When she thought of being in Vancouver for that long, only one person stood in her way. Troy.

"Well, yeah. I kinda like you." He nuzzled his nose into her hair, breathing in.

"Well, that's nice to hear."

And it was the truth, although the word *like* seemed weak when it came to her feelings for Luke. She knew she was falling for him, of that she was certain. Her feelings were strong the first time they locked eyes, and since that day months ago, she was feeling herself grow more and more attached with each day they spent together. It started as lust, but had grown to so much more than that. After late-night discussions and moments like this on the hammock, Elle knew that their sexual chemistry was just a portion of who they were together. Despite their differences, they complemented one another, and being with Luke felt simple, natural. He made her feel desirable and sexy. He understood her, possibly in a way that even Troy didn't. He understood her need to be in control, to be eased out of her comfort zone rather than pushed, and to do things in her own time.

"In fact," he continued, "*like* isn't a strong enough word. Not even close."

"Oh, really?" Elle asked, lifting her head from his chest to make eye contact. Luke's eyes were wet, his eyebrows pressed toward one another. "Wait, Luke . . . are you okay?"

Luke shook his head and laughed. "Yeah, yeah. I'm good. Great, actually."

"Then what . . . what's going on? You seem upset."

"I need to say something and it's something I've never said before . . . well, at least not to someone who's not a blood relative." Luke chuckled. His words sounded uncomfortable, nervous, vulnerable. Elle could feel his heart pounding beneath her fingertips. "I'm falling in love with you, Elle. I know it's crazy, and I know you're not mine . . . not entirely, but I feel it. And I believe if you feel something, then goddammit you have to *say* it. I'm falling for you. There, I—I said it."

Elle pushed her hands into the harsh fibers of the hammock, her heart racing and her cheeks blushing. She hadn't expected a declaration of love from the carefree actor. But his words were like a warm blanket around her body, around her heart and mind. They calmed her random thoughts and soothed her nervous heart. Despite the nagging of her brain telling her to avoid it, she was falling in love with him, too. But that didn't mean she was ready to verbalize it.

Elle paused. "You've really never said it before? Not to anyone?"

"Never. I told you, this is all new to me."

How is that possible? Elle thought. Women must have been throwing themselves at Luke for years. Not only was he incredibly easy on the eyes, he was charismatic and funny. The idea of being the first woman to evoke such emotion from him was mind-boggling.

"I have feelings for you, too." Elle paused. "Strong feelings."

Luke sighed and Elle knew he was relieved. "Then, be mine. *Just* mine."

Elle shook her head, conflicting emotions filling her as her stomach clenched with anxiety. "But you said . . . you said I was worth waiting for."

"I know what I said." Luke looked away, breaking eye contact. That simple gesture cut into Elle. She felt exposed, guilty. Her reluctance to walk away from Troy was evident, and it threatened to ruin everything she was building with Luke. "But I want you. I'm not sure I can share you much longer."

"Luke, I—what I feel for you is real. So real it scares me. But like you said before, I don't want to rush into a decision and live to regret it. I want . . . no, I *need* to sort this out. Figure out what I really need."

"I can give you *anything* you need. You just have to trust me."

"I do trust y—"

"And you have to let go of him, of the past," Luke interrupted, his words stern, and unyielding. "I can't do that for you."

Tears filled Elle's eyes and she pressed her lips to his in desperation. She couldn't lose him. That thought sent surges of adrenaline to her belly.

"I know. I just . . . I just need more time. Please be patient with me."

"Okay." Luke conceded her request, but his jaw ticked in frustration, betraying his facade.

"I mean it. You said I was worth waiting for . . . don't take that away. It'll break my heart."

"And what about mine?"

"I . . . I . . ." Elle stared into Luke's eyes. The possibility of her hurting him was unbearable. She'd rather experience a world of pain than subject him to any heartache. But she knew there was a chance it would happen. That she and Troy would find a way to move forward with their relationship and she'd be forced to walk away from Luke. Her stomach clenched again with that thought. The idea of walking away from Luke was oppressive, insufferable, cruel. It wasn't at all what she wanted.

"I never finished my answer."

"What do you mean?"

"In five years . . . I see myself acting, yes. But I also see myself with *you*. And I'm sure that scares you, but it's true. I see myself with you, a baby in your belly, and my ring on your finger. That's what I see and I'm not going to apologize for it."

Elle's heart fluttered and her mouth went dry. "I don't deserve you," she said, feeling her guilt consume her. But no matter the shame enveloping her heart, she couldn't do the right thing. She couldn't walk away to keep him from harm. She was falling in love with him, too.

"Yes, you do. And I deserve you. We deserve each other, Elle."

Elle pressed her forehead back to Luke's chest, running his words again and again in her brain. She imagined herself as Luke predicted. Her belly swollen, a diamond ring around her finger, and Luke at her side. They'd walk the red carpet together, Luke steadying her belly as she walked up the steps, never leaving her side. She saw them lying just as they were, in the hammock, wrapped in fluffy robes, their legs entangled, the cotton bed swaying in the summer breeze.

She saw their possible future.

And it was beautiful. Absolutely beautiful.

Whether or not it would come to pass was an entirely different story.

For another part of her brain imagined all of those things . . . but with Troy. Troy's hand on her belly, Troy standing at her side, his ring on her finger. She pressed her eyes tight, fighting the fantasy brewing in her mind. She hated herself—her indecision, her inability to walk away from her past.

She couldn't make a decision, no matter how much she was falling for Luke.

The truth was, she simply wasn't ready. And until she was, no answer could ever be the right one.

When Elle arrived at work the next morning, she found an unmarked copy of *Us Weekly* on her desk. No note, no explanation as to who had given it to her, but a Post-it marked a page inside. Elle turned to it.

An interview.

With Gina.

A glamorous shot of Gina adorned the two-page spread, but Elle's eyes jumped to the title of the article. "Love After Heartbreak: How Gina Romano Bounced Back." Elle's stomach flipped and her breath caught as she read the first lines of the article:

Gina Romano, the star of television drama Follow the Sun, *has had a rough year. After a tumultuous affair with her on-screen love, Nolan Rivera, that ended this summer, she has found love again with a new member of the cast, Luke Kingston. Luke, a rising actor, has helped the actress heal her broken heart and learn to love again. We caught up with the actress to discuss her Golden Globe nomination as well as*

*the new man in her life and the excitement of starring on the hottest
show on television.*

"No." Elle's heart sank as she read those words. There were two
possibilities: either Luke had been lying to her for months, and he
was balancing a relationship with both her and Gina at the same
time, even after she'd confronted him in his dressing room. Or
their showmance was in full effect, regardless of his proclamations
that he would turn Gina down, that he wanted nothing to do with
such nonsense. That he wanted his work to propel him to fame and
nothing else. Either way, he wasn't being honest with her, which
was the one thing she had always feared. Yes, she was torn between
Luke and Troy, but she was honest about it. Always. She gave Luke
an opportunity to tell her the truth about Gina when Perez Hilton
posted the photos of them together, but he denied it. He denied any
attraction or involvement with the actress.

So what was Elle to believe?

Less than twelve hours prior, he'd confessed his love. He'd seemed
so genuine, so nervous and sincere. Was he playing her? After all,
he was an actor. Was it possible his Oscar-worthy performance was
simply to keep her on the hook for more screen time or an extended
contract? Was he using her to advance his career while sleeping with
Gina on the side? The thought made her sick to her stomach.

She was falling in love with Luke, and the idea of falling in love
with someone who was playing you for a fool was reprehensible, dis-
gusting, and more than she could handle. As much as it pained her,
she read the entire interview. Gina not only claimed to be "getting
serious" with Luke, she also referenced his home on the beach and
alluded to "midnight swims" with the actor. Bile rose in Elle's throat
as Elle thought back to the night before, one of the most romantic
of her life. The thought of Gina eating Luke's homemade sushi,
swimming naked in the ocean with him, and cuddling beneath the

terrycloth robes with him on the hammock made her physically sick. The room started to spin and she gripped the edge of her desk to keep from falling to the floor in a heap.

Don't lose control. Don't lose control. Don't let them win.

Elle took a moment to calm herself, urging the spinning office to return to normal and her pounding heart to slow. A confrontation with Luke was necessary, inevitable, and needed to happen right then and there before she lost her nerve and walked away completely. She had to know the truth. Did he love her or was she only a pawn in his quest for fame?

Before she could change her mind, Elle sent him a text, asking him to join her in her office. He responded immediately saying he would be there in five minutes, that he'd just arrived on the studio lot. She glanced at the clock—forty minutes before the table read. She needed to gather her thoughts instead of following her gut, which was to lash out emotionally, to retaliate, to make demands with her heart. Normally, her mind was always the winner, the one in control. But with Luke, this was not the first time her heart battled to take over, that her emotions silenced her reasonable mind.

A quick knock at the door startled her. Luke entered the office with aviator sunglasses tucked into his t-shirt and his wavy locks mussed from the wind . . . or from Gina's hands. Elle realized she didn't know this man at all. And she couldn't trust him.

When he entered the room, his expression changed as he took in the sight of a distressed Elle. Her eyes burned and her hands shook. She pressed the *Us Weekly* to her chest until he closed the door, and then she threw it directly at his chest. He flinched, catching the magazine and looking stunned.

"What the hell? Baby, what's going on?"

"Don't 'baby' me. I want the truth. Right now, Luke. Enough is enough."

"I don't understand." Luke studied the cover of the magazine with wide eyes.

"Don't look so shocked!" Elle crossed her shaky arms in front of her chest, doing her best to stand tall with her chin tipped toward the ceiling. She couldn't let him see her heart was crumbling inside her.

"But I *am* shocked." Luke stepped toward Elle, placing his hand on her shoulder. She flinched at his touch and he pulled his hand away as if she were made of fire. "Baby, talk to me. Seriously, what the hell is going on?"

Elle cleared her throat, fighting to regain her composure. "Turn to the marked page."

"Fine." Luke turned to the page marked with a Post-it note. His cheeks turned pale as he read. "What the hell? Elle, you must know this is bullshit. All of it."

"No, I don't. Either you've been lying to me for months, or you lied to me weeks ago about the showmance. So which is it?"

"Neither." Luke's chest rose and fell with labored breaths. He stepped closer to Elle once again, and she stepped back, walking to stand behind her desk. "I swear to you, Elle, I told her no. And the only time I've even seen her outside of work was that one night you already know about. This has nothing to do with me. Nothing."

"Do you know how ridiculous this makes me feel? My God, Luke, I thought I was falling for you."

Luke closed his eyes and shook his head, crossing his arms in front of him. "Don't say that. Don't talk about us in the past tense. We're not over. This is just Gina having a tantrum, that's all."

"And why should I believe you? You're an actor, and a really good one. How do I know you're not playing me?"

"Because you know me. Think about this rationally, please. I didn't do anything but fall in love with you. I want nothing to do with Gina and never have. Don't throw us away because you bought a magazine."

Luke attempted to join her on the other side of the desk, but she hustled to the other side of the room, her guard fully up.

"I didn't buy it. It was waiting for me when I got in this morning."

"Don't you get it? She's trying to mess with you . . . with me, with us. Gina left that for you, she wants you to get pissed off. She wants revenge."

"That's ridiculous. I'm her boss! And I have nothing to do with her and Nolan."

"Whitney's your best friend, and Whitney slept with Nolan. She wants revenge and she'll drag us all down to get it."

Luke's argument made sense, and part of her wanted to believe him, to succumb to his reason. But she couldn't risk it—she couldn't risk being a pawn in their game.

"I can't listen to this. I have to go." Elle grabbed the magazine and stormed from the office, pushing the door to the side as she charged toward the hallway leading to the soundstage and dressing rooms.

"The table read starts in half an hour," Luke called out after her, but she blocked him from her mind. She'd had enough of Gina's horrible behavior and was ready to confront her, no matter the cost. She could hear Luke's footsteps behind her, but she didn't care. She could confront them together and end this once and for all.

Gina, dressed in a low-cut blouse and miniskirt, greeted Elle with a bright smile, a smile Elle hadn't seen from the actress in months.

"Good morning, Elle. How are you on this fine day?"

"Shut your mouth." Elle's nostrils flared as she stood before the actress, holding the magazine in front of her. "Care to explain this?"

The corner of Gina's lips curved up in satisfaction. "I don't understand. Did you not like my interview? It's great publicity for the show."

"Cut the bullshit, Gina. You left this on my desk."

"Um, no. I just got in, so I have no idea how you got your copy. But I also have nothing to hide. Luke and I agreed to do this to promote the show. Geez, if anything you should be happy."

"Love after heartbreak, huh?" Elle was seething as she glared at the actress.

"I know, right? What a great title. I bet it'll sell millions of copies." Gina placed her hands on her hips, a pompous smile still perched on her face. "Look, I'm sorry you had to find out this way, but I'd assumed you knew. I thought Luke gave you a heads-up. Anyway, just know we'll have to do some photo ops, and should probably go to the Globes together."

Elle's lip curled in anger as she contemplated a response.

"Are you deranged?" Luke snapped from behind Elle. "I'm not doing *that*!"

Gina scrunched her lips together and tilted her head to the side before walking to Luke's side, placing her hands on his arm. "Luke, seriously, you don't have to pretend anymore. It's all out in the open."

Luke pulled away from Gina, focusing on Elle. "She's lying, Elle. You have to believe me. This is all some sick, twisted game. I never agreed to this."

"Oh, please." Gina sneered, her fake smile erased from her face. "You could have told her. God knows you had plenty of opportunities. I gave this interview weeks ago. Don't blame me because you're a chickenshit."

"What are you talking about? I told my agent I wasn't interested in pretending with you. But you did it anyway! You're sick, you know that?" Luke's cheeks were scarlet and his chest was heaving up and down as he snarled at the actress.

"I'm not taking the fall so you can keep nailing the boss, Luke. Tell the truth."

"You're such a bitch," Elle snapped, offended by the insinuation. But what if it was true?

Luke pulled on the ends of his wavy hair. "Oh my God! You *are* deranged!"

Gina shook her head and flipped her dark hair behind her shoulder. "And what about you? You knew how this would play out, that poor Elle would be humiliated, but you went along with it anyway. You're breaking this poor woman's heart for the chance to be an A-lister. The least you could have done was tell her before it went to press."

Elle had no idea who to believe. Yes, Luke seemed enraged and confused, but perhaps he was just backpedaling, trying to figure out a way to cover up his scheme with his costar, trying to save his career. She tossed the magazine to the side, smoothed down her skirt and blouse, and regained her composure.

"Table read in less than thirty. I'll see you there."

"Elle, wait, please." Luke grabbed her arm, but she brushed him off, pulling her arm away from his grasp. "Don't go. I had nothing to do with this, I swear to you. Let's go back to your office, let's figure this out. I'll call my agent, I'll do anything. Just . . . you have to believe me."

Elle shrugged, her voice cracking. "I'm sure your Twitter followers will double by this afternoon. And more movie roles will follow. Not indie films, but the big stuff. That's what you've always wanted, right?"

"Elle, stop."

"See you in the conference room."

Elle slammed the door behind her, ran to her office, and locked the door behind her. She slumped into her leather chair and sobbed. Moments later, Luke knocked on the door.

"Please, think this through before you throw us away. I can't lose you, Elle, please."

"Go away. Please, just . . . let it be."

"You can't believe her, Elle, please. It's not true. I've never lied to you. Not once. And I never will."

Elle felt herself caving. She stood, tempted to allow him to enter her office. But she knew what would happen if she did. She'd succumb to his charms, she'd believe everything he said simply because she wanted to believe in him, in his goodness. She wanted to believe this wonderful, sexy man was exactly who he claimed to be. But her time spent in Hollywood had left her jaded. And she needed to put him to the test.

"If you don't leave, I'll call the police and they'll escort you out. And then I'll call the papers. Trust me, those *aren't* the headlines you want."

Elle waited with bated breath for him to call her bluff, to insist he'd gladly go to jail if it would prove his love and devotion to her. But when the other side of the door grew silent, she knew it. He left.

Everything suddenly became clear. Months ago, she'd suspected Luke was using her for his career, and now it felt as if every fear she had was confirmed. He didn't care about her. Not really, not enough. What he really cared about was fame, fortune, and headlines. No matter his proclamations of love, or visions of a future together. And she hated herself for buying into the fantasy. For allowing the images of them together, swollen belly, diamond ring, and lazy days on a hammock to travel from her mind to her heart. He was a gifted actor and nothing more. Nothing more.

Chapter 22

"A re you serious?"

"As a heart attack." Saul Greenberg, the president of the network, was smiling wide, leaning back in his chair.

Elle's leg bobbed up and down as she pondered his offer to create a new show for prime time.

"I'm thrilled, just thrilled at how you're running things down there. The viewers love it—our ratings have never been better. A time slot is opening up next fall. And I want you to present three pitches for a new drama to debut right after *Follow the Sun*."

"I can't believe this. How—how will I balance both shows?" Elle's arms, shoulders, even face were tense.

"You'll figure it out. There will be a significant salary bump, of course. And bonuses. This is a big deal, Ms. Riley. We don't do this for just anyone. You're a star—three Golden Globe nods. And number one in the Nielsens."

"What kind of show are you looking for, sir? Law? Medical? Something totally different?" Her mind was swirling, yet empty.

Saul cracked a smile and Elle wondered if he could sense her state of total panic. "We're open to whatever you can bring to the table. We'll start filming this summer. You'll need to hand over more of the writing to your staff, so you can balance both shows. Do you think you can do that?"

"I'm sure that can be arranged."

Saul chuckled.

Elle tipped her head to the side. "Sir?"

"Letting go of control is . . . well, it's not your strong suit."

"I promise to work on it."

"That's good enough for me." Saul rose from his seat. "Can you have those ideas to me by Friday?"

That's two days from now! Elle screamed inside her head. She inhaled deeply, knowing she'd figure out a way, and composed herself before rising to her feet to shake Saul's hand.

"Sure, I can do that." Elle reeled in her nerves, giving Saul her best confident smile. "Thank you for this opportunity, sir."

Elle left Saul's office and walked down to the parking lot, entering her car before whooping with glee and slapping her steering wheel with exuberance. She couldn't believe it. In several months, she could be the writer and show runner of not one, but two shows in prime time. The feeling was exhilarating.

The only problem was her empty brain.

No ideas, not one. She needed Rob. As much as his sage-like behavior sometimes annoyed her, he had definite skill when it came to coaxing the creativity from Elle when her nerves were shot. Quickly, she sent him a text informing him of her discussion and requesting a brief meeting in her office.

She returned to the studio lot and made her way to her office. Rob was waiting for her when she arrived.

"How excited are you?" Rob asked.

"I'm freaking out, Rob!" Elle paced her office. Her hands trembled and her mind remained blank.

"C'mon, you're a creative person. I'm sure you have plenty of ideas in that head of yours."

It was true most of the time. Elle's mind did wander at times, and she dreamed up new ideas. Fresh and exciting ideas that had nothing to do with her past. She needed to somehow tap into that now. The opportunity to create something completely from scratch was beyond exciting. It was the opportunity of her career.

"Thank goodness we're done filming this week. I can focus without Gina flaunting her showmance in my face."

"I really wish we could get rid of her."

Elle jerked her head back in shock. She didn't realize Rob shared her feelings of disgust when it came to their leading lady.

"Oh, c'mon," he continued. "We both know she's a shit."

Elle sat up straight in her chair. "I have a newfound respect for you."

"Listen, I have to go. Get those creative juices flowing. Get Whitney in here, she'll help you."

"Uh," Elle fumbled. "We're not in the best place."

"Oh, good Lord. I could never be a woman. I swear, there's always something."

"Guilty as charged."

"I'll see you tomorrow." Rob stood and walked to the door, turning once his hand was on the knob. "And Elle?"

"Yeah."

"Congratulations. I'm really proud of you."

"Thanks, Rob. That means a lot to me, seriously."

Rob gave her a quick wave before leaving her alone with her chaotic thoughts. She wanted to call Whitney . . . and Luke. But even though she reached for her phone, she placed it down on her desk, swarmed with conflicting thoughts. She and Luke hadn't spoken in a personal manner since she threatened to call the police and tabloids. And Whitney was MIA ever since their uncomfortable evening at the French bistro. She knew they would both be excited for her, but her feelings of excitement were overshadowed by the awkward state of each relationship. So instead she focused on what she could: the work. She needed three ideas.

A new show.

A new show.

A new show.

She was drawing a blank.

Whenever Elle was stuck, she did one of two things. First, she called Whitney for a brainstorm session over candy and/or cocktails. And if, like today, that wasn't an option, she retrieved her journal from the bottom drawer of her desk. Below her candy stash, a simple leather-bound book with a painted picture of an old-school typewriter and her initials sat for moments like this. She pulled the journal from her drawer, dusted off the cover, and scanned through her book ideas—ideas from long ago when she was starting her writing career.

When she opened the journal to the first page, her phone pinged with a text.

Elle glanced down at her phone. She couldn't take her eyes off the brief message from Troy. A proper response eluded her, and yet she knew it was necessary to respond sooner rather than later.

Are you avoiding me?

She and Troy hadn't spoken since their date at MacArthur Park two weeks earlier. Was she avoiding him? Not intentionally. Work was hectic, her relationship with Luke was at an impasse, and Gina was a royal pain in her ass. Not to mention she and Whitney were barely speaking. She was a mess, and adding Troy into the mix was an overwhelming thought. And, if she was being honest with herself, discovering that Amanda was Payton's mother was not helping things for her. Not at all.

No. Just really busy.

She stared at the screen, not wanting to be too dismissive in her reply. She wanted to see Troy. She wanted to spend more time with him—she was just lost. Truly lost, and she knew she had no idea what she wanted. It didn't seem fair to drag him into those mixed emotions, knowing he had mixed feelings of his own.

Did I just get the brush-off?

Never one to shy away from a confrontation, Troy was calling her out as usual.

Of course not. Dinner tonight?

The next reply came back so quickly she didn't even have time to place the phone back on her desk. The quick ping of her cell made her lips curl into a smile. Troy was eager to see her, eager to communicate. She liked that.

That can be arranged. 7:00? Chinese?

Elle pinched her lips together, remembering she needed to work on the pitch. This was too important to postpone. Her schedule the following day was packed with meetings, one in particular with the network stylist who was dressing everyone for the Globes. The show was in just two short weeks and everyone needed his or her attire. Arranging for sample gowns and tuxedos would take some time, and it was time to begin the process.

I just realized I need to work late. Any chance you can come here?

Elle clenched her teeth, worried Troy would again feel brushed off. When her cell pinged quickly, she breathed a sigh of relief.

I'll bring food. Kung pao still your favorite?

Elle smiled, flattered he remembered.

With fried rice, please!

You got it. See you in a couple hours.

Elle settled in, opened her notebook, and dove into her ideas of the past, hoping to find something for her future.

• • • • •

Elle smelled the delicious aroma of the food before she saw her dinner date. Troy knocked on her office door before entering. Elle was taken aback at how handsome he looked after a long day in a hot pizza kitchen. As usual, he was wearing a polo shirt from the restaurant with khaki pants and sunglasses. There was something sexy in Troy's simplicity. She couldn't quite put her finger on it. But his olive skin had deepened into a sumptuous tan, while natural highlights permeated his dark hair. When he removed his sunglasses, Elle peered into the gorgeous eyes she had missed for so long. When he saw her, he grinned, a dimple forming in his cheek.

Elle walked around the desk to greet him with a hug. He pulled her tight, wrapping his strong arms around her. Elle wasn't short. In fact, being five feet ten, she was much taller than most of the women at the network. But Troy towered over her at six feet four, and she enjoyed the safety of his hugs. She loved that the top of her head nestled into his neck. She smelled oregano as he pulled her close. She was convinced Troy was the only man who could make Italian spices smell sexy.

"I've missed you," she murmured into his chest, and she felt his arms pull her in just a bit tighter. It was a silent message received with no distortion. He missed her too. "I'm sorry you had to come down here, but I do have exciting news."

Troy pulled back, locking eyes with Elle. "Oh yeah? Tell me."

"Have a seat and I'll fill you in."

Elle walked to her desk chair and sat. Troy sat down as well, a warm smile on his face. Elle's stomach fluttered as she revealed her exciting news. "The network wants me to create another show. They'd air back-to-back starting next fall. It's an extraordinary opportunity."

"Wow. That's incredible, Rigby. What's the show about?"

"That's the problem. I have no idea. They need three ideas . . . by Friday."

"Whoa, that's . . . well, that's not much time, is it?" Troy grimaced. "Now I see why you couldn't go out."

"Exactly."

"Can I help? I mean, I know I'm not a creative type, but it could be fun."

"Yes." Elle nodded, blowing out a long breath and smiling. "That would be awesome, thank you."

Troy leaned forward, lifting the white cartons of food from the brown paper sack. "First, you need sustenance. Full bellies lead to productive minds."

"Where'd you hear that?"

"That's a Saladino original. It's how my mom got my sister to eat."

"I like it."

He shrugged, looking sheepish. "I'm glad."

Elle narrowed her eyes as she watched Troy open the steaming cartons of food. This Troy was softer, more approachable and less confrontational than the Troy she spent time with only weeks ago. Perhaps her absence made his heart grow fonder? Time would tell on that. Regardless, she was enjoying their time together already and was so glad he contacted her.

Elle reached for the nearest carton, peering into the container. "You remembered."

"How could I forget? You never let me order Chinese without crab rangoon. I can't vouch for this place, though. I haven't tried it yet."

"I have. It's good stuff." Elle had forgotten to ask him to purchase her favorite appetizer and was blown away Troy remembered anyway. They both remembered so much. But was that enough to move forward? She wasn't sure. Regardless, the gesture was important to her and she savored it with each bite of the crunchy wontons filled with sweet cream cheese and crabmeat.

"What about a hospital show? People love that stuff."

Elle grimaced. "There are so many of those, though. Don't you think?"

"True. I guess I shouldn't suggest one set in a law firm, huh?" Troy bit down on his bottom lip, widening his eyes and raising his eyebrows toward the ceiling.

"Yeah. I'd like to do something no one's done. Like *Follow the Sun*—it was the first drama set in a casino. I need another idea like that, but different."

"Gotcha. Hmm." Troy used his chopsticks to scoop a cluster of rice into his mouth. Elle watched with butterflies in her stomach as he chewed. She always loved watching his jaw muscles as he ate. Troy noticed her lingering eye and interrupted her gaze. "What? Do I have something on my face?"

Elle giggled behind her hand, which clutched the carton of kung pao chicken. "No, sorry. I just . . . I like watching you eat." She could feel her cheeks reddening with her revelation. Thank God they had known each other for more than two decades and he wouldn't think she was crazy.

"Oh, Rigby." He shook his head, a smug grin on his handsome face.

"What?"

"What am I gonna do with you?"

Elle's breath caught and her heart raced. They sat, staring at one another. Elle had no idea what to say to break the tension. But their staring contest was interrupted by a knock on her office door.

"Elle?"

Luke opened the door, his mouth dropping as he took in the sight of Elle and Troy sharing a meal in her office. "Oh, um . . . sorry to disturb."

Elle jumped to her feet, wiping her mouth with a napkin. "Luke, what—what are you doing here?"

"I'm heading out and I—well, I wanted to say hello. But obviously I'm interrupting, so—" Luke broke eye contact with Elle and her heart sank. She hated putting both of these men in such a precarious situation. Yes, she was honest with both of them. Each of them knew about the other and his presence in her life. But that didn't keep the guilt at bay. She and Luke were not on the best of terms, but they weren't exactly over either. Not officially anyway.

"Troy, will you excuse me?"

Troy closed his eyes and sighed, nodding as he looked down at the carton of food in his hands. Elle stood and followed Luke out of the office. When she closed the door behind them, Luke ran his fingers through his hair, looking perplexed, and agitated.

"So you made your choice then?"

"I didn't say that."

"You didn't have to, but at least I get it now. The thing with Gina was a great escape clause for you, wasn't it?"

"What are you saying?"

"You've been looking for excuses to push me away, Elle. Admit it—ever since we met. I'm using you, all I want is fame, I'm sleeping with Gina, I'm lying to you, the list goes on and on. But guess what? None of it's true."

Elle crossed her arms in front of her chest, feeling Luke's words penetrate her heart. The sincere tone in his voice made her question everything she thought she knew, everything she assumed to be the truth about the actor.

"You and me on that hammock—*that's* what's true, Elle. *That's* what's real. Even if you can't see it." He pointed toward the door. "You can hide in your memories, hide in your regrets. But I won't be a part of it anymore."

Panic spread throughout her body as she watched his eyes moisten. He was fuming, yes, but it was clear he was also heartbroken. The thought of Luke taking his affection, his love, away from her was unbearable. A lump formed in her throat. "What are you saying?"

"I'm done."

"What?" Elle shrieked, her eyes bulging, her heart plummeting to her feet.

"I can't do this. I've been so concerned about your heart, your feelings, that I've ignored my own. So I'm done. Call me when you come to your senses."

That final comment made irrational anger fill her from head to toe.

"Come to my senses?" she sneered. "Why don't you call me when you're done playing games, Luke? Call me when you're done being Gina's pawn, when you're done counting your goddamn Twitter followers, and seeking out paparazzi at the Ivy."

"Whatever." He shook his head, his lips pressed in a thin line. "Do you even know who I *am*?"

Elle drew her head back in disgust. "Oh. My. God. How big has your ego gotten? I'm shocked you even fit through my door!"

Once again, he shook his head, and with a snarl in his voice, he leaned in close. "That's not what I meant. But you just answered my question, didn't you? You don't know me at all."

Elle looked down at the floor. Conflicting feelings of anger and sadness swirled together, leaving her breathless and unable to protest Luke's claims. She knew him just fine, thank you very much. Just because he was in denial about his fame-seeking behavior didn't make her the bad guy. He knew about Troy—she was honest about that from the beginning. If he was willing to throw everything away over a couple of cartons of Chinese food, then that was on his shoulders, not hers.

"Have a nice dinner."

Luke pressed his knuckles into the door frame before turning his back on Elle and walking down the long hallway. Elle closed her eyes, anger and frustration growing by the second within her mind. She couldn't go after him since Troy was waiting in her office. And even if she did, she had no idea what to say. He said he was done—what was the point of chasing after someone who obviously gave up on her?

With a new sense of purpose, Elle took several deep breaths and entered her office, slamming the door behind her. Troy stood, concern plastered across his face.

"Is everything okay?"

"Everything's fine."

Troy took a deep breath and walked to Elle, taking her hands in his. "Listen, I suppose this is as good a time as any. I know I've been indecisive . . . I know I've put you through the wringer. And I know I should've told you about Amanda."

Elle looked away, unable to handle back-to-back confrontations. She felt as if the world were playing with her mind, with her heart. Was it possible she would lose both men in just a matter of minutes? If her temper took over as it did with Luke, that was a distinct possibility.

"It's fine," she said, looking away, doing her best not to be defensive and urging her tears to stay at bay.

"No, Rigby, I'm done with that."

She flinched at the word *done*. Hearing that word from Luke's mouth had pierced something inside of her, something that might never heal.

"What I mean is, I want to give this a real shot, a *real* chance. No more punishments or smug comments. No more passive-aggressive bullshit. I want to try to see what's still here between us."

Elle was stunned. Hope emerged from the heartbreak within her, and she managed a weak smile. Words failed her, but she stared at Troy with her mouth agape and tears building in her eyes. Tears of relief.

"I can't tell—are you happy? Disgusted?" A nervous laugh left his lips. "Put me out of my misery, Rigby. Say something, please."

Elle took a deep breath, looked into Troy's eyes, and said the first thing that popped into her head. "Want to be my date to the Golden Globes?"

Chapter 23

I don't know," Elle grumbled, turning her body in front of the full-length mirror. Pressed to her chest was a navy blue dress made almost entirely of lace, with a tight bodysuit underneath. "This is more suited for someone like Gina, don't you think?"

Eve, the petite network stylist with blonde hair and bright blue eyes, nodded in solidarity as she leaned against a table in the large conference room. For two days, Eve had set up shop in the room. Racks of designer dresses filled the room, and mirrors leaned against the gray walls.

"I suppose so, but you should consider something just as hot. What about this one?" She held up a black strapless gown, designed by Christian Dior, with a mermaid hem and a skirt comprised of elegant rosettes, a ribbon-like belt adorning the formfitting waist. Elle was drawn to the gown's sexy sophistication and exquisite fabric. It would reach the floor, and yet be just as sultry and seductive as the tiny lace number since the sweetheart neckline would accentuate her chest.

"I'll try it on." This was her second appointment with the stylist, and Elle had inspected over a dozen dresses in that time. This was the first she was actually considering for the Golden Globes, which was fast approaching.

"Now we're getting somewhere." Eve grinned, a dimple forming in her cheek as she handed the dress to Elle. "Where is Whitney? She was supposed to be here ten minutes ago."

Elle sighed. "She's probably avoiding me."

"Why's that?" When Elle cringed, Eve stopped herself, holding her hand out in a dismissive motion. "Never mind. I'm out of my element."

"No, it's fine." Elle slipped behind the makeshift dressing room composed of a portable curtain. She felt like Daniel LaRusso in *The Karate Kid* when he was wearing his shower curtain Halloween costume. "Things are just weird. You know how things go. We don't always see eye to eye."

"Um, Elle—" Eve attempted to interrupt but Elle continued.

"She's ridiculously stubborn, so—"

"Um, excuse me? I'm the one who's stubborn? I gave you my opinion and you shut me out completely."

Whitney.

Elle froze behind the curtain. Her bra was off and the dress was only halfway up her mostly naked body.

"Whit?" Quickly she pulled the dress to cover her breasts and waddled from the dressing room, constricted by the mermaid skirt. Perhaps this dress was not the right choice.

"Yeah, it's me, your stubborn ass of a best friend." Whitney rolled her dark eyes and crossed her arms in front of her chest. She glared at Elle, who sheepishly bit on her bottom lip and shrugged.

"I'm sorry, and you're not an ass. Can we just, I don't know, make up or something?"

"You're the one who left me alone in a booth after I got my heart trampled. You tell me." Whitney turned on her heels and walked to a rack of size six dresses. The hangers squeaked against the metal bar of the rack as Whitney tore through the dresses. Elle toddled across the conference room to join Whitney by the rack of clothes. Eve quickly pulled the zipper so the dress fit snugly around Elle's hips. The dress was comfortable, but her concern was Whitney. She had to make peace with her favorite person in the world.

"I screwed up, okay? I'm the stubborn ass. You were looking out for me, and I just—I didn't want to hear it."

"Fine. Whatever, it's done."

Elle grimaced. "It doesn't sound done." Whitney pulled a lilac chiffon dress from the rack and held it out for Elle, who immediately shook her head. "Doesn't go with your skin tone."

"True." Whitney returned it to the rack. "I didn't expect that from you, Ellie. We've always been brutally honest with each other. And this time, you treated me like the bad guy. I'm *not* the bad guy. I love you like a sister."

Whitney pulled a garnet Versace gown from the rack. Cap sleeves, godet pleats on the floor-length skirt, and a boat neckline; it was stunning and the perfect dress for Whitney. Elle nodded emphatically before responding. "I love you, too. I was wrong. I promise it'll never happen again."

"Good. Now tell me what's happening with the Globes. Has Luke bought a tux yet?"

Elle flinched at the question. She had no idea what Luke had done to prepare for the award show.

"Uh-oh. No. Tell me you two didn't—"

Elle nodded, looking up at the ceiling, refusing to cry over the man who placed a rather large hole in her heart. "He's *done* with me. Aside from work, I haven't spoken to him in over a week."

"Wait. He said you were worth waiting for . . . those were his *exact* words."

Elle grabbed the clothing rack, holding on for support. "I know. But I guess he's done waiting."

Whitney placed the gown back on the rack and wrapped her arms around Elle. "Oh, honey, I'm so sorry."

"Thanks." Her voice cracked with that single word and she knew the tears were coming. Quickly she retreated back to the makeshift dressing room. Eve unzipped the gown and Elle slid it from her body, placing it back on the hanger. "I'll take this one, Eve."

"Very good, Ms. Riley." Eve placed Elle's dress choice on a rack marked with index cards, labeling who would be dressed in which designer's gown. Whitney pursed her lips before retrieving the red gown and slipping behind the curtain.

"Maybe he just needs to cool off. I'm sure when he sees you on the red carpet, he'll flip. He'll remember why he's crazy about you."

"I don't know about that." Elle stood outside the curtain, dragging her fingers mindlessly down the polyester fabric of the curtain.

Whitney emerged from the dressing room and stood before the mirror. Eve zipped her up and placed her hand over her mouth. Elle stood behind her and managed a genuine smile as she took in the sight of Whitney in that dress. "Wow."

"Yeah?" Whitney asked, smoothing down the fabric and gazing in the mirror. "First one I tried. What are the chances of that?"

Eve glanced at Elle, then back at Whitney. "Slim to none."

"So tell me what happened. Why did he give up?" Whitney and Elle locked eyes while gazing into the full-length mirror. "*Something had to happen . . . right?*"

"He walked in on Troy and me . . . in my office."

Whitney turned, her eyes wide. "You weren't . . ."

"No, God no! We were just having dinner."

"You two certainly like to eat a lot," Whitney said with a sardonic laugh. "Pizza, Indian, and now . . ."

"Chinese." Elle closed her eyes, shaking her head. She and Troy did eat on their dates. First they flirted over food, then they argued, and they usually followed that up with a makeup session and vows to do better. History was repeating itself in a major way—that pattern was the story of their relationship, their dynamic. Add in some cherished Beatles songs, and you had Elle and Troy in a nutshell. She shook off that thought as she waited for Whitney to respond. But the outspoken beauty was gritting her teeth as she stared at Elle with conflicted eyes.

"Whit? What's wrong?"

"I'm afraid to say anything after last time. I don't want to fight with you."

"I won't get mad, I swear."

"Just be careful. You two have a history, an undeniably rocky history. Don't lose Luke over this."

Elle threw her arms up in defeat. "I don't have a choice, Whit. He's done. *Done.* You have no idea how much that word killed me. I have to move on, and Troy wants to give us a real shot. I'd be stupid to walk away from that . . . wouldn't I?"

"I suppose you're right." She shrugged. "I guess it's time to hang up my Team Luke shirt, huh?"

A weak laugh left Elle's lips as her eyes welled with tears. "Yeah, I think so. I'm sure he'll miss having you as president of the fan club."

As if on cue, Elle's phone pinged, and she raised her eyebrows for permission to leave the conversation. Whitney nodded and retreated to the dressing room as Elle checked her phone.

It was a text from Troy.

Can't stop thinking about you.

She smiled. Knowing she was on his mind was a comforting thought. One she cherished and appreciated. She pressed the phone to her chest just as Whitney emerged from the dressing room and handed the gown to Eve.

"Vegas?"

Elle nodded. "We've seen each other a couple of times since everything went down with Luke. It's been nice."

"Have you slept with him yet?" Whitney pressed.

Elle cringed at the question and shook her head. Out of the corner of her eye, she watched as Eve scurried across the room, busying herself with the hanging dresses. Obviously Whitney's frank nature was making her uncomfortable and Elle couldn't blame her. Elle was part of the conversation and her discomfort was through the roof.

"Not yet."

"How come?"

"We're taking things slow—figuring out what we want."

Whitney narrowed her eyes.

"What?"

"Well, I mean . . . what are you waiting for? Ten years of tension—you two must be going out of your minds."

Elle was shocked to realize she didn't feel that way at all. "It was like that in the beginning," she said, remembering the evening he pressed her against the brick of the Indian restaurant. "But not anymore. We're just being patient with each other."

"I see." Whitney's lips pressed into a thin line. Elle could read her mind easily. She wasn't buying it. But instead of getting defensive, Elle shared something she thought Whitney would appreciate.

"You'll meet him at the Globes."

Instead of an excited smile, her best friend glared at her. "Wait. You're *bringing* him?"

"Well, yeah."

"To the Globes?"

"Yes, Whitney. I'm bringing Troy as my date to the Globes."

"But Luke will be sitting at the same table. Don't you think that's a little cruel?"

Elle crossed her arms, tilting her chin toward the ceiling. "He broke my heart. Don't you think *that's* a little cruel?"

"Oh my God . . . you're trying to hurt him, aren't you? You're trying to make him jealous." Whitney's eyes widened, but instead of anger, she appeared proud of Elle. "You little tart! This is brilliant."

"No, you don't understand, I'm not trying to do *anything* to Luke. I just want Troy to come with me, to experience the Globes."

"Uh-huh." Whitney pursed her lips, then winked. "I understand completely. And just for the record, I'd do the exact same thing if I were in your shoes. If I could find a date to piss off Nolan, I totally would. But I'm afraid that's not in the cards. Mind if I borrow Luke?"

Elle glared at Whitney.

"Kidding, kidding!"

Elle knew there was no sense in arguing with Whitney over her intentions in inviting Troy to the award show. And if she was being honest with herself, there *was* a part of her that would delight in making Luke regret his decision to walk away from her. She didn't want to use Troy, or exact revenge. Her feelings for him were genuine, and she would never hurt him intentionally. But the hole Luke left was significant and the idea of regaining the upper hand in that scenario was too enticing to reject.

She could only hope sitting at a table with Luke, Troy, Gina, Whitney, and Nolan would not be the most uncomfortable four hours of her life. But somehow, she knew it would be exactly that.

Chapter 24

Luke sat in the limousine, his hands trembling as he gazed out at the mob of photographers surrounding the red carpet of the Golden Globes at The Beverly Hilton. The normally laid-back actor had dreamed of this moment for most of his life. He was a successful actor on the hottest drama on television, arriving at his very first award show. His hands should have been trembling with excitement and nervous energy over this monumental event in his professional life.

But that wasn't the source of his trembling hands. Instead, all he could think about was Elle. Gorgeous, headstrong, stubborn Elle. Three weeks prior, his temper allowed her to slip through his fingers. And tonight he would see her in some gorgeous dress, looking as hot as humanly possible, and he would want to take her hand in his, sit together at the table, drink wine, laugh, and celebrate the success of the show. And when the curtain closed and they retreated to the after-party at the estate of the president of the network, they'd lounge together on a couch near the pool, drinking champagne and toasting the awards received that evening. Elle would make a comment about how next year, Luke would be holding a statue of his own. They'd retreat to his home, where they'd cap off the evening with a late-night swim in the ocean and cuddling in his hammock.

But that wasn't going to happen.

None of it.

Instead, he was mentally preparing for an evening of uncomfortable glances and stifled conversation during the agonizing four-hour taping of the award show. If he was lucky, Elle would sit beside him and they would get past their fight and petty miscommunication. Elle would see Gina was crazy, that he never cooperated with her on any of her crazy schemes, and that his love for her was truer than anything else in his life. He loved her. And he'd never loved anyone before. Not like this.

And right then, he made the decision to win her back, to apologize for walking away. She was right—he told her she was worth waiting for and yet he abruptly stopped waiting. Well, not anymore. He would stand by her side and convince her they belonged together, even if it took all night.

Just as his newly confident self grabbed the handle of the limousine door, a swarm of photographers surrounded his vehicle, as if somehow they knew he was about to emerge. With confidence, he stepped from the limousine, doing his best not to flinch from the combination of the afternoon sun and the flashing bulbs of cameras. He raised his arm to give them a welcoming, friendly wave, just as Rob had coached him. A representative for the network wearing a brightly colored badge stood near a woman with a microphone, and he mentally prepared for a quick red carpet interview. He joined the two women, plastering to his face the most charming smile he could muster.

It was rather painless. The interviewer quickly asked him two basic questions about what it felt like to be a part of the show and to watch his costars be nominated for such prestigious awards. He could hear the cameras flashing all around him as he answered honestly. It was a tremendous honor for him to be a part of this evening, and a part of the show. He was looking forward to many more award shows to come.

"Great, thanks. We got it." The interviewer raised her arm and gestured for him to continue on his way. The network rep gave him a quick thumbs-up, and Luke walked to the next interviewer to repeat the process, with the rep following close behind.

After six or seven (he'd lost count) short interviews on the carpet, Luke was feeling confident in the process. He knew how to handle anything they could throw at him. That is, until a pesky host from the E! network shoved a microphone in his face.

"Luke Kingston," she said, waving her arms wildly as she approached. "We cannot even tell you how long we've been *dying* to talk to you," she bellowed, her eyes seeming to bulge from their sockets. Luke resisted the urge to cringe at her overly assertive nature and brash speaking voice.

"Yes, well, thank you." He gave her a forced smile, his lips pressed together.

"We're just dying to know. Where is Gina? Shouldn't she be on your arm?"

The *Us Weekly* interview was rearing its ugly head. After so many interviewers had skipped this prying personal question, he was dismayed to hear it asked at all.

He did his best to dodge the implication they were, in fact, a couple. "She'll be arriving soon, I'm sure."

"Ah, walking the red carpet separately. Sure, we see that all the time. So tell me . . . you have such great chemistry on the show, is that what led to your relationship offscreen?"

Luke cleared his throat and pondered the question. He could cooperate, go along with it, boost his career and Gina's and give hot gossip to the E! network's viewers. Or he could do the right thing, and publicly prove to Elle that he was hers and hers alone. He chose Elle.

"Thank you. Chemistry is a difficult thing, you know. And usually, when you have great on-screen chemistry, it doesn't translate off the screen. That's certainly the case with us. Gina and I are good friends and nothing more."

The interviewer froze, her mouth agape. Quickly, she recovered and asked a follow-up question. Luke's foot twitched. He was eager to escape this uncomfortable interrogation.

"So wait . . . you two *aren't* a couple? Weeks ago, she gave an interview for *Us Weekly* saying she found love again, are you saying she made that up?"

Luke nodded, looked directly into the camera, and smiled with confidence. "That's *exactly* what I'm saying."

The rep from the network glared at him from several feet away. She quickly dragged two fingers across her neck, insisting he wrap it up. He'd never been more grateful for a gesture in all of his life. Without batting an eye, he shook the interviewer's hand, saying, "You have a good evening."

When he walked to the network rep, he had no idea what to say. He knew he was in trouble.

"I don't know what the hell you were doing back there, but let's hope it works in our favor."

That response confused him. "What do you mean?"

"Love stories are good, but scandals are even better. Let's hope for some headlines."

Luke shook his head, holding his hand out abruptly. "Wait. That's not why I did it."

The rep raised an eyebrow and looked over her glasses at Luke. "I know that. But my job is to find the silver lining whenever any of you screw things up—so that's exactly what I plan to do. You can go inside now, you're done behind the microphone for tonight."

Taking a rather large sigh of relief, Luke followed a crowd of other actors, producers, and directors into the lobby of the large theater. When he reached one of the many entrances to the auditorium, he was greeted by a man wearing a tuxedo and holding a clipboard.

"Hello, I'm with *Follow the Sun*, I—" Luke began.

"Mr. Kingston, of course," the man said with a smile of recognition and deference. "You're at table nineteen, which is at the back of the first level, right next to the half wall. Some of your fellow cast mates have already arrived."

Luke still wasn't used to people recognizing his face or name. It amazed him every time and he was grateful for that. "Thank you."

"It's an honor to meet you, sir."

Luke smiled and extended his hand. The man placed his clipboard between his arm and side and shook Luke's hand with vigor before gesturing for Luke to enter the theater.

As he crossed the threshold, Luke took in the opulence of the theater. Chandeliers hung from the ceiling, and elegant velvet fabric lined the walls. He could hear the chatter of television and film stars meeting one another for the first time. His eyes caught a glimpse of the most famous couple in the world, sitting together at an empty table, enjoying a quiet moment. The actor brushed the brunette's hair from her eyes and she kissed the top of his hand. As starstruck as he was, taking in that private moment between two A-list movie stars, his focus was finding Elle. He could only hope she was sitting alone, or with Whitney, at their table. He could ask her to join him in the hallway, to have a conversation and start over.

Three simple steps led to the main floor of the theater. Before he could even make out the small card with the number 19 on the table, he saw them.

Elle looked just as stunning as he'd imagined. She was dressed in a black strapless gown that hugged her body and accentuated her gorgeous breasts. Her lips were ruby red, her hair was pulled up tight in a bun. She nearly took his breath away. But the man sitting next to her was the one who succeeded in knocking the wind right out of Luke's lungs. Her ex. The man who, Luke knew, didn't deserve another shot with the woman he loved. Ten years? Who goes ten years without speaking to another person and then expects another chance? He could barely let ten days go by without speaking to Elle. The idea of ten years astounded him.

Unwilling to let Elle see the disappointment and sadness written all over his face, Luke took a second to transform into character. Tonight he would be the aloof ex-boyfriend who couldn't be rattled. If he succeeded, it would be the performance of a lifetime.

If only he could have a moment alone with her.

"There he is." Gina rose to her feet, a cocktail in hand and a slur to her speech. "I was waiting for you. Here, have a seat."

The only empty seat at the table was squeezed between the obnoxious and clearly tipsy Gina and Whitney, the friendly casting director whom he always suspected was rooting for Elle and him to get together. Whitney placed her hand on Luke's shoulder and leaned in. "She's already bombed. Started drinking in the limo."

Luke shook his head. "Lucky me."

Whitney's expression changed, making Luke curious. Her eyes darted toward Elle and her date before locking with Troy's.

"Don't give up," she whispered so quietly her voice was imperceptible to anyone outside of their tiny bubble of conversation. Luke knew exactly what Whitney was telling him.

He smiled and placed a kiss on the top of her hand, like men used to do in the movies. He was touched she was clearly rooting for him. "I don't plan to."

Whitney's eyes smiled in a secret response as she nodded and took her seat. Luke glanced around the table, giving everyone a curt hello before sitting next to Gina. Once he did, his eyes fixed on Elle. She was fidgeting with her purse, avoiding eye contact with him. He smirked, feeling the gaze of Elle's ex upon him. Briefly, he made eye contact with Troy Saladino. Troy's eyes were dark, concerned, and insecure. For a brief second, they shared a glance before Troy leaned in to whisper something into Elle's ear. Whatever it was, Elle giggled softly, covering her mouth with her hand. Anger built within Luke, but he suppressed it, turning his attention back to the friendly woman to his left. Whitney smiled warmly.

"Quite the clusterfuck, huh?" She leaned in closer so only Luke could hear her comments. "I mean, this table is one tangled web of drama. Can I get you a cocktail or something? I'm headed to the bar. I'm too impatient to wait for the server."

"I'll join you." Luke stood, offering Whitney his arm. If Elle could bring her ex to the Globes, knowing they'd be seated together, he could certainly turn on the charm with her best friend. All's fair in love and war.

He glanced back just once before walking to the bar with Whitney. Elle was watching him, her chest rising and falling quickly and her cheeks turning a deep red. It was working.

Just you wait, he thought, knowing this was far from over.

After mingling with other stars from the network and polishing off his first cocktail, Luke escorted Whitney back to the table. Just as she reached her chair, she declared in a surprisingly less-than-subtle tone, "I'm not hanging up that t-shirt just yet."

Luke had no idea what Whitney was talking about, but apparently Elle did. He turned to see her, eyes wide, glaring at Whitney. Luke chuckled, knowing it was some sort of message in his favor. He'd take any support he could get.

Nolan interrupted Luke's enjoyment of the moment, tapping him on the shoulder. Luke never had any complaints regarding the man whom he was, for all intents and purposes, replacing on the show. In fact, he was grateful to the fellow actor for making his career happen.

"Can I have a word with you, Luke?"

"Um . . ." He glanced around the table, confused. "Sure?"

He walked with Nolan, who appeared frustrated and annoyed, to a relatively quiet spot near the bar.

"What's up?"

"Leave her alone," Nolan sneered.

Luke was at a loss. "Wait, hold up. Who are you talking about?"

If Elle had another man attempting to woo her, Luke would blow a freaking gasket. He could handle the ex, but Nolan too? What the hell?

"Whitney. I see how she's looking at you." Nolan's nostrils flared as he looked back toward table 19.

"I'm not interested in Whitney. She's just keeping me sane, dude." Luke placed his hand on Nolan's shoulder. "C'mon, let me get you a drink. You must be on edge tonight. Is this your first nomination?"

"Yeah. But man, I'm crazy about that girl. I didn't realize it when we were just screwing around, but now? Now, it's like . . . I'd do anything to get her back."

"I feel your pain, man, I really do." Luke looked back at Elle, who was leaning in, talking quietly with her ex. With every movement she

made toward the restaurateur, Luke felt less confident, less empow-
ered. He could only hope a little liquid courage would aid him in
staying the course.

The two men ordered their respective drinks before walking
slowly back to the table. "Sorry about that, I just—God, she drives
me nuts."

"Don't worry about it. But she *is* helping me at the moment, so try
not to take a little friendly banter as anything more than that, okay?"

"Trying to ruffle the boss lady's feathers, huh?"

"That obvious?"

Nolan chuckled, scratching the back of his neck. "A little. You
can take that guy."

Luke laughed, patting Nolan on the back, knowing he had no
intention of coming to physical blows with Troy Saladino, but he
appreciated the sentiment just the same. "Thanks, man."

"Ladies and gentlemen, please find your seats. Taping will begin
in ten minutes." The announcer's voice came booming over the
loudspeaker and attendees scattered back to their tables. The women
at table 19 checked their makeup and hair. The tipsy Gina tugged on
Luke's arm as she applied another layer of lipstick. She puckered her
lips, checked her teeth, and gave Luke her sexiest attempt at a smile.

True, Gina Romano was a beautiful woman . . . on the outside. But her personality was deplorable and Luke had absolutely
no interest in being dragged into her web of lies and delusion. She
jeopardized his relationship with Elle, and for that he would never
forgive her.

"I missed you. Come sit with me."

"I'm sitting." He glared at her, shaking her arm away from his.

"Fine, whatever."

"I won't be your photo op, Gina." His voice was husky and deep
as he scolded the actress. Within seconds, and without pondering

his earlier discussion with Nolan, he was leaning to his left. "Do me a favor," he whispered into Whitney's ear. "Switch places with me?"

Whitney raised her eyebrows, then looked around him toward Gina. "Sorry, pal. I have to draw the line somewhere."

And then it all seemed clear. Whitney and Gina had both been involved with Nolan. Of course Whitney wouldn't want to sit next to the drunk wreck of an actress. Luke nodded, and patted Whitney on the forearm.

"Of course, got it."

The lights blinked on and off, urging everyone to find their seats. Luke took a long sip of his gin and tonic, leaned back in his chair, and prepared to experience his first time at the Golden Globes.

• • • • •

"Motherfucker," Gina slurred rather loudly, when the winner of her category was announced.

"Gina!" Nolan hissed. "You can't look pissed on camera. Put a smile on your face."

"Screw you, Nolan. Don't tell me what to do. Ever!"

"Gina!" Elle hissed from across the table, her eyes stern and wide. "Enough. Listen to him and put a freaking smile on your face."

"Fine, whatever." In one fell swoop, Gina replaced her unglued expression with a calm, collected smile as she clapped along with the audience. The winning actress approached the microphone and the theater grew silent as everyone took in her gracious speech.

Whitney turned her head just briefly, giving Luke a wink. He was really starting to like her. He laughed into his cuff links, avoiding the daggers in Gina's eyes.

It would be hours before Nolan's category or the Best Drama category would be announced. Luke was feeling restless. Just as predicted, he and Elle shared several stolen, awkward glances. It wasn't enough. He needed time alone with her, away from Saladino and the rest of the crazy people at their table. He shifted in his seat, feeling his third gin and tonic doing its job. A warm buzz was spreading throughout his body, and he wanted nothing more than to enjoy his buzz with the woman he loved.

When the host of the show dismissed the cameras, Elle rose from her seat and Luke sat up in attention. "I'm going to use the washroom," she said to her date.

Feeling bold, Luke waited until she was just a few feet from the table before jumping to his feet and following her to the lobby. Her heels clicked against the marble floor of The Beverly Hilton lobby.

"Elle," Luke called. She turned, and the color drained from her face as her feet appeared glued to the floor.

"Luke, not now. Go back to the table."

"No, I need to speak with you."

Elle scanned the hallway before grabbing Luke's elbow and pulling him to a quiet corner near the empty entryway. Save for a couple of security guards, they were alone.

Elle's eyes were troubled, stressed. Luke didn't want to cause her pain. In fact, all he wanted was to make her happy, to bring love and joy to her life. Why couldn't she see that? Yes, he was being impetuous, yes, the timing was all wrong, but he didn't care. He needed her to know the truth.

"What do you want?" She crossed her arms in front of her chest. Gently, Luke pressed her into the wall, blocking her in with his hands against the wall. She looked back and forth between his arms that caged her in, then her eyes softened. Despite the harsh tone of her voice, her body language betrayed her.

"I had to talk to you."

"Fine." She looked around the hallway again. "Talk."

"Why did you bring him here?"

"Luke," she pleaded, her eyes welling with tears. "Don't do this now. You walked away from me, remember? You said you were done. And now you're all over my best friend. What in the hell do you want from me?"

"I never should've done that. My temper got the best of me and I was an asshole. But I'm not giving up, Elle. I didn't mean it."

"You say that now, but—"

"Do you want me to take out an ad in the newspaper to declare my love? I'll do it. Give an interview with *People*? No problem. Quit the show? Consider it done. I'll do whatever it takes to win you. Just tell me it isn't too late, Elle."

"I don't . . . I mean—"

Luke leaned in closer, their noses almost touching. "I'll *never* stop fighting for you."

Elle's eyes softened and her words came out in a harsh whisper. "You're . . . fighting for me?"

"Yes." He smiled, his fingers tracing a line down her warm temple and cheek. She closed her eyes at his touch. "And I don't give up easily, you should know that by now."

"Luke . . ." Her words trailed off and Luke nuzzled into her neck, planting feathery kisses on her silky skin. He wanted to stay there forever. Just the two of them, away from the craziness of the theater, away from the rest of the world that seemed determined to break them apart.

"Someone will see us," she murmured. He could feel her heart pounding underneath that sexy dress.

"Let them see. Let them splash it across the front page of the papers. I want nothing more than for the world to know I'm yours."

Elle opened her mouth to speak, and Luke traced her red lips with his thumb. "I have to get back to Troy. He doesn't deserve this."

"Fine." Luke pushed away from the wall, placing his hands in the pockets of his tuxedo.

"I need to use the washroom. Go back now, so we don't return at the same time."

"Whatever you want. But this isn't over."

Elle swallowed hard, nodding. He smiled to himself as he watched her walk to the ladies' room. His eyes followed the most beautiful woman in the world clicking her heels against the marble floor, and he had a thought. *Saladino damn well better have his game face on.*

Chapter 25

Tap. Tap. Tap.

Troy tapped his fingers on the white linen tablecloth as he stared at the door, waiting for Rigby to emerge. She and the actor had been gone for far too long and he was on the verge of straight-up exasperation. This entire environment made him ridiculously uncomfortable. The gowns, the tuxedos, the pretentious assholes seated at his table. One was drunk off her ass and staring at him with a sick grin on her face.

He attempted to ignore her, but she simply wasn't having it. "Hey, handsome." She waited for him to make eye contact. When he did, her next statement came out in a sing-songy tone, as if she was trying to make him feel even worse about his kinda-sorta girlfriend wandering off with her ex. "They've been gone an awfully long ti-ime . . ."

"Shut up, Gina," Whitney snapped. Troy took a sip of his scotch, attempting (yet again) to ignore the intoxicated star of the show, knowing she was probably upset about losing in her category.

"I'm ignoring you, whore." Gina's eyes stayed on Troy as she snapped at Whitney.

"Whoa!" Nolan interrupted. "There's no need for that language."

"Shut up!" Both women yelled at the actor, who raised his eyebrows and sat back in his chair with his hands up in the air, obviously retiring from the entire conversation.

Nolan nudged Troy in the arm. "I tried, man."

"I wonder if they're in the coat closet . . . or a bathroom stall," Gina said. "Either way, someone's getting nailed."

Whitney stood and glared at Gina. "I swear to God, if you say one more thing about my friend I will rearrange your freaking face."

"It's all right, Whitney. She's not bothering me." Troy attempted to defuse the situation, taking another sip of his drink, trying to calm his nerves. He offered Whitney a polite smile with his lips pressed into a thin line. "No big deal."

"Bitch," Gina slurred before taking another sip of champagne. Whitney rolled her eyes and started typing on her cell phone. Troy wondered if she was trying to reach Rigby, to let her know her absence was noticed in a major way.

"Enough," Rob the director said between clenched teeth. Troy could tell his patience was wearing thin with Gina's antics. "Reporters and bloggers are all over this place."

Gina perked up, a smug look on her inebriated face. "Hey, as long as we're making headlines—"

"I mean it, Gina." Rob bared his teeth at the actress. "The last thing we need is bad press at the Globes. Get yourself under control . . . right now."

Kingston returned to the ballroom, and despite the fact his appearance was not disheveled in any way, Troy wasn't convinced nothing had happened. Trusting Rigby was not his strong suit. He knew he was one to hold a grudge—and he held one against her for a decade. Weeks ago, he promised her he was done with that, promised the grudge would end to give them a real chance. But as he watched the actor casually return to the table, take a sip of his drink, and lean back in the chair to talk quietly with Whitney, Troy's insecurities bubbled to the surface, and his old friend the grudge yelled at him. Loudly.

She's not yours. Never has been. Even when she walked down that aisle.

Troy gritted his teeth, waiting for Rigby to return to the theater. A beautiful television star was holding an envelope and introducing nominees for Best Actor in a Drama Series.

"This is it," Nolan said, nudging Troy.

"Good luck," Troy said, noticing Rigby standing by the door, unable to return to her seat while an award was being announced. They locked eyes and she offered a smile. Skeptically, Troy returned it. He had no intention of ruining her big night, no matter how conflicted he felt inside. He watched as she pressed her interlaced fingers toward her chest. She wanted Nolan, and the show, to be rewarded for their hard work. He could tell she was holding her breath as her eyes remained glued to the stage. God, she was beautiful.

Nolan's name was announced as the winner, and the standard music began to play. Nolan rose to his feet, shaking Troy's and Rob's hands before walking to the stage. Instead of watching the actor, though, Troy's eyes darted back to Rigby, who was bouncing with excitement on her toes. Troy was so proud of her, of the world she created for these characters, of the recognition it had garnered her. She deserved every drop of success Hollywood had to offer her. As he watched her, he listened to Nolan's speech.

"Wow. What an honor. First of all, thank you to the Hollywood foreign press for this incredible honor. Also, I need to thank the woman who created Desmond and Molly and everything that goes into this show. Even though this is my final season, I'll always be grateful to Elle Riley for giving me this chance on one of the best television shows ever written. I want to thank my agent, my publicist, and our director, Rob. Gina, what can I say? It's been one hell of a ride, sweetheart. And lastly, to Whitney Bartolina . . . thank you for inspiring me, baby. This one's for you!"

Troy turned his attention to Whitney when he heard that final sentence and was baffled when Whitney didn't seem pleased with the dedication. In fact, she seemed annoyed as she rolled her eyes and shook her head, diving back into her cocktail. Troy couldn't figure these people out. He couldn't imagine how he would feel if Rigby thanked him in a speech heard by millions. But he liked to think he'd feel grateful rather than irritated.

"This blows, I need a smoke." Gina stood, her legs wobbly as she passed Rigby on her way to the smoking terrace. Troy, although concerned the terribly inebriated actress might get herself into even more trouble, knew it was not his place to do anything about it, especially since Rigby was walking toward him with a satisfied grin on her face. Her expression was contagious and he found himself smiling right along with her.

"Oh my God, he won," Rigby boomed when she returned to the table. "This is amazing!"

She and Whitney exchanged an awkward glance and Troy became curious. Then he noticed Whitney and Nolan weren't even sitting together. That dedication was starting to seem odd. Troy resigned himself to the fact this group would continue to confuse him—he'd never quite understand their dynamic, nor did he care to. Rigby was his focus, not them.

Rigby settled in next to Troy and he placed his hand on her thigh. "Congratulations. You *know* he won because of you." And it was the truth. It also wasn't lost on Troy that Nolan's character was based on him. Troy was, for all intents and purposes, the character of Desmond, and he couldn't help but feel proud for inspiring her to create such a character. Even if he was cloaked in heartbreak.

She kissed his cheek, smiling with gratitude. "Thank you for saying that."

"It's the truth." He smiled, moving his hand from her thigh to wrap around her shoulder, pulling her close. He could feel the actor watching his movements, and he didn't care. He wasn't giving up so easily. He and Rigby had a history Kingston couldn't possibly comprehend.

"Only a few more awards until Best Drama. Now that Nolan's won, I'm jumping out of my skin." Rigby hopped up and down in her chair, showing her vulnerability and excitement. As usual, it was infectious and Troy wanted her to take home that award more than anything. She deserved it.

Nolan returned to the table, hugging Rigby and Rob, and shaking hands with Troy and Luke. He approached Whitney, attempting to pull her in for a hug, but she pushed her hand into his shoulder and mumbled, "We need to talk."

"What's that all about?" Troy whispered into Rigby's ear as the two made their way toward the lobby.

"Long story. I'll tell you later, okay?" she said, looking sheepish as she peered at Whitney through the corner of her eye.

Troy kissed her forehead, not wanting to cause her any stress. Clearly, Whitney's unhappiness became hers as well. That was always something he adored about his longtime love. She internalized the feelings of those around her. Regardless of her driven nature, she was quite talented at putting herself in the shoes of others—something Troy himself admittedly struggled with. It was difficult for him to see outside his own comfort zone, his own emotions. He tried, especially when it came to Rigby, but clearly he came up short.

As they settled in for another award announcement, Troy's mind drifted back ten years, as it did frequently whenever she was near. The anger consuming him had dictated his actions. Even though, at the time, he loved her more than he loved another human being on the planet, he managed to treat her as if she didn't exist within a day of her confessing she couldn't be married.

What he heard that morning in Las Vegas was she couldn't be married *to him*. Because, deep down, he knew in his gut, that was exactly the case. After all, he always felt Rigby's feelings for him could never and would never match the intensity of his own. And so, when she made herself sick the morning after their wedding, the wedding he tried so hard to make perfect for her, he knew in his gut he was correct.

She didn't love me enough. Not nearly enough. Not the way I'd always loved her.

For weeks, she reached out to him. She came to his apartment almost every day and he looked through the peephole, seeing her distraught features, her bloodshot eyes. But he couldn't put himself in her shoes. All he could feel was his own pain, his own disappointment and anger. He wanted to believe she loved him, but the truth of the matter was, he couldn't do it. Each time she arrived at his door, he'd look through the tiny window the size of a thimble, take in her expression, and press his forehead to the door, his hands against the wood. Then, he'd take a deep breath and retreat to his bedroom, closing the door and blaring his music.

He started sleeping with Amanda less than two weeks after returning from Las Vegas. He hated himself for leading her on, but he was inexplicably drawn to his ex-girlfriend during times of heartache. And if he was being honest, there was a part of him that wanted Rigby to know he was seeing Amanda again. He knew how to hurt her, and he knew how to do it well. She was right when she asked about Amanda looking through the peephole. He sent her to the door just once, when he was feeling especially angry and full of resentment. He wasn't proud of that, or the fact that he'd gotten her pregnant. Payton, however, was someone he would never regret. He was blessed to be her father, no matter the circumstances.

When Rigby slid the annulment papers under the door, he knew it was over. She'd given up. He was finally free of his attachment to her, or at least that's what he told himself.

Even now, he feared, despite the miles or time apart, he might never be free of her. Time, space, distance—none of it seemed to make a difference. And so, when she materialized in his restaurant months earlier, he let his guard down, albeit slightly. And now he was seated next to her during the pinnacle of her career—just minutes away from a possible Golden Globe win. With each smile that crossed her face, with each squeeze of her hand with his, he was letting go of that anger, of that pain. He was forgiving her—something he didn't know he was capable of. And it felt nice.

Now, if he could only get visions of her with Kingston out of his head. He was in no way naive when it came to that situation, or the fact the actor clearly affected her. After hours sitting at a table with the two of them, the tension was palpable. He noticed the stolen glances, the way she avoided looking across the table.

Troy wanted to laugh at the irony of the situation. For years, his anger and resentment were the biggest barrier placed between Rigby and himself. And now that he was finally ready to forgive, to break down that mammoth of a barrier and move on with her, creating a future together as a couple, he was faced with a different obstacle. One named Luke Kingston, a man who'd entered her life only months prior.

Perhaps he'd missed his chance. Perhaps ten years was just too long.

But he wasn't ducking out so quickly, even though his old friend The Grudge was urging him to. The thought of being humiliated again was horrible. But missing his one shot with Rigby was even worse. So he would wait to hear it from her. Until that moment, if and when it happened, he would enjoy his time with her, squeezing her hand, and pulling her close as she enjoyed the biggest night of her life.

Chapter 26

A nd the Golden Globe goes to . . . *Follow the Sun,*" the legend-
ary film director announced from the stage as he clutched
the envelope under his arm and clapped his hands. The crowd
erupted in applause as the announcer continued over the loudspeaker. "Accepting this award on behalf of the show is Elle Riley,
creator, head writer, and show runner of *Follow the Sun.*"

Elle jumped to her feet as every nerve in her body stood at attention. Her hands clasped over her mouth as the air in her lungs stood
still. Troy stood to embrace her, a look of pride on his handsome
face. Trembling, she wrapped her arms around his neck, squeezing
him hard, grateful he could be there to share in the moment. A
moment she never dreamed possible. Her show was deemed by the
Hollywood Foreign Press Association as the best drama on television. What a staggering, humbling honor. Before she stepped away,
Troy opened her tiny handbag and retrieved the speech she had

prepared weeks earlier. She thanked him, knowing she would have completely forgotten to bring it with her to the stage.

Everyone at the table rose to his or her feet, shaking hands and exchanging hugs, joining her as she walked to the stage. Just before her unsteady legs attempted to climb the tiny flight of stairs, a familiar hand took hers in his own, to guide her gently to the top. Relief poured through her body, grateful for his assistance. The last thing she needed was to fall flat on her face in front of a thousand members of the industry.

"You did it!" Luke boomed over the applauding audience once they reached the large expanse of stage. Whitney, Rob, and everyone else at the table, aside from Troy, gathered around her as the heavy golden statue was placed in her hands.

She stood before the microphone and looked out into the massive audience. Tears of amazement and gratitude brewed in her eyes as she leaned in to deliver her speech. She cleared her throat and began.

"I can't believe I'm standing here," she said off the cuff before she wiped her brow with the back of her quivering hand and looked down at her note cards. The thick paper bounced between her trembling fingertips. "It's an honor and a privilege to be a part of this show. First and foremost, to the Hollywood foreign press—it was such an honor to be among those nominated tonight. I'm delighted to work with the cast and crew of our show each and every day. Nolan, Gina, and Luke, you make this show what it is—you each bring so much talent and creativity to the table and we couldn't do it without you. Rob Morris, Whitney Bartolina, and everyone else who makes this show possible each week, thank you for your tireless work and for supporting me with each storyline we've undertaken. And finally, thank you to a very special man named Troy who came to support me tonight. You're the reason I'm standing here, whether you know it or not. So thank you. Thank you so very much."

The lights were so bright Elle was unable to find Troy in the audience, let alone make eye contact with him. But she could only hope he was touched by her speech. It was because of their love story that *Follow the Sun* came to be. He deserved recognition, even if it was painful to accept.

They were guided offstage by the award presenter. When they were out of sight, Luke wrapped his arm around her waist, pulling her into his strong chest. Within seconds, he lifted her by her waist and twirled her in the air. Her fingers gripped his shoulders as she threw her head back in absolute joy.

When he lowered her to the floor, Elle, who was smiling from ear to ear, looked into Luke's bright eyes. They were backstage and the production crew was shuffling this way and that. It seemed everyone was moving in fast-forward motion as they stood together, their eyes connecting as Luke beamed with pride.

"I think this is the best and worst day of my life," Elle said, smoothing down his disheveled hair. Luke took her hand in his and pressed it to his chest. His heart was thumping wildly beneath his tuxedo.

"Focus on the good. Everything else will work itself out."

Elle wanted to be as optimistic as Luke often was. She wanted to view the world as a place filled with endless opportunities and limitless potential. She wanted to ignore the turmoil building within her as she was torn between the two men in her life. Celebration seemed almost impossible when she felt this way. No matter what she did, someone would be hurt. Wouldn't he?

As if he somehow read her thoughts, Luke pressed his lips gently to her forehead and sighed. "I'll stay out of the way. But that doesn't mean I'm giving up. This was your story, the two of you, and you should celebrate together. So for tonight, I'll give you your space."

Luke released her hand and started to walk away. "Wait," she called after him, her voice urgent and filled with nerves. "Will you be at the after-party?"

He smiled. "Of course. Wouldn't miss it."

Relief came over her as she nodded and lifted her hand to blow him a kiss. In a silly, overly dramatic form, Luke pretended to leap in the air to catch it just in time. Elle giggled as he placed it in the pocket of his tuxedo. He patted the fabric, and for just a moment, he looked sad. His smile was replaced by a contemplative gaze. He raised his hand, gave her a subtle wave, and disappeared into the swarm of production assistants and staff who were preparing to announce the final awards of the evening.

•••••

"We're so impressed with you, Elle, and I want you to know we've been giving your show ideas much thought." Saul Greenberg, the network president, had cornered her beside the pool. Troy was seated next to her, his hand on her thigh as they listened to Saul, a tall, portly man, encourage Elle and her success at the award ceremony. Elle knew awards such as these were a major factor in renewed contracts and future opportunities. She was thrilled Saul was pleased.

"Is that right?"

"Indeed." He took a drink of his cocktail, wiping his lips with the back of his hand. "In fact, I probably shouldn't tell you this, but since this is my fifth drink, I don't really care. We like them all— we're having trouble deciding."

"Well, maybe you can increase your entire fall lineup," Elle joked, nudging him in the elbow. Saul erupted in laughter.

"You never know, young lady." Elle cringed at being referred to as a young lady. She was thirty-five freaking years old. She forced a smile, however, knowing that Saul a) was drunk and b) could make or break her career with just one phone call. "Just keep doing what you're doing, and the possibilities will be endless."

"Thank you, sir." Elle stood and smoothed down her party dress. She and Whitney had changed into shorter, more comfortable cocktail dresses before arriving at Saul's estate. "I'm going inside to use the ladies' room. Troy, can I get you something to drink?"

"You know"—Troy stood and took Elle's hand in his—"my glass is getting low. I'll get our drinks while you use the washroom."

"Great." Elle squeezed Troy's hand. "It was a pleasure speaking to you, Mr. Greenberg. You have an absolutely gorgeous home."

Saul raised his glass and winked before leaning back into his soft outdoor armchair. Elle and Troy quickly retreated into the house.

"I don't really need to pee. I just had to get away from him. He was really making me uncomfortable."

Troy sighed. "Same here. I'm glad you said something. I wasn't going to pull you away from him, or anyone from the network. C'mon, let's get another drink."

It felt like they had been drinking for almost eight hours, and yet, Elle never reached more than a delightfully steady buzz. Thank goodness she remembered to eat, and food was plentiful at the awards show and now at Saul Greenberg's enormous mansion. When they reached the indoor bar, Troy ordered two glasses of scotch, handing one to Elle. They toasted the evening and the success of the show before linking arms and strolling through the expansive first floor of the home. Cast, crew, and executives from all of the network's shows were walking through the elegant estate. Elle and Troy made their way to the empty foyer to escape the loud music at the back of the house, where most of the partygoers were

drinking, eating, and celebrating. Marble floors and two winding
staircases led to the second floor.

"God, this place," Troy began, taking a sip of his scotch. "I can't
even imagine. I thought your place was huge, but this is . . . well,
it's like a compound."

Elle giggled, nodding. "I think I'd get lost here."

"Should we go back outside? They have a dance floor, ya know."

One thing Troy and Elle were good at was dancing. Back in
college, they actually took swing dance lessons with a few of their
friends and learned several routines. In each one, Troy would flip
Elle's entire body over, until she landed back on her feet. Swing
dancing led to salsa, which led to ballroom dance. The one place
they never argued was on the dance floor.

"Ahh, do they now, Mr. Saladino?" Elle placed one hand on her
hip. "Do you still have your moves?"

"I guess we'll find out, won't we?" Troy offered Elle his arm,
a flirtatious grin on his face. Playfully, Elle puckered her lips and
narrowed her eyes, looping her arm through his and allowing him
to lead her back outside. The warm breeze of the evening swept
through her hair and down her back. The evening was turning out
just lovely.

"Kingston!" a voice shrieked from inside the house. "Where is he?
Where is that rat bastard?"

Gina.

Tearing through the crowd of partygoers, Gina searched wildly
for Luke, who was talking with a small group of men near the pool.
Elle watched as he craned his neck, making eye contact with Gina.
And then he rolled his eyes as she stormed toward him.

"The E! network? How could you *do* that?"

"Calm down, Gina," Luke responded, his voice low, so as not
to draw more attention to them. But Gina was having none of it.

"Calm down? I will not calm down! You screwed me! Now the whole world thinks I'm a liar!"

"Knows," Luke corrected her. "The whole world *knows* you're a liar."

"Screw you, Luke."

Elle watched in awe, not having any understanding of what they were talking about. But she'd be lying if she said she wasn't curious. In fact, *curious* didn't do her emotions justice. She was dying to know. Without even realizing it, her feet inched toward them until her toes reached the concrete around the pool. Across the glistening water, she watched as their argument continued.

"You need to sleep this off." Luke touched Gina's elbow, but she pulled away.

"I don't need to do *anything*! My publicist just spent the better half of this party screaming at me, you asshole!"

Whitney approached Luke and Gina, looking embarrassed at Gina's ridiculous display. "What the hell is going on?"

"Him. He told E! News I lied."

Whitney crossed her arms in front of her chest. "You did, didn't you?"

Gina looked exasperated, flailing her arms and throwing her head back and screaming into the air, "Of *course* I did! And if this idiot were smart, he would've just gone along with it! Now I'm the laughingstock of Hollywood!"

Luke shrugged, his words stern and unwavering. "I told you I wasn't interested, Gina, but you did it anyway. What the hell did you expect? I'm not your puppet."

"Oh, that's right." Gina threw her head wildly from side to side before locking eyes with Elle across the pool. "You're *her* puppet! Isn't that right, Elle?"

Luke grabbed Gina's elbow. "Do *not* bring her into this."

Elle's heart raced as she watched everything transpire, doing her best to process what, in her heart, she already knew to be true. Luke had nothing to do with the *Us Weekly* article or a showmance of any kind. It was Gina. All Gina.

"Or what?" Gina pulled away from his grasp, crossing her arms in front of her chest.

Whitney took a few steps to stand beside the actress. "Oh for God's sake, shut *up*!" With one swift nudge from Whitney, Gina's heels wobbled over the edge of the pool until she plunged into the water. She screeched as her arms splashed about. Most of the attendees watched as Gina popped back to the surface. Once she did, Elle, Luke, and everyone else near the pool looked to Whitney with mouths agape.

"What?" Whitney raised one shoulder, her hand resting gently on her hip, like it was no big deal. "It's the shallow end."

Elle pressed her hand to her mouth, her chest heaving with laughter. She wanted nothing more than to run around the pool and tackle Whitney with a grateful hug. But she refrained. Instead, she watched as Nolan walked to the steps of the pool, offering Gina his hand. Surprised by his compassion, Elle smiled. The actress attempted to pull him into the pool with her, but Nolan anchored himself with the handrail, shaking his head at her as he guided her up the steps.

She was soaked, her chiffon dress like a second skin on her body. Elle curled her lips underneath her teeth, her hand still blocking her mouth as she watched the actress, who looked ridiculous. One of the waiters brought her a towel, wrapping it around her body and guiding her into the mansion.

Elle stood, watching Luke from across the pool. When his eyes found hers, he smiled—a smile Elle could only describe as relieved. She finally knew the truth—but that didn't make their situation any less precarious. He polished off his drink, placed it on a server's tray, and gave Elle a salute, bidding her good night. Her stomach tied itself in knots as she watched him hug Whitney and shake the hands of those around him, before turning and exiting the party.

"Well, that was interesting." Troy's arms were crossed in front of his broad chest. "Poor girl."

"Poor girl? Do you know the hell that *poor girl* has put me through? The lies she's told, the damage she's done?"

Although true, her words were venomous and Elle regretted them the second she finished uttering them. She was backing herself in a corner with Troy, forcing him to learn more than she wanted him to know about her failed relationship with Luke.

"Still," Troy said, shaking his head, "she didn't deserve that."

"She'll dry off and be fine. But the damage she's done . . . it's so much more than a ruined gown. Trust me."

"I guess I'll have to," Troy replied with a furrowed brow. "Because I know almost nothing about your life, Rigby. I'm on a need-to-know basis, I guess."

Elle turned on her heel and crossed her arms in front of her chest. "Excuse me?"

"Listen." He ran his hands through his hair before placing his hand behind her back and leading her to a quiet spot near the dance floor. "I realized tonight I know almost nothing about your life, and that sucks."

"That's what happens when you disappear for ten years."

Troy flinched. She'd finally said it. Finally said what she had been dying to say for months. Conflicted relief flooded her body. The words, albeit satisfying, were weapons, aimed to inflict pain. She knew it, as did he.

"Let's not do this here, Eleanor."

Elle rolled her eyes. "Don't say my name as if you're scolding me."

"I'm *not* calling you Elle."

"And why not? What would be the harm?"

"Because that's not who you *are*—it's who you want all of them to *think* you are."

Enraged, Elle's eyes widened. "And what is that, exactly? A success? A Golden Globe–winning show runner? Is it so difficult for you to see me as anything but the bitch who broke your heart?"

"No." Troy looked up at the darkened sky. "Look, I didn't mean that, I just . . . why do I feel like we always veer off course? We're fine one minute, bickering the next. I hate it."

"I hate it, too."

"All night long, I've watched you. I've watched you and Kingston—and don't even get me started on your little disappearing act."

"Nothing happened. I wouldn't do that to you, Troy. Never."

"But you wanted to, didn't you?"

Elle had no response. The truth would be too painful. Troy was slipping through her fingers and their fight was heading in such a speed, she was powerless to stop it. She just had to hold on, take her lumps, and do her best to survive it.

"For God's sake, Rigby, just tell the truth. What do you want?"

"I don't know!"

"Let me rephrase. Who do you want, Rigby? Who?"

Elle closed her eyes tight. "Luke," she whispered, unable to look Troy in the eye. "I want Luke."

"I knew it." Troy's voice cracked.

"I was falling in love with him before you resurfaced in my life. And that love . . . it won't go away, no matter how much I try. It consumes me."

"I don't know what to say." Troy bared his teeth before pressing his lips together tightly. His eyes avoided hers as they stood in the moonlight.

"I'm so sorry, Troy. So very sorry I dragged you into this."

"Was this some sort of revenge or something?"

Elle shook her head, quickly, back and forth, back and forth. Shocked by the question. For months, she'd wondered the same thing about Troy's intentions—never, for even one minute, did she consider he might question her motives.

"Absolutely not. I promise you with all that I am."

"Then what?" Troy's face fell, his eyes soft and pleading. "What do you want from me?"

Elle hesitated as she thought the question through. "I want to be forgiven."

Troy said nothing. He turned and walked in the opposite direction. Elle gasped, wondering if those would be the last words she'd ever say to him. Her eyes grew wet as he walked to the DJ's booth. Confused, Elle watched as he leaned in and spoke into the DJ's ear. The young man behind the booth nodded and Troy shook his hand.

Troy returned to Elle and they stood in awkward silence for a moment before he offered her his hand. Elle was confused, at first, but placed her fingertips in the palm of his hand and followed him to the dance floor. The familiar notes of "Here, There and Everywhere" filled the air. She stared at Troy in wonder.

"One last dance, Rigby?"

Slowly, they swayed as their song filled the air. A lump formed in Elle's throat as she tried to imagine what else to say to Troy. Her mind was swirling and her heart was racing. She knew she was, ultimately, saying good-bye to one of the most important people in her life. The possibility of them remaining friends after reopening so many wounds was unlikely and she knew it. But, she was desperate for his forgiveness. As they danced in silence, she looked up at Troy, waiting for him to break the silence. Finally, he did.

"I forgive you," Troy murmured, pulling Elle closer. "But only if you'll forgive me."

Elle pulled back, her eyes meeting his with confusion. "I don't understand."

"You've always been the girl who was just out of my reach."

"That's not true."

"Just hear me out," Troy insisted. "I knew it at the campsite, and the bar when we finally got together. Hell, I knew it when you walked down the aisle."

"How could you think I didn't love you?"

"That's not what I mean." Troy shook his head. "I know you loved me. But it wasn't the same. Even today, I felt it . . ." His words trailed off.

"What do you mean?"

"All night, I watched you, even when you didn't know I was paying attention. I saw the way you look at Kingston. You never looked at me like that, Rigby. Never."

Elle's eyes filled with tears. "I never meant—I mean . . . I just . . ."

"It's okay." Troy smoothed her hair down before pressing his forehead to hers. Together, still swaying to the music, they cried below the stars. "But I need you to forgive me. At every stage of our lives, I pushed you. At the time, I thought I was doing it for your own good, to make you realize how much you loved me and that we belonged together. But I get it now. I was fooling myself and doing my best to fool you, too."

"Don't apologize for loving me," Elle whispered.

"I have to." Troy shook his head. "I pushed too hard. I didn't want to see the truth."

Elle placed her hand on Troy's cheek, brushing his olive skin with the tips of her fingers. "But you loved me just the same. Don't apologize for that. I'm honored that you loved me, Troy. Honored."

Troy cupped her face with his hands, and placed a gentle kiss on her lips. The last kiss they would ever share.

"Should I take you home?"

"After the song ends, okay? I want one last dance with you."

And there, under the twinkling lights hanging above the dance floor, Elle and Troy finished the song, holding one another close, purging themselves of their mistakes, their anger, their pain.

And it was there, under those lights, that Elle was finally free.

Chapter 27

Elle watched from her front porch as Troy climbed into his car and backed out of her driveway. She clutched her Golden Globe. The award was much heavier than she'd anticipated, just like the night on which she'd won it. The idea of never seeing Troy Saladino again was a painful one, but she knew a friendship couldn't be forced. He needed to heal and move on. And so did she.

Elle watched his car's taillights as they drifted away from her house. Quickly, she unlocked her door, placing the Globe on her mantel. Poor Linus was begging to go outside, so she slid open her back door, allowing him relief. She sent Luke a text while she waited.

By the time she changed out of her gown, and wrangled her warmest coat and favorite pair of fuzzy boots, there was still no text from Luke. She sent another.

When she reached her car, she checked her phone again. No replies. She drove to Luke's new home in the Pacific Palisades. She rang his doorbell five times.

"Come on," she muttered. "Be home, be home."

Finally, after the sixth ring, she accepted he wasn't. Suppressing the questions popping up in her brain wondering where he was, she opened his gate and retreated to his deck, making herself comfortable on the hammock until he returned.

The stars were bright, and as she stared up at the vast sky she continued to text the man she was crazy for, hoping he'd respond, hoping he'd come home, hoping she'd figure out the perfect thing to say to reclaim his love.

●●●●●

"Elle?" The bright sunlight pierced her eyelids as a warm hand pressed her cheek. The distinct smell of coffee permeated her senses. "Elle, baby, what are you doing here?"

Groggy and cold, Elle opened her eyes, blinking roughly at the merciless sun as it streamed down from the cloudless morning sky.

Then she remembered where she was. The memories came together like a brightly colored mosaic and she remembered everything. Now Luke was greeting her with a cup of coffee in hand and a worried expression affixed to his chiseled face. He perched himself next to her on the makeshift bed, sweat dripping from his brow. He must've just finished his morning run along the beach.

"I—I came to see you, after the party. I must've fallen asleep."

"Did you ring the bell? I was here." Luke's brow wrinkled as she studied him.

"Yes, many times." Elle rubbed her eyes with the back of her hand and yawned. "Where were you?"

"Sorry, I guess I was out like a light. Or my ears were still ringing and couldn't process the sound waves." Luke chuckled and ran his fingers through his wavy locks as the morning breeze fought to press his unruly hair to his forehead. "Are you all right? Did something happen?"

"I—I'm fine." Elle gripped the hammock with her hands, swinging her legs to land on the wooden deck. She was now sitting shoulder to shoulder with Luke and her heart began to pound. She couldn't ignore the voice screaming it was too late. That voice poisoned her past with Troy. She was constantly questioning herself and acting out of fear. She couldn't do that with Luke and was determined to finally silence that horrible voice for good. She breathed in, preparing to profess her love to Luke. She also knew he deserved a sincere apology for the way she had handled herself since Troy reentered her life.

"Coffee?" Luke offered her his cup. Elle took a sip of the steaming, slightly bitter yet sweet drink of the gods. She closed her eyes and enjoyed the soothing sip, knowing it would help her to organize her thoughts properly. She stole one last sip before handing the cup back to Luke.

"I said good-bye to him," Elle said, searching Luke's expression for a response, but his face was guarded. Elle knew she needed to elaborate. "For good."

The corner of his mouth perked into a half smile. "Is that so?"

"Yes. This is where I belong."

Luke's furrowed brow returned, causing a crease to form above his nose. Elle hated that she'd put him through so much with her indecision.

"At first, when you didn't answer your door, my gut reaction was to go home, to chicken out, to sleep it off and see you at work. But then I remembered what you said."

Luke licked his lips. "About what?"

"This hammock. You and me on this hammock—this is what's real, this is what's true."

Luke ran his fingers through her wild, disheveled hair. "I did say that, didn't I?"

"And suddenly, there was nowhere else I could handle being. I had to be here . . . right here, in this spot."

"Well, that's nice." Luke's lack of expression was worrying Elle. He promised he'd fight for her and she hoped he still would.

"I couldn't see it then." Elle, filled with anxiety, rubbed her legs with her palms as she spoke. "I mean, I wanted to, but something held me back. Does that make any sense?"

"You didn't trust me," Luke said softly.

"I was an idiot. Deep down, I knew you were telling the truth, I just . . ."

Her words trailed off as she watched Luke scratch the back of his neck. She was messing this up completely. She needed to be bold, daring. She needed to prove herself to him once and for all.

"If this is going to work, you'll have to trust me, Elle."

"I know. I promise. I let my past dictate how I treated you and that will *never* happen again." Elle peered into Luke's eyes, but he had broken their eye contact and was looking down at her lap. "Luke? What's wrong?"

He said nothing in response. In fact, he was blatantly ignoring her as he took her hand in his. He squeezed her fingertips in his grip, and just as he did months ago on their very first date, he raised it to his lips and placed a kiss inside her palm.

"Forgiven," he said.

Stunned, Elle lost her breath as she stared into the eyes of the man she loved. She couldn't believe how forgiving, how trusting Luke Kingston was. And despite knowing he was sincere in his sentiment, she still had so much to say.

"I mean, I was insecure, confused. I didn't know what the hell I was thinking half the time, and—"

Luke laughed, taking her chin between his fingertips. "Elle, did you hear me? It's all in the past."

"As simple as that? I was horrible to you, Luke."

"Horrible? Far from it." He brushed her bangs from her eyes. "You never expected to see him again, especially just as we were getting to know each other. You didn't plan any of this, you just did the best with the cards you'd been dealt. And I'm glad you took the time to figure this out. You were drowning."

"I was?"

"Your entire life—your career, the show, it was all based on the hell you went through. It was your story, Elle."

"Was," Elle said with newfound confidence. "It *was* my story."

"Exactly." Luke wrapped his arms around Elle, pulling her close.

"Thanks for not giving up on me. When I thought you had, it crushed me."

"It crushed me, too."

"There's more, though. There's more you need to know."

Luke shifted his body to face Elle on the hammock. He rubbed her back with his hand and she sighed at his gentle touch.

"I never slept with Troy." Elle quickly caught her poor choice of words. "I mean, since he came back into my life."

Luke shook his head, closing his eyes and holding his hand out in front of him as if to stop her. "That's not my business. You're a grown woman, and we weren't exclusive. It's fine, really."

"No, you need to hear me because it's the truth. We were taking it slow. We'd get close to it, and then I couldn't go through with it. My feelings for you kept me from being completely intimate with him."

Luke bit down on his lower lip before giving Elle a coy smile. "So . . . these feelings you mentioned."

Elle returned the smile, realizing she hadn't yet said the words. Weeks ago, he told her in this exact spot how he felt. But Elle hadn't reciprocated the words. Not exactly. She'd held back. But Elle was done holding back her feelings for Luke.

"I'm in love with you, Luke. Only you."

For just a moment, they were quiet before Luke pulled her in for a kiss. His strong lips brushed against hers with an urgency that drove her wild. "Only you." She whispered it again and again between each kiss.

"And I love you. I've loved you since the moment we first met."

"You have?"

"Mmm-hmm. I told you, I've never felt like this before. And when you experience something at thirty-five years old that you've never felt before, you know it's time to pay attention. I've never stopped paying attention to how you make me feel."

"And you fought for me," Elle murmured with a smile. "I'm sorry I didn't do the same."

Luke recoiled, placing his hands on her thighs. "Sure you did."

Elle scanned her memories, looking for a time when she'd fought for Luke, but she came up short. Clearly, he was just giving her the benefit of the doubt.

"I seem to remember a very hot session in my dressing room where you took what you wanted."

"That was just jealousy." Elle shrugged it off.

"I disagree. Every time you would get upset, every time you came crashing into my dressing room demanding answers over Paris Hilton or my supposed showmance with Gina, you were fighting for me, Elle. For us."

"Perez."

"Hmm?"

"Perez Hilton."

"Oh, that's right." He chuckled, rising to his feet and pulling her with him. "What did I say again?"

"It doesn't matter," she said with a smile.

"The point is, we fought for each other—both of us. And it all worked out, didn't it?"

"Focus on the good," she repeated his words from backstage the night before, "and everything will work itself out."

"Exactly."

And just as he did the night before, he grabbed her by the waist and lifted her into the air. The California breeze danced in her hair as he spun her around the deck. And for the very first time, she let go of his shoulders, and her arms reached toward the clouds. She was letting go, learning to be free, and enjoying every second with the man she loved so very much.

Luke returned her to the deck, placing a kiss on her forehead. And then, without warning, he stripped himself of his shirt and shorts, tossing them onto the hammock.

Elle scanned the neighbors' houses, wondering if anyone could see her naked boyfriend. "What are you doing?"

Luke wiggled his eyebrows. "C'mon. Let's go for a swim."

Epilogue

SEVEN MONTHS LATER . . .

Elle relaxed into the cool leather of the limousine seat, her hands interlocked with Luke's. His foot was tapping relentlessly against the floor of the car and he was fixing his bow tie . . . again.

"First nominations can be nerve-racking. But you've got this in the bag. You have to know that."

Luke grunted in response and Elle couldn't help but giggle.

It was Luke's first time attending the Primetime Emmy Awards, and unlike at the Golden Globes, they were proudly attending this show together. *Follow the Sun* was nominated for Best Drama Series, and Luke was nominated for Best Supporting Actor in a Drama Series. Elle couldn't help but celebrate when Gina failed to receive a nomination. It was business as usual at the studio, only now Luke and Elle were able to ignore Gina and her antics, knowing she was a severely unhappy person who was going to ride out her contract.

"Easy for you to say, Miss Golden Globe winner." Luke smiled, wiping his brow. "I bet next year, you'll be nominated for *both* shows."

"That would be incredible, wouldn't it?"

Once the filming of season four had wrapped, Elle quickly started writing her new show, *Give Me Shelter*, a drama revolving around a woman in the witness protection program, struggling to make a new life for herself. Whitney was recruited for casting, and a pilot was shot. During that time, Luke was filming an independent movie in Vancouver. Elle split her time between California and Canada. It was exciting for her to sit on the sidelines, watching Luke portray a character who was nothing like David McKenzie. He pushed his limits with the role, pouring himself into the character, and the result was phenomenal. Yes, Elle was biased, but she watched in awe as Luke dazzled his director and fellow cast mates with his talent. The film was still in the editing process, but Elle was confident it would garner him much-deserved attention.

And now, it was the end of August and they were just minutes away from arriving at the Nokia Theatre. And because she'd never seen him like this, Elle was starting to worry about Luke's nervous state.

His cheeks were flushed, his palms were sweaty, and he wouldn't make eye contact with her. Granted, they hadn't attended the Globes together, but she couldn't imagine he had been this nervous. Something was wrong.

"Are you feeling okay? You look like you're coming down with something." Elle shifted in her seat, pressing the back of her hand to his forehead. He felt warm, but not feverish, which left her even more confused.

Luke shook his head abruptly. "No, I—I'm great. Better than great, actually."

Elle shifted in her seat and her chiffon dress, the color of daffodils, tickled her knees as she moved. "Maybe you need a drink. The driver said there's champagne in the fridge."

"I know. I ordered it."

"So have a glass."

Luke shook his head, clearing his throat. "No, I ordered it for a reason."

Elle tilted her head in confusion, placing her hand on Luke's thigh. "What are you talking about?"

"To celebrate."

"Feeling awfully confident, huh?" Elle laughed. She wished she could join in his confidence regarding their chances at a win. "That was a quick change. Two minutes ago, you looked like you might puke."

"No," Luke said with a laugh. "I mean, yes. But . . . aw, hell. Here goes . . ." He turned his body to face Elle and then continued. "I've revised my five-year plan."

"What are you talking about?"

"I can't wait that long." Luke pursed his lips and shook his head. "I want you to have this now."

Elle watched as Luke reached into his pocket, removing a small velvet box. Butterflies swarmed her belly as she looked at the box, then into Luke's beaming eyes, then back again at the box. "Oh my God, Luke!"

Luke slipped off the leather seat, kneeling in front of Elle with the box perched in his hands. "When you asked about where I see myself in five years, what did I say?"

"You saw yourself with me." Her breath caught as she remembered that night on the hammock. "With a ring on my finger and a baby in my belly."

"Exactly." He opened the box to reveal an exquisite solitary diamond on a platinum band. He removed the ring from its velvet case. "My beautiful Elle, I've waited thirty-five years to feel this way about another person. To feel like I can't breathe without you near me. To feel like I'd do anything in the world to make you smile, to make you feel happy, content and loved. Yes, we're very different, and of course we don't always see things the same way, but we strengthen one another, we make each other better people."

"Yin and yang."

"Yes," Luke agreed. "Exactly."

"I feel the same way about you, Luke. I love you so much."

"Then I have something very important to ask you."

"Okay." Elle sniffed. "I'm ready."

Luke laughed, his eyes watering and beaming with pride. "I want to spend the rest of my life with you, Elle Riley. Will you please wear my ring, be my wife, and make my life complete?"

"Yes!" Elle shrieked inside the limousine, holding out her trembling hand. Luke slid the ring on her finger before taking her hand in his and kissing the inside of her palm. Elle sank to her knees opposite Luke, and wrapped her arms around his shoulders.

"I love you, Luke," she whispered through her tears. "Only you."

They remained on their knees, locked in a comforting embrace, as the limousine came to a stop in front of the theater.

"Are you ready for this?" Luke asked, wiping the moisture from her cheeks just as the door to the car was opened.

"Let's do it."

Luke took her hand and guided her out of the limousine. Hand in hand, they walked the red carpet, smiling for the flashing cameras and stopping to give brief interviews. Just as they were about to enter the theater, Luke turned to Elle.

"Are you sure you wanna go in there? I mean, we could just jump back in the limo and celebrate in style."

"Don't be silly. I don't want to miss your first win."

"I've already won, Elle." Luke kissed her, the red carpet beneath their feet. "I've already won."

Acknowledgments

Thank you so much to my editor, Maria Gomez, for believing in this story from the very start and for all of your support during the writing and editing process. I feel so lucky to work with you!

Thank you to my agent, Jessica Watterson, for your continued support. It means so much to have you in my corner. Thank you for everything that you have done to make *Red Carpet Kiss* a success!

Thank you to my developmental editor, Lindsay Guzzardo. I have truly enjoyed your insight and ideas. You made the editing stage FUN! You pushed me in the best possible way and I'm so grateful to you for that. It was a pleasure working with you on this project and I hope to work with you again in the future.

Thank you to my beta readers: Deb Bresloff, Pamela Carrion, Megan Kapusta, Allison East, Laura Wilson, Sharon Cooper, and Jennifer Merkley. Sharing chapters with you was my favorite part of writing this book. I loved the Team Luke vs. Team Troy debates and all of your wonderful and constructive feedback. You all helped to shape this story and I can't thank you enough for that!

Thank you, Deb Bresloff, for all of our awesome brainstorming sessions regarding Luke, Troy, the Beatles, etc., etc., etc. This story wouldn't have been the same without your awesome input. I am so grateful for your unconditional love and support. I am one very lucky girl.

Thank you to Beth Ehemann for all of your awesome brainstorm suggestions, support, and encouragement. I love that we are now Montlake sisters. How awesome is that?

Thank you to Janna Mashburn for all of your love and support. You've been supporting me since the beginning of my writing career and I am forever grateful for your friendship.

Thank you to my writing family. You know who you are and I love every single one of you. I'm so happy we're still together and going strong.

Thank you to my husband, Chris, for always loving and supporting me—watching the kids when I needed to write somewhere without hearing the word *Mommy* and for always reminding me that I make you proud. I love you so very much.